THE HAMMER
IS STRONG WITH
THIS ONE

JEFFREY POOLE

Jeffrey Poole's Epic Fantasy Books
Bakkian Chronicles:

The Prophecy

Insurrection

Amulet of Aria

Disneyland Debacle (short story)

Winter Wonderland (short story)

Tales of Lentari

Lost City

Something Wyverian This Way Comes

A Portal for Your Thoughts

Thoughts for a Portal

Wizard in the Woods

Close Encounters of the Magical Kind

The Hunt for Red Oskorlisk (short story)

May the Fang be With You (Pirates trilogy #1)

The Hammer is Strong with This One (Pirates #2)

These are Not the Stones You're Looking For (Pirates #3)

Blast from the Past

Dragons of Andela

Harness the Fire

Strike the Spark

Clear the Water

Mysteries by J.M. Poole
The Corgi Case Files Series

18 delightful cozy mystery novels featuring corgi sleuths, Sherlock and Watson

THE HAMMER IS STRONG WITH THIS ONE

Tales of Lentari, Book 8

JEFFREY POOLE

Secret Staircase Books

The Hammer is Strong With This One
Published by Secret Staircase Books, an imprint of
Columbine Publishing Group, LLC
PO Box 416, Angel Fire, NM 87710

Book layout and design by Secret Staircase Books
First Secret Staircase paperback edition: February, 2024

First Secret Staircase e-book edition: February, 2024

* * *

Publisher's Cataloging-in-Publication Data

Poole, Jeffrey
The Hammer is Strong With This One / by Jeffrey Poole.
p. cm.
ISBN 978-1649141675 (paperback)
ISBN 978-1649141682 (e-book)

1. Lentari (Fictitious location)—Fiction. 2. Epic fantasy fiction
3. Dragons and mythical creatures—Fiction. 4. Time travel—Fiction.
I. Title

Tales of Lentari : Book 8.
The Hammer is Strong With This One
Poole, Jeffrey, Tales of Lentari epic fantasy series.

BISAC : FICTION / Fantasy/Epic.

813/.54

For Giliane —

There's never a dull moment, my dear. For that, I am eternally grateful! Don't ever change, babe!

Acknowledgments

I may be responsible for the story, but there are many people who help bring the story to the readers. First and foremost, I always have to thank my wife, Giliane. She continues to be my inspiration and I truly consider myself blessed to have her by my side.

I have to thank the members of my Posse. They are the ones who take time out of their busy schedules to help me polish the story as much as possible. Jason, Wendy, Debbie, and Elizabeth, just to name a few. My mother, Diane, is also still there, as she continues to point out my constant dislike of commas, and how I still have a tendency to make a single sentence as long as a full paragraph. And, to my Secret Staircase Books beta readers: Susan Gross, Sandra Anderson, and Paula Webb. Thank you for helping get these new versions all cleaned up for re-release.

And to you, the reader. Thank you very much for all your support and continuing my series. It means more than you ever know.

Now, let's see what those pesky pirates have been up to!

J.

Table of Contents

Chapter 1 - Mystery Mentor

Quietly, while the rest of his companions argued amongst themselves, a lone figure slipped away into the darkness. Here, many feet below the surface of the ground, in a dark, dank cavern, he crept slowly, choosing his steps with care. Nearly a thousand feet below the surface, the tiniest of noises would sound like a veritable thunderclap. The last thing he wanted to do was to alert any of the men to his absence.

Flinn, captain of the infamous pirate ship *Emberbrand*, grunted with irritation. His men were under the impression he knew where he was going. In truth, he hadn't a clue. He was just as much in the dark—literally—as the rest of them, but he was desperate to keep that bit of information safely under wraps.

He needed advice.

Therefore, he was sneaking away to consult his most prized possession, an item no living man knew he possessed.

This was something so powerful, and so valuable that, should it become known he had it, even his loyal crew would turn on him. In a heartbeat. Without a second's notice.

Farther and farther he slinked, looking for a suitable place to consult his Stone. If his crew ever discovered their captain wanted to talk to an inanimate object, the last thing he'd have to worry about was being ridiculed. Strung up, fed to the fishes, or being hand-delivered to his enemies were only a few of the colorful choices available to a pirate should this particular secret become known.

Flinn reached inside his coat pocket and palmed the object. This talisman, he had learned, was called an Alchos Stone and at one time had belonged to one of the four Ancients, beings who had witnessed the birth of the land. While he didn't yet know which of the Ancients his stone had belonged to, he *did* know that even he, who had possessed the stone for several years now, hadn't come close to realizing its full potential.

The ability to conceal was the first skill he had learned the stone possessed. Simply being in contact with the stone would render him, and anything else he was in physical contact with, invisible. That included not only men and weapons, but vessels. His beloved *Emberbrand*, the terror of the Seven Kingdoms, would disappear from sight should he touch any part of the ship while holding the stone. How else had he been able to avoid the prying eyes of the Lentarians and make his escape?

Captain Flinn frowned. He really hadn't wanted to disclose this special ability, but that damn fire thrower had forced his hand. Even as they had sailed away from their last encounter with the damned Lentarians, concealed even from prying wyverian eyes, his crew had rounded on him and demanded answers. It had taken every ounce of his persuasion to convince the men that the situation was under control and he was simply using a spell cast by a wizard, created at his behest. Thinking quickly, Flinn had thrust his hand into one of his coat pockets and pulled out whatever was there, which was two gold coins, a silver snuff box, and a twisted piece of metal that had broken off his favorite dagger's hilt.

"Do ye see this here?" he said, holding the various items aloft. "Do ye have any idea what they are?"

Several men opened their mouths, ready to answer.

"Of course, ye don't," Flinn hastily continued, before anyone could speak. "They be spells. Spells, I tell ye! And do ye know where I got 'em?"

"You stole them?" one pirate had tentatively asked.

"Of course I stole 'em," Flinn sighed with mock exasperation. "I be a pirate, be I not? Silence yer tongue, Arik. As I was sayin', these spells have been cast by a powerful wizard, so trust me when I be sayin' I have the ability to protect my own crew."

It hadn't been the best explanation nor had it been the most plausible, but at least it had silenced the men. Temporarily. Flinn gave a decisive grunt. If the crew knew the value of what was waiting for them at the end of this journey, he was quite certain he would have a mutiny on his hands.

A drop of liquid fell onto the bridge of his nose. Captain Flinn angrily glanced up. The cavern was so big that he could no longer see the roof. He could see, though, that the cavern's ceiling dipped low in several places. As such, he could see many stone stalactites stretching dozens of feet down from above, appearing like oversized teeth ready to bite down on whomever was foolish enough to pass underneath. Flinn touched the tip of a finger to the liquid and then gingerly put the finger in his mouth.

Water.

Pure water, filtered by hundreds of feet of rock and sediment, dripped throughout the cavern. It had been his bad luck to walk right under a steady stream. Not liking water for anything other than quenching his thirst—when ale was not available, of course—Flinn stepped around the stone formation reaching up from the ground. The stalagmite was nearly two dozen feet tall, and was easily a dozen feet in diameter.

Beyond the stalagmite, out of sight from the path he had been following, Flinn spotted a dark opening. It was the mouth of a small cave. Rejoicing in his good luck, Flinn checked to see if the coast was clear before ducking inside.

Once he was concealed within the tunnel, Flinn sat on the closest rock, reached into his inside pocket, and retrieved the tightly wrapped stone. Only when the layers of fabric had been removed, and the stone was lying, exposed, in his open hand, did Flinn breathe a sigh of relief. Holding the object felt good, natural. Whenever he was in contact with the stone, it seemed all his troubles melted away.

That brought a frown. Staring into the depths of the enormous sapphire, Flinn briefly wondered if the shiny blue jewel might be affecting him in some fashion. Shaking his head, and laughing off his concerns, he sank down to the floor and stared at it.

Waiting.

Within moments, the huge fist-sized sapphire began to glow. The light it emitted was enough to dimly illuminate the small cave. Eagerly leaning forward, Captain Flinn waited as patiently as he could.

"Speak."

The voice was faint and barely audible over the dripping water. He cupped his hand around the stone and held it aloft, as though he had captured the world's most fragile soap bubble. The captain stared into the depths of the glowing jewel and scowled.

"Where are ye leading me? I told ye before that I do not care to be underground, and naturally, that's where ye insisted we need to go. If the dwarves have the blasted hammer, as ye have said they do, will they not eventually bring it to the surface? Why couldn't we get it then? We can wait a week or two. We may be pirates, but we are patient."

"If the events of today remain unchanged," the soft voice intoned, *"then that which you seek will not see the light of day for another three years."*

"Blast. How much longer must we be down here?"

"That is up to you."

"Are we headin' in the right direction? Will ye at least tell me that?"

"Yes."

"Yes? Yes what? Yes, we be headin' in the right direction,

or yes, ye can answer the question? Which is it?"

"*Yes.*"

Captain Flinn took several deep, calming breaths.

"Listen, mate. This whole damn kingdom is no doubt lookin' for us right now. Time be critical. Every last second counts. Now, are we headin' in the right direction?"

"*Yes.*"

Flinn breathed a sigh of relief. "Good. That's good. Will this hammer be easy to acquire?"

"*No.*"

"No? No? Why not?"

"*Those who possess that which you seek are cunning, crafty. This will not be an easy task for one unfamiliar with the terrain.*"

"What's so special about this hammer?"

"*Possession of the hammer is critical for success.*"

"Why?"

"*Possession of the hammer is critical for success.*"

"Ye already said that, mate. I need to know why this hammer be critical. And don't say—"

"*Possession of the hammer is critical for success.*"

"Ye sound like an old parrot I used to have. Fine. How do we retrieve the hammer?"

The stone was silent, content to softly glow in Flinn's outstretched hand. Flinn cursed silently. The stone's silence always meant the same thing: it was up to him to figure it out. There was no point asking it the same question over and over. If it didn't want to answer, then the stone would certainly *not* offer an answer.

Flinn suddenly smiled. A thought had just occurred. This was a subject he really hoped it would be able to answer.

"How do I defeat the Fire Thrower? He and I have jhorun that are equal in strength. How do I defeat him?"

"*Seek ye not the Protector's wrath.*"

"What? Say again?"

"*Seek ye not the Protector's wrath.*"

"Aye, that's what I thought ye said. What does that mean? What protector? Who's the protector?"

The Stone refused to answer.

"Fine. Ye wish to keep yer secrets, then so be it. Tell me

this. How are we supposed to get out of here?"

"None by one, down by two."

"What? Why do ye insist on speaking in riddles? What is that supposed to mean?"

The stone fell silent once more. A few seconds later, the soft blue glow gently faded away, leaving its owner glaring at it. Flinn gave it an angry shake.

"What the ruddy hell is that supposed to mean? Get back here and explain yerself!"

"Captain?" a voice called from the distance. "Captain? Where are you?"

"Blast," he hissed.

Captain Flinn hastily wrapped the stone and thrust it into his coat pocket while rising to his feet. He hurried to the mouth of the cave, eager not to be seen exiting it. However, in his haste, he didn't see a dark figure crouching on the other side of the huge stalagmite which concealed the mouth of the cave. After a few moments, the anonymous eavesdropper fell into step behind the captain, but kept far enough back so that his presence was never known.

"What is it?" Captain Flinn demanded as he rejoined his men. He glanced around the giant cavern and saw all of them lounging on the ground. "What be this? On yer feet! We have much to do!"

"We don't even know where we're going," one of the men whined, as the crew slowly climbed to their feet. "We've been traveling for days now. Can you not give us an idea where we're going?"

"I have already explained this to ye before," Flinn snapped. "We need a very special hammer. It can only be found deep beneath the ground. That's all ye need to know. Shut yer trap, follow my orders, and ye will be jus' fine. Do ye understand?"

There was a chorus of mumbles and grunts.

"And besides," Flinn continued, as he angrily eyed his men, "we only started this blasted journey underground at sunrise. That be less than six hours ago. Stop yer complainin'."

The grumbling of the crew finally tapered off and it became quiet. Too quiet. Flinn looked around the vast cavern and sighed. He singled out his first mate and called him over.

"Yes, Captain?" Rusty, quartermaster and first mate of the *Emberbrand*, said. "What can I do for you?"

"Have the men split up. There must be another set of stairs leading down. We need to find 'em."

"There are more stairs?" Rusty groaned. "Are you sure, Captain?"

"Do ye see this hammer laying around anywhere?" Flinn dryly asked. "Do ye see any dwarves? Nay, this be nothing but a stopping point. The journey continues."

"Very well, Captain. Men, you heard him. Spread out. Search for another way out. And no, Puck, the stairs we just came down on don't qualify. Report to me should any of you find anything. Is that understood?"

"Aye, Q," the men echoed.

"Good. And I told you, don't call me 'Q'. Only the captain can call me that."

"Brown-nose," one of the men muttered.

Flinn noticed the frown on Rusty's face, but cared not. Dealing with the crew was Rusty's responsibility, and therefore, his headache. He had more important things to worry about, like how quickly they could find this damn hammer and return to the blessed open skies of the surface.

"I found something!" one man cried out, from somewhere to the left.

"Who was that?" Flinn asked Rusty in a low voice.

"It sounded like Casimir."

"Where is he? I cannot see a bloomin' thing down here. Where's Mister Alquin? He be the one with the superior eyesight."

"I'm here, Cap'n," Alquin's voice said, from his right.

"Can ye see Casimir?" Flinn asked, as he squinted in the darkened cavern. "It be too dark to see anything."

"I can see well enough," Rusty contradicted.

"Not enough to tell me who spoke," Flinn returned. "Mister Alquin, lead the way."

"Aye, Cap'n."

It still unnerved him, Flinn angrily thought, as he and Rusty fell into step behind Alquin. Things he didn't understand tended to set him on edge. How could it be that anyone besides Alquin could see anything in the faint light down here? This cavern was probably the largest underground cave he had ever stepped foot in, and judging by the grueling trek down—what felt like thousands of stairs—they were nowhere close to the sun. And, unless his nose was telling him lies, there was also water nearby—stream, or a pond, or some body of water. So how could there be any light down here? Granted, it wasn't much, but it did allow them to see that the cavern had stalactites strewn across the ceiling and matching stalagmites dotting the floor. Thankfully, they could easily see their way around them, but more than one of his crew had cracked their heads on low-hanging stalactites when they hadn't been paying attention.

Flinn stepped close to the wall and ran his fingers along the surface. A faint, bioluminescent glow appeared on the tips of his fingers. Flinn studied the substance closely. It felt gritty, as if whatever was growing on the wall was slowly eating into the stone surface.

Flinn slowly scanned the great cavern. Could that be the source of the illumination? Some foreign substance growing on the surface of the rocks? He grunted. He didn't know, and he didn't care.

By the dim light he carefully moved toward Casimir, who was nearly fifty feet away and waving at them. The pirate was standing next to a stone pillar, which he ducked behind, followed closely by Puck and Grenden. Then they heard a great splash, followed almost immediately by another. And then another. It would appear that the source of water was directly behind the stone pillar.

"Where are all the men?" Flinn demanded, as he turned to Alquin. "Yer jhorun provides ye with nocturnal vision. I can smell water, and I heard the splashes. There must be a lake. Find the men. I don't trust this."

"Of course, but I don't…" Alquin trailed off as he squinted his eyes. Then he pivoted in place. "I'll be damned, Captain. Aye, I do see water. You're right. It's just over that ridge. I … I found the men, Captain. It looks like they have found the water, too."

"And the splashes?" Rusty asked. "Did some of our crew fall in?"

Alquin nodded. "Aye. I can see Casimir in the water, along with Puck, and Jino, and Grenden, and…"

"The crew decided to go for a swim," Captain Flinn snapped. "I get it. Who told them they were allowed to shirk their duties? Q, deal with this, or else I will."

"Of course, Captain. Although, may I point out that this might be what the men need? A breather? Perhaps if we let them blow off some steam, they'll be in better moods. None of them, myself included, particularly care for being underground. This may be a blessing in disguise. What do you say? What harm could befall them?"

"What harm?" Flinn snapped. "How about my sword's blade? Is that harm enough for ye?"

"I'm just looking out for the men, Captain. If you want me to pull them back, I will do it."

About ready to give the order, Flinn thought better of it.

"Forget it, Q. Ye could be right. The men might do well to cool off. Let them dally, but not for long. I wish to spend only as much time as needed down here. Be that understood?"

"Completely, Captain. And thank you."

"Whatever. They be yer problem now, not mine."

Rusty pulled his tunic out from his belt and drew it over his head.

"What the blazes are ye doing?" Flinn demanded.

"That water looks too good to pass up, Captain," Rusty explained, as he tossed his tunic to the ground. Then he pulled off his boots. "It's been at least two weeks since my last bath. I think I'll join the men for a swim."

"Ye have twenty minutes, Q," Flinn warned. "No more."

"Understood. Lads, make way! Here I come!"

"Captain!" one of the men called from the surface of the water. "Captain! Will you be joining us?"

Flinn approached the water's edge and surveyed the small lake. In the darkened cavern, he was barely able to make out its dimensions. He'd be able to walk around the entire lake in an hour. While nowhere as grand as the lakes Flinn had witnessed in his many years, it was still a remarkable size for being below the surface of the ground. So, the question was, what was a lake this size doing hiding from the sun?

The sound of splashing water suddenly escalated into shouts and peals of laughter. Flinn glanced over his shoulder in time to see one of the men push himself out of the water and land—unceremoniously—on the back of another, effectively dunking both.

"Blast it all, Puck," Jino exclaimed, the moment he surfaced. "You will pay for that. How dare you dunk me? I—"

Jino was abruptly cut off as another pirate sprang onto his back and pushed him back under. Sputtering, Jino broke the surface, swearing as only a pirate could. Then he was dunked again. And again.

"You lose your advantage in the water, don't you?" Puck mercilessly teased. "Perhaps you've boasted about your physical prowess one too many times?"

"I will get out of here eventually," Jino vowed. "What will you say then, miscreant?"

"I will look you straight in the eyes and say … what's that?"

Jino blinked his eyes a few times and glared at Puck. "What's *what*? Your pathetic attempts at stalling won't stop me from knocking some much-needed sense into you."

Puck shook his head. "No, I'm serious. What's that thing? On the back of your neck? It's blue, slimy, and utterly revolting!"

Fully expecting a ruse, Jino reached behind his head and felt along his neck. His eyes widened as his fingers brushed by a slimy lump at the base of his neck. Then, he felt the tiniest of pricks, as though he had been jabbed by a thorn.

"What is it?" Jino practically bellowed. "Get it off me! Now!"

"I ain't touchin' that thing!" Puck cried, as he scrambled to put distance between them.

Jino suddenly pointed straight at Puck and let out a shout of alarm.

"You've got one on your arm! No, your left arm. It's … er, Puck? Don't panic, but there's two on your left arm and one on your right!"

The playful shouts coming from the water rapidly switched to screams of terror. Nearly a dozen men were now frantically swimming for the shore. The moment they felt solid ground under their feet, the strip-tease began. Tunics were flung to the ground. Undergarments were hastily yanked down. Exclamations of shock and horror echoed raucously throughout the cavern.

"Get it off of me, Cap'n!" Puck whined, as he caught sight of Captain Flinn watching the antics from the shore.

Puck's body must have had at least twenty of the engorged blue slugs on him, with the vast majority stuck to his back. Flinn shook his head, took several paces back, and rested his hand on the hilt of his sword.

"Ye got yerself into that predicament, mate," Flinn began, "and ye can get yerself out of it. Them things look like pech, do they not?"

"I don't care if they are blood suckers or not," Rusty bellowed, as he emerged from the water and conducted his own strip tease. "I don't want 'em anywhere on me! Get them off of me. Somebody? Anybody?"

"Might I suggest ye ask Casimir to lend a hand?" Flinn casually suggested. "Fear be a powerful motivator. Behold. Casimir shed all his new *friends*."

The men descended upon their one companion who could use his jhorun to evoke fear. They stood about, hopping up and down on one foot, while each waited their turn to rid themselves of the blue parasites. Grenden, who was responsible for the medical well-being of the crew, stooped to retrieve one of the blue slugs. Holding it by its tail, Grenden studied the creature as it writhed and twisted in his hand.

"Be that a pech?" Captain Flinn asked, as he approached the *Emberbrand*'s doctor.

"It sure looks like it," the normally composed crewman replied, suppressing a shudder. "Bah. I could never stand these things. These may be blue, but they're just as disgusting as the green pech we have back home."

"Ramifications?" Flinn asked.

"Ramifications?" Grenden repeated, puzzled. "Oh. From the pech? Well, that depends on the total number of worms that attached themselves, Captain. I would think lessened energy, from blood loss, would be most prevalent. We'll have to watch each other very carefully, in case anything else appears."

Flinn grunted once and nodded.

"I can't wait until we can go home," Flinn heard one man say to another. It sounded like Puck. "I don' wanna be underground anymore. I hate it here."

"Do ye think I like this any better than you?" Flinn demanded, growing angry. "We be here for one purpose only, Puck: the hammer. Once we have it, and *only* when we have it, will we return to the surface. Do I make myself clear?"

"Completely, Captain."

"Does anyone else want to lodge a complaint?" the captain asked, raising his voice so that it echoed in the great cavern. After it became clear no one else wished to say anything, Flinn grunted and pointed at the sodden heap of clothes on the shore. "Get dressed. We be leavin' here in five minutes."

"But our clothes are wet!" Puck complained.

"Whose fault is that?" Flinn challenged. He turned an angry eye on Rusty and then stalked away.

The ship's quartermaster hurriedly dressed, groaning when he stopped to wring out his soaked underclothes, cringing when they made contact with his skin. A quick check of his companions indicated they all felt the same.

"I hate it down here," one of the men quietly grumbled.

"Watch your tongue, Jino," Rusty advised. "You don't want the captain overhearing you, do you?"

"I thought we'd be back on the surface by now," the *Emberbrand*'s best fighter complained. "I'd much rather be out under the open sky."

"As we all would," the quartermaster agreed. "The sooner we get our hands on this hammer, the sooner we can leave. Focus on the task at hand, pirate. That's all that matters now."

Jino nodded glumly.

Ten minutes later, the men had joined the captain on

top of the ridge. Flinn was gazing around the cavern with an intense look of concentration. Someone finally nudged Rusty on the shoulder. The quartermaster nodded and took a deep breath.

"Er, Captain? Could I bother you a moment?"

"Ye already are."

"Okay, well, could I bother you again?"

"Blast it to the heavens, just speak yer mind, Q. What is it?"

"What are you looking for, Captain?"

"The way out of here."

There was a collective sigh of relief from the men.

"I be looking for the way *down*, not up," Flinn clarified.

The sighs switched to groans.

"Can I help?" Rusty asked, in a hushed tone.

"What do ye think *none by one, down by two* means?" Flinn asked, curious to hear his quartermaster's answer.

Rusty shrugged and shook his head. "Nothing, Captain. Why do you ask? Where did you hear that?"

"Where I heard it be not important. Look around. What does it mean to ye standing in this accursed cavern?"

Rusty thoughtfully stroked his goatee as he considered.

"Well, if we're to assume you're looking for a way out of this cavern, and that way isn't up, then that would suggest there'd have to be another tunnel somewhere in here that leads down. Maybe two? 'None by one, down by two' might suggest there are more than one tunnel?"

Surprisingly, Flinn grinned and nodded. "My thoughts exactly."

"The tunnel must be hidden, Captain. The door leading down from the surface was a rock. A huge boulder. I'm willing to wager the way out of this cavern is also disguised."

"So, how do we find it?" Alquin asked, overhearing the conversation.

Two more of the men stepped forward. Grenden and Von both looked as though they had something to say. Flinn pointed at Grenden first.

"You. What are yer thoughts?"

"I think our quartermaster is right. Who would've

known the dwarves in this land could make their entrances blend seamlessly into the surroundings? We're looking for a disguised door."

Flinn grunted once and then pointed at Von.

"Even if we were to split up and check different parts of this blasted cave, we could easily spend a year or two looking for this hidden door."

"What are ye suggesting, mate?"

"You knew these Lentarians would steal back the fang," Von began, "so you replaced the one on your belt with a replica. Then you knew which stone held the hidden door back in that valley. We trust you, Captain. We all do. You would never lead us astray."

"Brown-noser," one of the men squeezed in between coughs.

"What's yer point?" Flinn demanded. "What's yer suggestion?"

"You must have an idea what we need to do," Von said.

"Would ye be suggestin' I be withholding information?" Flinn asked. A dangerous glint had appeared in his eye.

"No, Captain," Von began, as he held up his hands in mock surrender. "I'm just sayin' you have some of the best luck I have ever witnessed. I was hopin' you'd give us some suggestions where to start. Maybe close your eyes, spin around a few times, and then point at something. We'll check wherever you end up pointing. What do you think?"

"I think you be crazier than the fire thrower," Flinn muttered.

"It couldn't hurt to try," Rusty suggested. "It'll give us a place to start."

"Yer all nuts," Flinn grumped. "Fine. I'll do it."

The captain closed his eyes, spun in place three times, and then threw out a hand and pointed. The men fell silent as they all squinted in the direction Captain Flinn was pointing.

Flinn slowly opened his eyes. He pointed toward the opposite end of the cavern from where the original tunnel had deposited them. He squinted his own eyes to see if there was anything remarkable in that direction, but unfortunately, his eyes couldn't focus on anything that far away. But, there was someone here who could.

"Mister Alquin. What do ye see in that direction? Anything?"

The men fell silent once more as Alquin stepped up onto an outcropping and peered at the far corner of the cavern. His eyes widened with surprise. As quick as a heartbeat, Flinn appeared by his side.

"What is it? What do ye see?"

"I see the mouths of two tunnels. I cannot believe I didn't see them before."

It was Flinn's turn to stare. Two tunnels? *None by one, down by two.* He had asked how to get out of the cavern. Could that refer to the tunnel that would lead them out of here? Was Grenden right? No exit in the first, but an exit *down* could be found in the second?

It was worth a try.

"Make for the tunnels," Flinn ordered. "Step on it."

"How did you do that?" Rusty whispered in his ear, several minutes later. "I had no idea that Von's suggestion would work so well."

"I have no idea, Q," the captain admitted. "However, I will not argue the point. It be the first lead we have since we got in this wretched place."

"Do you think we'll find a way out?" Rusty quietly asked.

Flinn shrugged. "We shall see."

Nearly thirty minutes later, they reached the other side of the cavern. Alquin peered anxiously into the mouth of the first tunnel.

"Tell me what ye see," Flinn demanded. "Be there a way out? Be there stairs?"

"Nothing, Captain," Alquin reported. "This tunnel dead-ends."

"Fine. We check the other. Let's move."

Five minutes later, Alquin had reported that this one ended abruptly, too. Flinn cursed to himself. He was so certain that this was going to work!

"Captain!"

The voice was faint, as though it was calling to him from far away.

"Aye! Who is this? Who speaks?"

"It's Alquin, Captain," Rusty announced. "He's still in the second tunnel."

...*down by two*...

"Back to the second tunnel," Flinn ordered. "Me thinks it deserves a second look."

Flinn and Rusty pushed past the curious men and headed down the short, incomplete tunnel. Alquin was staring at a spot on the heavily scarred wall, holding a lit torch.

"Where did he get a torch?" Flinn quietly asked Rusty. "I didn't see any before."

"Perhaps he found it? I don't know, Captain. All the men carry tinder boxes, so it wouldn't be impossible to light a torch, provided one was found. Alquin, what do you have? What did you find?"

Alquin pointed at a nondescript section of wall, at his own eye-level. "Do you see this?"

Flinn scowled. "It be rock, mate. This whole damn area be nothing but solid rock. What about it?"

"This bit of rock turns, Captain!"

That got everyone's attention. Intrigued, Captain Flinn leaned close. He motioned for Alquin to show him. In response, Alquin hooked three of his fingers into three small indentations in the rock surface, then rotated his hand clockwise.

A small section of the rock suddenly spun in place. Encouraged, Alquin spun the rock dial a few more degrees. Suddenly, they heard loud clicks and clacks, as though machinery which hadn't been used in years had suddenly been pressed into service.

The heavily scarred and chipped tunnel wall retracted smoothly into the surrounding wall, revealing a steep stone staircase cut out of solid rock, descending into the depths of the earth.

Flinn was exuberant. However, the men all collectively groaned.

The captain grinned and slapped a hand on Alquin's back.

"Well done, Mister Alquin. All right, lads, let's get to it. Those stairs aren't gonna carry us down."

Chapter 2 — Pirate Pursuit

They've got to be here somewhere. It's not as though they could disappear right from under our noses. They're hiding. They've got to be. I just hope they're not using their Alchos Stone to do it. We'll never find them if they are."

"We'll find them," Sarah promised. "They're going to turn up somewhere. It's just a matter of time."

Steve scowled as he paced. After a few moments, he looked up at the open blue sky. He could really use a dragon right about now.

"Pryllan? I don't suppose you're in the area, are you?"

Silence.

"You're actually speaking to her?" Sarah asked. "Shouldn't you be, you know, doing your mind meld thing instead?"

"Mind meld? That's *Star Trek*, dear. I think you mean telepathy."

Sarah rounded on Steve and put her hands on her hips.

"Isn't a mind meld where one of those Spock aliens puts his hand on another person and then they share their thoughts? Is that, or is that not, what you're doing with Pryllan?"

"Oh, okay. When you say it like that, then yeah. That's kinda like what we're doing."

"Look at that. The King of Nerds has just been proven wrong."

Steve laughed as he looked admiringly at his wife. "And how does that make you feel, dear?"

"I don't wanna talk about it."

"Mm-hmm. I'm so proud of you."

"Yeah, that's peachy," Sarah grumped.

Pryllan? Can you hear me?

Of course. I heard you the first time.

Why didn't you say something?

Because our conversation should not be overheard by other ears.

Oh. What's up? What's the problem? The only person with me right now is Sarah. I don't keep any secrets from her.

Ah. I didn't know who was within earshot.

Pryllan, what's going on? You're getting me a little concerned now.

I am just leaving my nest, on my way to help you. I was concerned about Pylaria. I do not wish it known that the Dragon Lord and his mate have both left their nest at the same time.

Wait. What about Pylaria? I know you're not thinking she's old enough to fend for herself.

Do not worry about Pylaria. Kahvel has assigned a protector for her.

A dragon nanny? How cool! Who did he pick?

Nanny? I am unfamiliar with that word.

Umm, it means someone who helps with a youngster.

Ah. Very well. I accept your definition. Aye, Kahvel acquired a 'nanny' for Pylaria. You have met them before, I recall.

Yamira and Lamira, the female.

Impressive. How'd you manage that?

They volunteered. I will be arriving at the castle soon. Will you be ready?

Kahvel wishes these human pirates to be found

immediately.

I couldn't agree more, my friend. Okay. Sarah will head inside the castle to brief Mikal. I'll be waiting at the dragon cave.

Excellent!

* * *

Ten minutes later, they were airborne. Castle R'Tal had long disappeared from sight, as had the coastline. Dragon and rider were now well out to sea, soaring over open water as low as comfortably possible. The last thing either of them wanted was another close encounter with one of the gigantic oskorlisk.

"Where would you like to focus our search?" Pryllan asked as she banked south, toward the distant Selekai Mountains. "This body of water is many leagues in size. We could search for hours and find no trace of the human bandits or their vessel."

"I honestly don't think they'd venture too far from the coast," Steve answered, as he turned to look at the thin distant line which represented land to the west. "They're here for a reason. They may have the fang, but I'm pretty sure that's not the only thing they want. No, they're out there. Somewhere."

"And if they are using the Alchos Stone to conceal themselves?" Pryllan inquired.

Dragon and rider gasped with alarm as a sudden gust of wind appeared out of nowhere and pushed down at them with frightening speed. Pryllan was forced to dip her wings and fly even closer to the water than she wanted. Steve ignited his hands and prepared for the worst.

The worst never came.

"I don't see him," Steve said, as he hurried from one side of Pryllan's body to the other. "What about you? Can you spot him?"

"I believe it was just an errant gust of wind," Pryllan returned. "I do not believe the human windbag was responsible."

"Human windbag," Steve chortled. "I love it."

"Is that not what he is?" Pryllan asked, confused. "I heard

you describe him in this manner."

"Oh, no. You're totally right. *Pleasepleaseplease* keep referring to him in this manner. It makes me smile every time."

"As you wish."

"How's Pylaria doing? I'll bet she's growing like a weed, isn't she?"

"I'm not familiar…"

"She's growing very fast," Steve quickly interrupted.

"Aye. Kahvel noted that she has already tripled her birth weight."

"How quickly does a dragon reach their full adult size?" Steve asked.

Pryllan approximated a shrug. "It can vary. Pravara attained her adult size by her second year. I have heard it can happen in as little as one, but it is not common. Pylaria is…"

An unfamiliar voice interrupted, asking Pryllan's location.

Both Steve and Pryllan stiffened with surprise. Another dragon had joined the search? Was this Kahvel's doing?

"It's no one you know," Pryllan assured him. "Frankly, I am astonished that he has volunteered."

"Who is it?" Steve wanted to know.

"Caius. He's probably one of the oldest, and fiercest, wyverian warriors we have. He has seen more battles than many of us combined."

"A dragon bad-ass. Nice."

I'm pleased to meet you, Caius.

Silence.

"I should also mention Caius is not overly fond of humans," Pryllan added.

"What? Seriously? Aren't we all allies?"

"Caius tolerates humans because he serves the Dragon Lord, and Kahvel has obviously ordered him to lend us his aid."

"So, is he searching for the pirates, too?"

"Aye. I just relayed to him the area we have searched. He is headed south, and will search the southern shores of the great sea."

"Copy that. So, maybe we should head to…"

Both Pryllan and Steve heard the voice of yet another dragon.

Samara?

"Samara?" Steve whispered.

Pryllan nodded. "Aye. He was Rhamalli's mentor. For the second time, I find myself surprised. Samara is a valued member of our community and hasn't participated in an extracurricular activity for several years."

"Then why has he started now? For that matter, why has Caius?"

"I'm not sure," Pryllan admitted. "I can only assume Kahvel has asked for volunteers to come to our aid."

Of course, I have, my love, Kahvel's powerful thought came. *You are flying over a dangerous area. I want Wyverian assistance nearby.*

I am not alone. Steve is here. He will not allow me to come to any harm.

Steve, you will watch over Pryllan?

You can count on it, buddy.

Good. You two should know that I have dispatched two dozen dragons to come to your aid.

Steve felt the shock ripple through his wyverian friend. "I take it that's a good thing?" he quietly asked Pryllan.

The huge green dragon could only nod.

We appreciate the help, Kahvel. We should easily be able to keep an eye on the eastern coast with that many dragons in the air.

Pryllan. Steve. It seems you will have even more assistance with your search.

Intrigued, Steve leaned forward. *Oh? Who?*

The Shealk. Lord Phaedren has informed me his shealk are searching the West Coast. Nice.

I wonder why all of a sudden Lord Phaedren was so eager to help search.

Lord Phaedren is familiar with the Alchos Stones. His shealk will not underestimate the power of these stones.

Got it. Be sure to thank them for us, okay?

I will.

"This is turning into one mother of a manhunt," Steve murmured, once Kahvel's presence faded from his mind. "It's almost as if the whole damn kingdom is on high alert. I can't even begin to imagine what will happen if Flinn manages to get his hands on that power hammer first. We've *got* to find him before that happens."

"What good will it be to him?" Pryllan asked, as she dipped her right wing to turn east. "I was under the impression only certain dwarves can wield that hammer."

Steve nodded. "That's right. I didn't even think about that. Unless Captain Windbag has a Narian dwarf on his crew, I can't imagine what he's going to do with that hammer. It must weigh over a hundred pounds. Hey, what do you know about that hammer?"

"What little information we have was gleaned from Rhamalli, the wyverian who accompanied the dwarf search party during their quest to find Nar. He has witnessed the hammer in action. This hammer, it would seem, has the power of a hundred hammers, or more. Breslin, the current owner of the hammer, has used it effortlessly, without tiring. That has to be significant, don't you think?"

Steve shrugged. "It still doesn't explain how Flinn is going to make off with it, or how he plans on using it once he has it. Maybe he wants the spiraled ruby?"

"Perhaps. Maybe … Steve, where are you now?"

"Hmm? What kind of question is that? I'm on your back, just ahead of the junction of your wings. Why do you ask?"

"Because if you're just ahead of my wings, then who—or what—is near the base of my tail? I can feel another presence."

"What?"

Steve whirled around and ignited his hands, expecting the worst. What he found had him snorting with laughter. Straight ahead of him, perched precariously on Pryllan's flank, and with both wings extended, was an adult griffin. It spotted his flaming hands and had a look of alarm on its avian head. The wings were extended and it looked as though it were ready to jump off at a moment's notice.

"Who are you?" Steve demanded. "What are you doing here?"

The griffin nodded. "Fire Thrower. You are known to

me, as is your wyverian companion, Pryllan. I am Auberon."

"Auberon," Steve acknowledged. "It's nice to meet you. Umm, I have to ask, why are you on Pryllan's rump?"

"I was sent by my Prime. We offer our assistance."

"Your Prime? Would Pheris happen to be a member of your flock?"

Auberon nodded. "Aye. Pheris is one of our newly appointed Elders. The Prime learned of your desire to seek out a renegade band of humans, and he volunteered our flock."

Steve cringed. "Oh, sorry. I didn't mean to draft you guys into service."

"Fear not, Fire Thrower. What can you tell me about these humans we seek? How many are there?"

"Uh, there are probably two dozen pirates, although I don't think there'd be that many on land. They're looking to steal something from the dwarves." Steve went on to explain about the hammer and the lost city of Nar.

"Logic would suggest they would keep their excursion small," Pryllan added.

Nice. I hadn't considered that.

The griffin is an ally. I sense no malice.

"So," Steve continued, "I would think we'd be looking for no more than a dozen pirates, heading north to the valley of the dragons. Four dwarf clans call the Bohanis home. There will be doors leading underground."

"And how do you know they aren't traveling south?" Pryllan asked. "Granted, we know the location of the hammer, but how would they know this?"

"All I have to do is reference your nest. How did Flinn know how to find it or the fact you had the fang? I'm telling you, they have outside help. Someone is giving them instructions on where certain things can be found."

"Your assumption is that, based on your observations, they will know how to locate a dwarf door?" Pryllan asked.

"Yes."

"What if they've already located one of the dwarf doors?" the griffin asked, ruffling its feathers. "If so, then all this searching will be for naught."

"I'm willing to bet the use of a dwarf door by a group of humans would not go unnoticed," Steve said.

"If you find anything, look for the nearest dragon and ask them to relay a message to us."

"The dragons can relay messages without being in contact with one another?" the griffin asked, amazed. "If a dragon can initiate contact with another dragon, without being in speaking range, then could you not ask if anyone has witnessed a human using a dwarf door in the past day or so? As you said, there should be wyverian eyes watching that valley at all times."

"Son of a biscuit eater," Steve swore. "I should've thought of that. Pryllan? Can you…"

"I've already relayed the question," Pryllan softly told them. She gently banked right in order to follow the Zylan River west, toward the opposite side of the kingdom. "I am awaiting a reply."

"In the meantime, I will begin our search. Farewell. May the winds of fortune never diminish." Auberon leapt lightly off of Pryllan's back and was gone.

Bemused, Steve sat back on his makeshift seat and chuckled. With two dozen dragons, the seafaring shealk, and a large flock of griffins searching for Flinn and his crew, they should have these pirates located before the end of the day.

Pryllan's body suddenly tensed. Steve sat forward but couldn't see anything amiss.

"Pryllan? Is everything all right?"

"I … now who is on my back besides you?"

"What? Is it Auberon again?"

Steve started turning in his seat when a voice surprised him.

"Who's Auberon?"

Gareth, acolyte wizard extraordinaire, was sitting nonchalantly near Pryllan's tail. Gareth was sixteen years old, lived in Verdayn, and was quite possibly the strongest wizard Steve had ever encountered, save Balthor the shealk wizard, Gareth's father. The young wizard nodded at Steve and eyed the passing ground far below.

"Hey there, Gareth. That was a helluva entrance. How'd

you get up here?"

"Well, it was pretty easy," Gareth began. "You see, I had to write a spell which could not only pinpoint the exact location of…"

"That's okay," Steve interrupted. "I take it you have some news, otherwise you wouldn't have popped up on the backside of a dragon."

Gareth grinned. "You bet I do. I found your pirate ship."

"What?" Steve demanded.

"What?" Pryllan echoed.

What? Kahvel mentally said, all at the same time.

"You all seem so surprised. It wasn't that difficult. I just had to … you probably don't care about which spell I used, do you?"

It was Steve's turn to grin, "No, not really. The only thing that's important is that you found them. "Nicely done!"

I agree.

Kahvel, is that you?

Aye. Proceed.

"Gareth, where'd you find it? Was the captain on board?"

"I didn't see the captain. I did see some crew on board, and they seemed unaware of my presence. I believe that they don't know I have figured out how to counteract the jhorun that's providing their camouflage protection."

"Where were they? Are they on the move or has the ship been moored?"

"They're tucked away in an inlet just north of the castle. It's perhaps less than two miles from Castle R'Tal."

"Those sneaky devils," Steve groaned. "They must know we're searching for them. What better place to hide the ship than right under our noses?"

Do we attack?

No. You know what? I've got a better idea.

And that is?

We do nothing.

"Why are you making that face?" Gareth inquired. He turned to Pryllan and pointed at Steve. "You saw it, right? His eyes were closed and his lips were moving, as though he was talking to someone."

"He *was* talking to someone," Pryllan clarified. "He's talking to my mate."

Gareth stammered, "The Dragon Lord? He's not still mad at me, is he?"

"Why would you say that, young wizard? Have you done something which would raise the ire of the Dragon Lord?"

"No!" Gareth exclaimed, as he held up both hands in a universally recognized symbol of surrender. "Of course not! It's just that … well … I know he doesn't like me that much."

"Continue to render assistance like you have been doing and his anger will pass over time."

"So, what do you think we should do?" Gareth asked.

"What does Mikal think we should do?" Steve countered. "After all, he *is* the king."

"I, er, haven't told him yet."

Steve's eyebrows shot up. "You haven't? How long ago did you find the ship?"

Gareth shrugged. "About ten minutes ago."

"And you told us first? Why?"

"I don't know. You were the first person I thought I should inform."

"Okay, pal, I'm flattered. However, this is something that needs to be told to the king."

"Very well." Gareth started to draw imaginary symbols in the air.

Steve held up a hand. "Wait a sec. Gareth, what are you going to tell Mikal?"

Gareth's brow furrowed. "That we found the ship. Is that not what you want me to tell him?"

"No, you're right. You need to tell him. However, I'd also suggest you tell him to not do anything."

An excellent plan—illusion. Inaction will ascertain the vessel remains where it is, where we can silently observe.

"Exactly, Kahvel. Exactly."

"Exactly what?" Gareth wanted to know. "What did he say?"

"The Dragon Lord agreed with my suggestion to not do anything. If we let on that we know where the pirate ship is, they'll probably move it."

"And then we'll have to conduct the search all over again," Pryllan added.

Steve nodded. "That's right. So, if we do nothing, then the ship stays put, and we can keep an eye on it."

Gareth was nodding. "I see your point. I'll inform Mikal. Oh, if I happen to see the captain on the ship, I'll be sure to let you know."

"How was it you were able to teleport onto a moving dragon's back?" Steve asked. "I've been wanting to know ever since you got here."

Gareth smiled cryptically at him, drew a few imaginary symbols in the air, and vanished.

"I'm glad he's on our side," Steve mumbled.

Pryllan grunted once. "Agreed."

Agreed.

"Yep. Pryllan, how long does it take to get an answer from the Collective? Does this mean that no one saw a human using a dwarf door in the valley?"

"I have not yet received a response," Pryllan admitted.

You asked for information from the Collective and have not had a response? One moment, I will deal with this.

Almost immediately, answers to her question began flooding the Collective. Sadly, the answer was 'yes'. Steve felt Pryllan's dismay.

"I take it the answer was an affirmative. Damn it. Well, do we know which door was used?"

"Aye. It's the same door you used during your first adventure to Lentari. A small band of humans found and used the door a few hours ago. From what I've been told, they knew precisely where and how to open the door."

"How the hell is that even possible?" Steve groaned. "Someone has *got* to be helping them, but who?"

Pryllan gently told him, "We have bigger issues to consider. Beloved, are you still monitoring?"

I am.

"I believe you may *now* call off the search. Please let all participating species know that the renegade humans have been located."

I will. I will also keep my brothers observing from afar.

"I would keep your dragons patrolling the valley, but out of sight. Those pirates will have to return Topside sooner or later."

Valid point.

"Do dragons have nocturnal vision?"

Aye.

"Perfect."

Warn our earthen brethren—the human windbag is formidable. The dwarves will be no match for him.

"That's a good idea. And, just let me say for the record that I love it when Pryllan and Pravara call Captain Flinn 'windbag'. But when you do it? Priceless. Pryllan? Take me back to the castle. I need Sarah. We need to get a message to Borahgg, fast."

"Will Sarah be able to deliver a message to the dwarves in time?" Pryllan asked as she banked sharply to the right, leveled off, and increased her velocity.

Steve nodded. "Yeah, she can, but I don't think we'll need to use her jhorun this time. I remember hearing somewhere that Maelnar created a new portal last year and connected it to the castle. We can be there in no time flat *and* spare Sarah's jhorun. Something tells me we're gonna need every drop of power we can get."

Chapter 3 — Calm Before the Storm

Captain Flinn looked down at the bustling dwarf city from his perch. They had just emerged from the tunnel. In complete silence, Flinn lay on his stomach, with his spy glass in his hand.

It seemed almost a shame, the captain thought. Look at them. So peaceful, so ... so ... normal. They couldn't possibly know what they possessed. Well, what they didn't know couldn't hurt them. It'd be his extreme pleasure to relieve them of their unknown treasure.

"What's the plan, Cap'n?" Puck whispered, as the pirates watched the bustling activity in the city below them.

"This be not what I expected to find down here," Captain Flinn murmured. "Maybe a few dwellings, perhaps a network o' caves, but this? This be just as large as Aarszan!"

Casimir nervously cleared his throat. "So, you're saying that you want to go back, Captain? Well, that'd be okay by us.

We just have to…"

"There be no going back," Flinn flatly declared. "Not without that hammer. For someone capable of exuding fear to others, you seem to be full o' it, mate."

"Stop your whining, Casimir," Rusty added, giving a mighty sigh. "Think about it, man. It took us three long hours to get here from the big cavern. That's three hours going down, which means we'd have to climb upstairs for a solid three hours to go back. Are you sure you really want to do that?"

"But how are we expected to find anything in that?" one of the men whined.

Flinn growled. Damned if it didn't sound like Puck again. That crewman needed a serious attitude adjustment.

"You don't think we came all this way without having a plan, do you?" The quartermaster eyed his captain and lowered his voice even further. "You do, don't you? Captain, you have a plan to get this hammer you want so badly?"

Flinn was silent, and everyone else fell silent, too.

What the captain had been about to admit was that he wasn't too sure how they were going to locate the hammer. What he really needed to do was consult a certain item, however that was out of the question since he didn't have a secluded place to unwrap the stone without revealing its presence.

"I do, indeed, Q. Behold."

Flinn reached inside his coat pocket and withdrew the small velvet pouch once more. Opening it, he drew out a handful of items—spells purchased from a spellcaster back in the port city of Aarszan—for way more gold than he cared to admit. He placed them on the ground before his crew and carefully selected one in the shape of a shield. Muttering the incantation which he knew would activate the spell, he held his breath and remained utterly still.

"Is somethin' suppos'd to be happenin', Cap'n?" one of the men asked. "Maybe that spell will … Cap'n? Hey, Q! Where'd the Cap'n go?"

Flinn smiled. The spell worked!

"Captain?" Rusty called out, as loudly as he dared. "This

isn't the best time for you to disappear. Where are you?"

"I haven't moved, idiots," Captain Flinn grumbled.

As Flinn had predicted, the men were properly spooked.

"The captain is invisible?" Flinn heard Grenden ask. "That's impossible!"

"Not for a spellcaster," Flinn argued. "Now still yer tongues. Nobody move. I'm heading toward Q."

Suddenly, Rusty vanished, drawing gasps of alarm from the crew. Hushed conversations erupted, but were abruptly cut off as one of the men suddenly keeled over in pain.

"I said, shut yer damn traps before I shut 'em for ye!" the captain's voice snapped.

"I be testing the limits of this spell, lads. I think I have it now. If ye be in physical contact with me, then ye will share the benefits of this concealment spell. That's how we avoid detection by the dwarves. The rest of you men, stand fast. I will be touching each of ye momentarily."

Several of the men snickered. Rusty suddenly reappeared, standing directly before Casimir and Puck.

"Moving around will be difficult," Rusty cautioned.

"How so?" Flinn's voice demanded.

"We can't see our own feet," Rusty pointed out. "Have you ever tried to walk around when you can't see where you're going?"

"Blast," Flinn's voice came out of thin air. "An excellent point, Q. Men, be prepared. If we work together, we can get this done. Now, everyone join hands."

Several men began grumbling.

"Link up," Rusty ordered. "Join hands or you'll be left behind."

The men reluctantly grasped hands. Rusty approached Grenden and took his open hand. Moments later, he felt Captain Flinn grab his.

Just like that, all the men were invisible. Flinn checked the tunnel landing and grunted appreciatively. There were no signs of him or his crew. Stepping carefully over a strange blue disk embedded within the rock floor, Flinn started walking down the slope, toward the city.

"Be silent!" Flinn hissed. "If these dwarves hear voices

coming out of thin air, they'll know something is amiss. Our mission's success be based on secrecy. Now, from here on out, I will do the guiding and the talking."

Flinn heard a chorus of soft 'ayes' coming from behind. Nodding, Flinn moved out again, and the men moved along, somewhat clumsily.

Blast. He hadn't figured moving while concealed to be an issue, but Rusty was right. This wasn't going to be easy. The slightest hiccup could easily reveal their presence in the city. Progress, as much as he didn't want to admit it, would be slow.

Directly ahead, he could see a cavern so immense that it made the one they had come from pale in comparison.

Emerging into the huge cavern, Flinn could now see the overall layout of the city. Set in a perfect circle, the dwarf city of Borahgg was comprised mostly of small rectangular buildings with thatched roofs. Each building looked as though the tiniest of gusts could knock it over and each, he also noted, had at least three chimneys.

Flinn grunted. The only thing he cared about was which of these infernal buildings held his prize. There, near the middle of the city, the buildings were larger, and several had circular domes for roofs. Perhaps that would be where they could find the hammer?

A clamor sounded from behind them. A group of dwarves had emerged from the tunnel and were chatting animatedly amongst themselves as they made their way down the slope toward the city. Laughing and joking, the group of four dwarves approached his own little group, and if he didn't do something quick, they would be discovered.

"Against the wall," Flinn quickly ordered. "And be silent, no matter what happens."

The dwarves appeared outfitted with tools and implements, as he had expected. Each dwarf had an axe strapped to their back and each, he also noted, wore crisscrossing straps across their chest. Flinn squinted at the straps. What did they contain? Knives? Gear?

The dwarves passed them by, all without suspecting a thing. They stepped over another of the bright blue disks that had been set into the floor and moved off. Then, and only then, did Flinn breathe a sigh of relief. Perhaps, just perhaps, they might be able to pull this off after all.

CRACK!

Startled, Flinn muffled a curse and gave a quick glance behind him. Jino, his best fighter, and admittedly, not the wisest griffin in the flock, was now visible, picking the blue disk off the ground. Flinn growled a curse. Why would a shining blue disk be capable of producing a sound that could be heard across the cavern?

"Blast it to hell, Jino! What the blazes are ye doing'? I said no treasure until we get what we came for. Did ye not understand me the first time?"

His strongest fighter looked longingly down at the blue disk, shrugged, and then flung the object back toward the mouth of the tunnel. A second, louder clang erupted the instant the disk touched the ground. Captain Flinn cursed with disgust.

At once, a clamor erupted from the city. Hundreds of footsteps were headed their way. Dwarves swarmed out of their houses. All of them, Flinn noted with dismay, appeared armed and ready for combat, and they were headed straight toward their concealed location.

"Jino, I'll skin ye alive for this! Whoever was holding onto Jino, take hold again. Hurry!"

"We need to move, Captain!" Rusty anxiously whispered, as Jino vanished from sight. "Right now!"

Flinn thrust his free hand inside his jacket and contemplated wrapping it around the huge sapphire he carried with him. But, before he made physical contact with the stone, his hand paused. Flinn scowled. As dire as the predicament was, he still was unwilling to reveal the existence of the Alchos Stone to anyone, including his crew.

Thinking quickly, Flinn glanced up and noticed hundreds of stalactites hanging precariously from the ceiling far above. He chose a stone spike that looked precarious and blasted a jet of super-condensed air at it. The impact thundered noisily above their heads. Flinn hit the stalactite again, as hard as his jhorun could.

The stalactite tilted to its left, cracking and splintering, trembled for a moment, then dropped straight down. There was a collective gasp of relief as the stone icicle narrowly missed them.

"Who is it?" Flinn heard a gruff voice demand. "Who struck the signal stone?"

"I don't know," another voice said. "Someone must have, though. The signal stone was activated. It wouldn't have gone off by itself."

Three dwarf soldiers, replete in dark leather armor, rounded the bend first. They saw the fallen stalactite and came to a stop. Several necks craned up as they peered at the cavern roof high above their heads.

"Now how do you suppose that happened?" one of the dwarf soldiers asked, scratching his head. "Stalactites don't simply fall from the roof like that."

Another two dozen soldiers appeared, fully armed, and walking in perfect lines. They came to a halt within inches of the disguised pirates. The leader of the group, wearing armor consisting of a mix of silver and gold, paused at the mouth of the cave and swept a few broken rocks out of the way. He picked up the blue disk-shaped stone and tilted his head to look up at the ceiling, more than a hundred feet above their heads.

"False alarm," the dwarf finally decided. He turned and handed the disk to a subordinate. "See to it that it's properly replaced. And do a stability check on the cavern roof. If any others are loose, knock them down."

The second dwarf nodded and the group of dwarves began to disperse. Flinn waited an additional ten minutes before he allowed himself to take a breath of relief.

"That was close, Captain," Rusty whispered. "Did you see how fast those small people arrived?"

"They're dwarves, Q. And aye, they clearly know what they're doing. We had better not be detected. Pass word down the line. If Jino so much as *thinks* about stealing something that would give us away, tell him it'll be my pleasure to lop his hand off at the wrist."

"Understood, Captain."

"Did ye hear me, Jino?" Flinn asked, raising his voice just enough to be heard.

"Aye, Captain."

"I mean it, mate. Keep that free hand of yers in yer pocket. Be that understood?"

He heard Jino groan. "Aye. No taking anything. Got it."

The last of the dwarf soldiers was just disappearing around the base of the hill. Flinn tugged on Q's hand, indicating he wished to follow.

Flinn increased the pace again, anxious to not lose sight of the soldiers. Armed dwarves meant more than likely those soldiers were going to report back to someone in charge. The odds were in his favor that dwarf might have the hammer or know its whereabouts. Either way, he had no desire to wander aimlessly around the streets of this accursed city any longer than he had to.

"It'd be easier if the Strathos would just create another portal that'd link to Foronlir."

Flinn drew to an immediate stop. Unfortunately, no one could see him, so this caused a comical pileup as each pirate ran into the next. Rusty smacked into Flinn's back so hard that he pushed the captain a few steps forward.

"Be silent!" Flinn hissed. "Listen!"

"I heard that he is," a second dwarf's voice stated. "I heard Maelnar is planning on interconnecting all the dwarf clans together via portal."

"You heard nothing of the sort," the first voice sneered. "Why would we want to link Borahgg to one of the Kla Snakkoth's cities? Or to the Kla Luthur? It's a bad idea. We have a hard enough time seeing to the organizational needs of our own two cities. The last thing we need to worry about is another clan's."

"It's not your decision to make," the second voice snapped. "We are dwarves. We stick together, regardless of which clan we call home."

"Pah."

"I heard," a third voice chimed in, "that our great sister city wasn't supposed to exist at all!"

"You and I both know those are nothing but rumors," the

first dwarf angrily announced. "You do not possibly believe that, in another time, we of the Kla Guur were all living in just one city, do you? There aren't enough resources. No, the absence of Foronlir, in an alleged alternate timeline, is just an old wizard's tale. Besides, do you know where that rumor originated? With the humans. That alone should tell you all you need to know."

"But I heard…"

"Enough of this matter, Kurke. They are stories only. Treat them as such."

"Did you hear that, Captain?" Rusty quietly whispered. "There's another…"

"Will ye shut up?" Flinn angrily snapped.

The dwarf at the rear, Kurke, hesitated and looked back, directly where the pirates were concealed, and tugged on his beard. After a few moments, the dwarf shook his head and hurried to catch up with his fellow guards.

"Did ye see how close that was?" Flinn growled. "The only way we will be successful in getting that hammer is if ye all pay attention and follow orders. Be that understood? So, ye have questions do ye? Well, belay them for now. We have more important matters to attend to."

For the next hour, the pirates followed the group of dwarves, believing them to be returning to an official locale, like a barracks, or maybe a governmental office. Unfortunately for them, they quickly learned that the only thing they were doing was following a group of dwarves on patrol. They marched past vendors, street after street of foundries, and then—surprisingly—marched past the shores of a great dark lake where not a single sailing vessel could be seen. In fact, Flinn was shocked to learn that each dwarf seemed to hate the water with a passion, and steered clear of the shore as much as possible.

Finally, as they began their second pass of the area where vendors held sway, Flinn pulled his group to a stop. Only when the patrol had disappeared from sight, and after he and his crew had ducked into a narrow alley, did he relinquish his hold of Rusty. The rest of his crew appeared instantly, looking very much like a group of school children who had been told to hold hands so they wouldn't become lost.

"I did not say any of ye could speak!" Flinn hissed out. "Be silent! And do not move, 'cause we will be concealing ourselves again as soon as we figure out where we're going."

"I don' wanna follow them dwarves no more," Puck whined. "They were jus' leadin' us in circles, Cap'n!"

"Do ye not think I figured that out?" Flinn angrily retorted. "We just wasted an hour of our time followin' them little soldiers around. We could've been…"

"Dwarves," Rusty corrected.

The interruption drew Flinn up to his full height. He glared at his quartermaster and scowled. "What was that, mate?"

"Umm, er, you called them little soldiers. They're dwarves. I just thought you might want to know."

"Do ye think I care what them people call themselves?"

Rusty shrugged. "It's not important, Captain. You were saying?"

"Aye, I was saying. If ye don' let me finish what I was sayin', then I will be personally cuttin' out yer tongue. Be that understood?"

Flinn scowled again as he noticed his first in command had essentially shrugged off his threat. One thing a pirate captain could never do, Flinn knew, was to appear too soft. The men needed to fear him, and fear him they would.

Making a mental note to come up with harsher punishments in the future, Flinn tiptoed to the end of the alley and knelt low. His men followed closely. After a few moments of silence, a commotion appeared out on the street, which caused Flinn to curse with disgust and hastily grasp the activated concealment spell once more. He held out his left arm just as his right closed around the tiny shield. In a split second, the alley appeared as empty as it had been prior to the pirates' arrival.

A group of twenty underlings appeared, attended closely by two adults. A third of the youngsters were chatting merrily away, while another third were singing some type of song, which, to Flinn's ears, seemed to repeat itself over and over. The remaining six or seven children elected to walk in silence, with their heads down low.

"This is going to be so exciting," one of the adult dwarves exclaimed. Flinn blinked a few times as he stared at the speaker. The adult looked like a male, but the voice that had come out was undoubtedly female. What trickery was this? What kind of lives did these small people live under the ground?

"It's just a tool," one underling sighed. "If I wanted to see another tool, then I'd ask my father, who must have nearly a half dozen."

"That's nothing," another child exclaimed. "My father has a foundry which must have nearly a dozen tools, all of which serve a different purpose. Top that!"

"Now, now," the adult was saying, in the comically high-pitched voice that belied his appearance. "There's no point in arguing. Nowhere is it said that each family should have more tools than the next."

"I'm sure mine has the most of all," a third child haughtily added. "My father has two anvils in his workshop. Two! Can anyone beat that? No? That's what I thought."

Flinn suddenly felt a presence directly behind him and then heard a soft whisper in his ear. "Let us be off, Captain. They're nothing but children. We need to find this hammer."

"Be silent! There's something about ... Shut up and listen!"

"Anyone?" the second adult was saying. "No one has seen the hammer before? Does anyone know what significance this hammer holds?" This voice also sounded like a female, even though the voice didn't match the appearance. What was with the adults around here?

"They're women," Flinn breathed, as he finally deciphered the mystery of the voices. "Dwarf women must have beards, too!"

"Eww!"

"Shut yer mouth, Casimir. I've seen yer wife. Ye have no grounds to complain."

"He's right," the doctor, Grenden, added. "I've heard about..."

The unmistakable sound of steel being drawn immediately

silenced all conversations. After a few moments, the sword was returned to its scabbard.

"But it's so far away!" a small voice whined. "Why can't we just wait until it comes to Borahgg?"

"Sure sounds like Puck is out there with those youngsters," someone mumbled, eliciting snickers from the rest of the men.

Flinn also fought the urge to laugh, so he let that one act of defiance slide.

"The Narian Power Hammer will only be in Foronlir for another day or two," the first adult was saying. "Its owner, Master Breslin, son of Master Maelnar himself, will be reclaiming the hammer as soon as he returns from Topside. We don't know when he'll make the hammer available for study or display again."

Flinn gripped Rusty's arm excitedly. Yes! This was the break they were looking for! The children were on their way to see the Narian Power Hammer! All he had to do was simply follow. How perfect was that?

The silence from the street hit him as hard as the last time he had one too many ales in Perz and had fallen—face first—onto the floor. The children! They were gone! Of all the blasted luck! Where could they be?

Flinn had no sooner headed into the street when he heard a loud clang. With a curse, he glanced back and saw Jino on the ground, rubbing his jaw. Nearby was a metal pole, and it was still vibrating.

"Stop messin' around, man," Flinn snapped.

"Puck, grab his hand. Let's go!"

Just ahead, Flinn caught sight of the group of underlings, straggling along. Catching up to them hadn't been too terribly difficult. Trailing behind, undetected, was another matter. Flinn sighed again as he heard yet another clatter. Several of the underlings turned to look behind them. Thankfully, once they had seen only an empty street, their attention drifted.

They were definitely headed in the right direction, Flinn decided, as the street started to fill with people. However, it was becoming increasingly difficult to move without bumping into someone. Cursing silently, Flinn increased the pace until they were just a few feet behind the children. Thankfully, the rest of the adult dwarves seemed to give the school group a wide berth.

Nearly twenty minutes later, they approached the front entrance to one of the large domed structures Flinn had seen from their perch. Leering excitedly as he stepped foot indoors, Flinn quickly cast his gaze around the room, taking notice of all the exits. The captain narrowed his eyes as he watched the two adults lead the children through the rows of chairs, angling toward a closed door on the far side of the auditorium. He yanked Rusty's hand, to catch up.

Standing in front of the closed door, the two adults waited patiently for the group of underlings to gather in front of them.

"Just behind this door," the first adult was saying, with her distinctively female voice, "lies the portal. Now, who amongst you have ever traveled through the portal?"

Five underlings raised their hands.

"Did you find the experience unpleasant?" the second adult asked, addressing the five children holding their hands up.

Five children collectively shook their heads no.

"Do you see, class? There's nothing to fear. This will be just as harmless as stepping from one room to another. Now, are we all ready?"

So, this building did not contain the hammer. The pirates watched, in utter silence, as the door opened, revealing a much smaller chamber. There, up against the far wall, visible through the open doorway, was a set of large doors. Each of the doors, Flinn noted, had to be at least ten feet tall. They also appeared to be made of solid stone. This was the portal? This wasn't what he was expecting at all.

One of the dwarf women—Flinn shuddered as he caught sight of the tightly braided beard—stepped up to the portal. With her back facing the expectant children, the adult waited a few moments before finally stepping back.

A few seconds later, the portal hummed to life. The two large doors shimmered, as if the surface of the stone had started rippling. Flinn nodded appreciatively. Whatever she had done, the portal was now active. To him, it looked as though the large doors had simply opened, allowing someone to pass from one room to the other. However, having prior experience with Lentarian portals, Flinn knew the small chamber visible through the open door was probably located many leagues from their present location.

And it was where they needed to go.

"Come," one teacher commanded. "The portal will not stay on indefinitely. Let us be off. We have a lot to see today."

The group of underlings filed through the portal two at a time. Flinn tugged on the hand he was holding and rushed to the portal, just as the last of the children disappeared from sight. Taking a deep breath, he looked at the similar stone chamber on the other side of the portal and stepped through.

"We made it!" Flinn heard Rusty exclaim. "We must now be in … oomph!"

Flinn's punch to the quartermaster's midsection had the desired effect.

"No one speaks until I allow it. Now, move out! We have to catch up to them kids."

"As I was saying," the pirates heard, as they caught up to their unwitting guides, "Foronlir is perhaps half the size of its sister city, Borahgg. Would anyone like to venture a guess why that is?"

Nearly a dozen hands rose into the air. The adult singled out one of the underlings—a young female.

"Because Foronlir isn't as old?"

"Well done, Murilyn. Full marks. Now, here's a difficult question. Ten extra points for anyone who knows. Think about this before you answer, because it is a devious question. Who founded Foronlir?"

Only two hands were raised, and Murilyn was one of them.

"Yes? Thekkon, you have an answer?"

The male dwarf child paused for a moment before answering.

"It's a trick question, 'cause only Council Elders can create another city. You're trying to trick us into thinking someone else was responsible. So, my answer would be whoever was on the Council at the time. I happen to know Master Maelnar has been on the Council for centuries. My father said so."

"Is that your final answer?" the adult female asked. A smile had formed on her face.

"Aye. Master Maelnar."

"Incorrect," the adult reported. She turned to Murilyn. "And you? What is your answer?"

Located less than a dozen feet away, concealed within their spell of invisibility, Flinn rolled his eyes and silently groaned. Not only were they forced to follow school children, now they were being subjected to their lessons? Yet again, he fervently wished this particular journey was over. Just show him this blasted hammer so he could properly steal it, thank you very much.

Murilyn smiled knowingly, her hand held aloft unwaveringly.

"It wasn't a Council Member, ma'am."

The teacher clapped her hands together delightedly. "Well done, Murilyn! Well done! Do you know who it was? What role in society they held?"

The girl nodded. "He was a security chief, and his name was Selwyn."

The entire class halted, nearly causing Flinn to bowl over a row of students. The second teacher approached the female underling and bowed.

"Very impressive, Murilyn. I don't suppose you know why this security chief was given such an important task, do you?"

The child nodded eagerly. "I do indeed! He is Aislinn's father! My father has told me the tale numerous times. Aislinn was dying. Her one final wish was to ride the back of a dragon. A human arranged the ride, in exchange for something that only Selwyn could get. Because of Selwyn, the dragons and dwarves became allies."

Both adults applauded the answer.

"Quite correct, young Murilyn, although you left out a few key points. Selwyn's act of defiance, which was the theft of an athe crystal the human wanted, is what caused the dragon to allow the rider."

"Actually," the other adult contradicted, "it was the

human's doing."

"What was?" the first adult asked.

"You wanted to know why the dragon allowed the rider. It was the human's doing. He was friends with the dragon, and arranged the ride. Several members of the Council witnessed the end of the ride, which was what prompted the peace talks."

"And you know this how?" the first adult asked.

"Who bloody cares," Flinn grumbled to himself.

"My mother was one of Aislinn's childhood friends," the second teacher answered. "They still keep in touch."

The group resumed moving. The children—and pirates— were led to a series of ornately carved buildings, each larger than the next. The closer they moved toward the buildings, the more people they saw. Progress became difficult. On more than one occasion, an invisible pirate would bump into an unwitting dwarf, who would turn to see what had collided with him. Not finding anything, the dwarf would resume his trek to wherever he was going.

Flinn gritted his teeth in frustration. There were too many damn people here! Didn't those school teachers say Foronlir was smaller than the previous city? Why, then, were there so many people present?

The answer manifested itself as they finally neared their destination. A structure unlike any Flinn had ever seen lay before them. Gigantic, and rising all the way up to the cavern roof, the building looked as though it had been carved out of a single block of stone. Nine great carved arches were on the ground level. Each arch contained a doorway, which looked as though it led in a different direction. Carved into the stone above each archway was a creature, acting as guardian to their individual passages. Some were familiar. Very familiar, Flinn thought with a scowl, as he saw a dragon coiled above the first archway. One was a large humanoid figure, covered with oversized muscles. Another was a small quadruped, loosely resembling a horse, but with *two* sets of wings. And the others? Well, he'd never seen any of them before in all his years of travel.

Right about then, Captain Flinn noticed several people

heading for the small space separating each archway from its neighbor. What he had thought were large stone columns were, in fact, cleverly carved spiraled staircases, leading up to the second floor, some type of communal space, where dwarves were sitting on benches, reading scrolls spread out across tables, and having hushed conversations amongst themselves.

Flinn craned his neck upward. Past the second story were more windows, evenly spaced apart and uniform in size. The higher he went, the fewer windows he saw.

The teachers led the group of students to the farthest arch on the right. Over the ninth archway was a creature that looked like a large bug with … Flinn squinted as he studied the monster … at least eight legs. It looked large, mean, and the stuff of nightmares. Of the archways, Flinn noted, this was the one that seemed to be the most frequently used. He yanked on Rusty's hand and hurried to catch up. This building was much too large for his liking. He did not want to get lost in there. When the time came for him to permanently *borrow* the hammer, he had to know they could all safely beat a hasty retreat.

"You're now entering the Ninth Hall," one of the teachers was saying. "How many of you have been here before?"

One child raised her hand: Murilyn.

"What is this place?" one boy asked. His voice echoed loudly back at him.

"This Hall is dedicated to all things Nar," the second teacher proudly added. "Currently undergoing excavation, the lost city of Nar has been yielding extraordinary things for several years now. Realizing that our people needed a place where we could all gather and study the remarkable findings unearthed in Nar, four separate clans came together to decide how to display the artifacts. This, young master, is every dwarf's paradise. Welcome to Myrm."

The young boy scoffed, unimpressed. "You're telling me that this is just another school, but for adults? Why would every dwarf consider this a paradise? More like a terrible nightmare, if you ask me."

"Well, I think it's paradise," Murilyn huffed as she beamed

a smile at the teachers. "There are all kinds of treasures inside."

Flinn stiffened with surprise. A smile slowly appeared on his face. Now they were talking his language!

"I don't care about their ruddy armor," another underling retorted, also a boy. "That seems to be the only thing they're known for. They don't even have good weapons. My father can make a better shield."

"I guarantee you he could not," the first teacher answered. "But you are quite correct, young master Herdag. The Narians were not known for their weapons, but for their armor."

"See?" Herdag sneered, as he turned to his small group of friends. "What did I tell you?"

"What the Narians were also known for," the second teacher continued, casting a frown at the young underling, "were their tools. They possessed a technology allowing them to create tools that were unparalleled in power. Take the Power Hammer that we are going to see. It's the only one known to exist, and it is unmatched in power. It can pulverize the hardest stone with naught but a slight tap from the hammer. It allows its owner to wield the hammer for hours on end without becoming fatigued. Our best blacksmiths have been studying the hammer for years and we are no closer to unlocking Nar's metallurgical secrets than we were the first day it was announced the lost city had been discovered."

Nearly ten minutes later, with the pirates closely following the school group, they arrived at their destination. There, sitting on a stone dais in the middle of a small, nondescript chamber, surrounded by eight golden stanchions, was the hammer.

The teachers beckoned the children closer and began pointing out the various parts of the hammer.

"Do you see how the hammer is resting upside-down on its head? Would anyone care to venture a guess as to why that is?"

Flinn promptly ignored the school group and focused on the hammer. He felt Rusty's grip tighten in anticipation of what was to come. He pressed his hand, still holding Rusty's, against his quartermaster's chest, as a sign of warning. The message came through loud and clear: no action until he authorized it.

"Four distinct pieces," Flinn heard one of the teachers drone on. "Head, counterweight, handle, and helix."

Keeping to the outskirts of the small chamber, Flinn and his men quietly circled the hammer. There didn't seem to be any type of security precautions in place. What luck! Were these damn dwarves that trusting? There had to be something in place to prevent what he was about to do. He just had to figure out what that could be. The last thing he wanted were surprises. There was too much riding on the success of this mission to allow for failure now.

Captain Flinn noticed the sparkling ruby on the head of the hammer. He wasn't sure who had thought it best to put a jewel on the side of a hammer, but it didn't matter. He only wanted the hammer. The men could have the ruby. All he needed to do now was to clear the chamber so his men could get to work.

"Tell Casimir he's up," Flinn quietly whispered to Rusty. "I want this room cleared. Pass it down."

He heard his quartermaster repeat the order, and then the soft whispers faded away. Within moments, the teachers decided it was time to move on, even though they had only been studying the hammer for a few minutes. As soon as the chamber was clear, Flinn released Rusty's hand.

His men instantly appeared. Flinn pointed at the two entrances and snapped his fingers.

"Grenden, Puck, cover the entrances. Alert us if anyone approaches. Casimir, be ready to blast 'em with yer jhorun if they say someone be comin'. Now, Jino? Yer up. Get the hammer. The sooner we be away from here, the better."

Jino quickly hopped over the stanchions and then cautiously poked a finger at the hammer. When nothing happened, and no alarm began to sound, Jino grinned, gripped the hammer handle tightly, and lifted. The hammer rose off the dais, but was almost immediately pulled out of the pirate's hand, as though it was tethered to the ground by an invisible chain.

Muttering a vile curse, Jino was able to catch the hammer

before it fell. Jino carefully placed the hammer on the ground as quietly as he could. Flinn was about to let out an angry retort when he saw Jino grasp the handle and struggle to lift the hammer a few feet off the ground. In fact, it looked as though the hammer was starting to slide out of his grip, no matter how tightly Jino gripped the handle. Was that what the stone meant when it advised it wouldn't be easy to acquire the hammer?

"Is it heavy?" Flinn worriedly asked, as he strode over to the dais.

"I've never lifted a hammer this heavy," Jino reluctantly admitted. "It's all I can do to keep this blasted thing from falling back to the floor."

"How long do you think you can last?" Rusty anxiously asked.

"Long enough to get this out of here," Jino snapped. "And that's only if we move, like *now*!"

"Ye heard him, lads," Flinn said. "We be leavin'. Casimir, we need yer power most of all. Don't squander it. Use it only as it be needed. Grenden, Puck, behind me. Alquin, bring up the rear. Von, help Alquin."

The pirates hastily retreated from the chambers, retracing their steps. Flinn, keeping a worried eye on Jino, began to curse. Judging from the way Jino was sweating, he wouldn't be able to carry the hammer much longer. Was this really necessary? What good was a hammer if it couldn't be wielded properly?

Flinn scowled. He must have been mistaken. There was no way this Power Hammer could be what he was searching for in this blasted city. Making a hasty decision, Flinn opened his mouth, intent on telling Jino to forgo the hammer. Whatever he had believed could be accomplished by possessing that hammer, he had to have been mistaken.

His inside jacket pocket suddenly grew warm. Surprised, Flinn thrust a hand into the same pocket which held his Alchos Stone. As soon as his hand was cupped around the stone, he heard the voice in his head:

TAKE THE HAMMER.

It be too blasted cumbersome, Flinn angrily thought. *It'll slow us down. No, it must be abandoned now while we can still escape!*

TAKE THE HAMMER.

"Blast it to hell and back. Jino, give that here."

"Captain, I do not think—"

The profusely sweating pirate gratefully passed the hammer off, then froze as he stared at Captain Flinn. Flinn was holding the hammer upright as though it wasn't any heavier than a feather.

A smile slowly spread across the captain's face.

Chapter 4 — Unexpected Twist

W hy can't we just use the portal?" Steve huffed with irritation. "Mikal, didn't you say the portal could now link directly with Borahgg? Wouldn't that be the easiest way to warn them?"

The young king nodded and then sighed. "Aye, it would. However, proper protocols must be followed. We cannot arrive unannounced and uninvited. To do so would be a serious invasion of their privacy."

Steve turned to look at his wife, who was sitting at Kri'Entu's private desk. "Any luck?"

Sarah held out her hand and a paper materialized on it. She opened it and quickly scanned the contents. She sadly shook her head. "No. It's still my original message. No one has added anything to it."

"Someone seriously needs to invent the telephone here," Steve grumbled. "I mean, there's *got* to be a better way to send a message to another part of the kingdom."

"That doesn't help us right now," Sarah sighed. She pushed

back from the desk and rose to her feet. "There's something wrong. I've never had a message ignored before. Let's look at the facts. We know the pirates are already underground, heading straight to Borahgg, home of Maelnar. Now, all of a sudden, we lose all contact with the city? What are the odds of that? No, Steve is right. We need to get there and we need to do so *now*. Mikal, there must be something we can do to get their attention."

Mikal reached into his pocket and retrieved a small, carved figurine of a dragon. A water dragon, Steve noted, from the long, sinewy shape of the creature. Mikal knocked the figurine against the surface of his father's desk three times.

"What are you doing?" Steve asked, curious.

"Signaling Gareth," Mikal answered. He held the tiny form of the shealk up so everyone could see it. "It's one of his spells. Gareth gave this to me earlier this year as an easier way to contact him. If the spell is activated, he's alerted, and he'll know there's a problem."

A slight breeze appeared. Indoors. The hairs on Steve's arm suddenly stood straight up and he could feel an electric charge in the air. Moments later, a crackling white ball of pure energy appeared. It hung, suspended, in the air for a few seconds before it rapidly expanded, and then flashed. When the spots disappeared from Steve's vision, he could see that the apprentice wizard was now in the Antechamber.

"What news do you have?" the acolyte wizard immediately asked. "What can I do? Well, what do you need me to do? What? Why is everyone staring at me?"

"Your entrances are very impressive," Sarah told the teenager. "I'm very glad you're on our side."

Gareth offered a sheepish smile and shrugged.

"Do we need to notify Shardwyn, too?" Steve asked. "I hate to bring it up, but I don't want to step on anyone toes by not at least giving him a chance to…"

"Shardwyn is incapacitated," Gareth interrupted. "He's fallen sick, so he's currently bedridden."

Sarah was instantly sympathetic. "Poor thing. Is there anything we can do?"

"Stay upwind from his tower," Gareth softly answered.

"In fact, I created a spell to keep a strong breeze blowing from his tower to the Great Sea."

"He smells?" Steve asked, confused. "That's nothing new."

Gareth bit his lip. "His, uh, ailment forces him to, er, keep a chamber pot by his bedside."

Steve winced. "Eww. I didn't need to know that. He's got the trots. That's just great."

"That's where Lissa is," Mikal explained, indicating his young wife's absence. "She's trying everything she can think of to offer him some relief, only nothing seems to be working."

"It's so bad that not even Lissa can cure him?" Steve asked, amazed. "I didn't think that was possible."

"It's not life-threatening," Mikal quickly added. "At least, that's what she tells me. Whatever the cause, it has thus far eluded her."

"That is one bright kid," Steve observed. "If anyone can figure it out, she can."

Mikal nodded appreciatively. "I would agree. Now, Gareth, you're here because we need to send a message to Borahgg."

Confused, Gareth looked over at Sarah.

"She's already tried," Steve answered, before Gareth could ask. "She's sent numerous messages, but they've all been unopened."

"Use the portal," the teenager suggested.

Steve instantly beamed. "That was my suggestion, too."

"We can't, you nitwit," Sarah admonished, giving him a punch on the arm. "Didn't you hear Mikal? We can't arrive unannounced. We have to let them know we're coming first. So, how do we do that? Gareth, any thoughts?"

"Where have you been sending your messages?" the young wizard asked. His eyes had closed, as was the case whenever he was working spells in his head.

"Maelnar's private office," Sarah answered. "When that didn't work, I tried the big room where the Council of Elders meet. So far, nothing."

"How big is the chamber where their Council meets?"

Gareth wanted to know.

Steve held up his arms, spread as far apart as he could get them. "Huge. That place can probably hold every single dwarf who lives in the area."

Gareth nodded and started chanting.

"That's encouraging," Sarah softly whispered to Steve. "That means he's got something up his sleeve."

The three of them waited, in utter silence, for several minutes. Both fires were crackling merrily away in the Antechamber, casting a welcoming warmth to the whole room. Finally, after close to five minutes had passed, Gareth opened his eyes.

He was frowning.

"That can't be good," Steve groaned. "Out with it, kid. What'd you find out?"

"Well, I created a locator spell, and modified it to ... you really don't care about that. I don't know where Maelnar's office is—I could have searched, but we don't have the time—so I focused on the big chamber where the Council meets. It's the middle of the day, so there should have been someone there. I created a spell to locate a familiar and then added a few layers to translate what they were seeing into something I could use."

"All that in just a few minutes?" Steve breathed, amazed. "Damn, kid. You're good."

"That was easy," Gareth admitted. "Trying to figure out what I was looking at was the hard part. I found some type of creature, lurking about in a nearby tunnel. I took control of it and made it venture into their city. Whatever this thing was, I felt its reluctance. It truly thought I was placing it in mortal danger, so I then added a layer for protection. If there is some type of predator nearby, I wasn't going to jeopardize my familiar by making it do something it ordinarily wouldn't do."

"Smart," Steve and Mikal both echoed. Each gave the other a grin and then bumped their fists together.

"What were you able to learn?" Sarah wanted to know.

"That the city appears to be empty," Gareth sullenly reported. "If you're sending messages, it's no wonder no one is answering. I had this creature wandering the streets, looking for some signs of life. Nothing. I couldn't find a single dwarf. Maybe they're hiding? Maybe they've evacuated the city? I honestly don't know."

Steve turned to Mikal and frowned. "Well? What do you say? Now do you think there's enough evidence to warrant an uninvited visit?"

Mikal nodded as he sat down at his father's desk. "Aye. It would seem our allies are in grave danger. I, for one, will not stand idly by." Mikal uncorked a bottle of ink and hastily scribbled a note. He handed it to the closest guard. "Give that to Captain Pheron, on the double."

The guard nodded and hurriedly exited the room.

"I can teleport us there," Sarah announced. "I can put us right inside the Council Chamber."

Mikal shook his head and activated the hidden wall behind the desk. "Save your jhorun. I'll give you the Borahgg portal key. You never know what you're going to find once you get there."

"I wonder what those damn pirates are looking for this time," Steve wondered aloud. "Gems? Weapons? You'd think they'd have enough of that type of thing already."

"How do you know they're not looking for something else?" Sarah countered.

Steve shrugged. "Such as?"

Sarah shook her head. "I'm not sure. Think about it. They knew the dragons had that oskorlisk fang. They knew more about its properties than we did. Who's to say they know something we don't?"

Gareth was nodding. "Lady Sarah makes a good point. What would the dwarves have that the pirates would want? So much so that they're risking capture?"

"I still say it's for the jewels," Steve decided, after a few moments of silence had passed. "I've seen some of the gemstones they mine down there."

Their armor.

Steve stiffened with surprise. A gentle, soothing feminine presence had appeared in his mind. He smiled. He'd recognize her telepathic connection anywhere.

Pryllan! Hello! I didn't know you were listening!

I tuned in once your mate said 'dragons'. It is akin to someone saying your name in a crowded room.

"Pryllan is listening," Steve softly reported.

Sarah smiled. "Hello, Pryllan. I'm glad you're here. We could use all the help we can get!"

A correction: I am not there. I am at my nest, caring for Pylaria. I'm listening through Steve's senses.

"So, Pryllan, what were you saying about the armor?" Steve wanted to know.

I was suggesting that, perhaps, the renegade humans are searching for dwarf armor. I have heard stories about how valuable armor found in Nar can be.

"What's so special about that armor?" Steve asked, once he had finished relaying Pryllan's response.

Gareth snapped his fingers. "Of course! Narian armor has got to be the most sought after, highly desirable armor in existence. It's impenetrable, uncrushable, and impervious to any weapon known to exist. For all we know, it might even be impervious to jhorun. I'd love to find some and run a few experiments on it."

"But it's *dwarf* armor," Sarah pointed out. "Wouldn't it be designed for a much smaller person? Pirates are human-sized, not dwarf-sized. That armor would do them no good."

A very valid point.

"What's so special about this Nar place?" Steve wanted to know. "I've heard the word in passing."

Mikal looked at Gareth and held out an arm in open invitation.

"Well, I'm no expert," Gareth began, "but based on what I've heard, Nar was a dwarf city that flourished thousands of years ago. Their technology surpassed what is in use today. Most specifically, Narian metallurgical techniques were so far advanced that, as I mentioned before, their armor became worth its weight in gold."

"Sounds like our version of Atlantis," Sarah decided.

"I wonder what kinds of weapons they have," Steve mused to himself. "Wouldn't a Narian sword or axe look good up on the wall back at our place?"

Sarah shook her head. "You have a sickness, dear. Just because you don't have one doesn't mean you need to track it down and put it up on the wall."

Steve raised a hand and waggled a finger at his wife. "Cookbooks. Don't get me started on all your cookbooks. You know as well as I do that a collector never stops collecting, dear."

"Dork."

"Snot."

Mikal gave a loud cough. Everyone looked over to see him holding up a familiar pewter box. Inside, Steve knew, was a collection of sparkling crystal keys. Portal keys, made by Maelnar himself. Apparently, there was a brand-new key in there that would link the castle's portal to the one inside Borahgg. Both husband and wife briefly wondered about the color.

As everyone proceeded toward the smaller, adjacent portal room, Gareth tapped Steve on the shoulder. "Just so you know, Nar wasn't known for making weapons. Sure, a few swords and shields were recovered, but there wasn't anything spectacular about them."

Steve's face promptly fell. "Awww. Say it ain't so."

Sarah approached and threw an arm around Gareth's shoulder. "Oh, honey. You just made my day. Good. Keep dissuading him from trying to hang any more weapons up on my walls and you'll be forever in my good graces."

Gareth grinned, looked over at Steve, and tried to wipe the smile off his face.

"I really don't think there's anything in Nar that'd interest you," Gareth was saying, "unless you like tools."

Steve hesitated, and then shrugged. "Sure, what guy doesn't? Wrenches, socket sets, drills, saws, and pretty much anything that'll fit in my tool box. Why? What kinds of tools are we talking about?"

"They were known for several," Gareth cheerfully supplied. "The most important and well known is the Narian Power Hammer. Did you know there's only one in existence? Ow!"

The wizard painfully rubbed his forehead, having walked head-on into the back of Steve, who had come to an abrupt stop. For that matter, so had Sarah and Mikal, who had been just about to open the door into the portal room. As one, they all turned to Gareth.

"What's the matter?" Gareth asked, as he turned to look at his friends. "Why is everyone staring at me?"

"This hammer," Steve began, as he fought to keep the exasperation from his voice, "what can you tell us about it? Why is there only one?"

"I heard it was found in pieces," Gareth exclaimed, as he walked around Steve and opened the door for Mikal, whose hand had stopped inches from the portal room's door knob. "The hammer can be wielded for hours without the user showing any signs of fatigue."

"Wait, wait, wait," Sarah said, holding up a hand. "This hammer? We've seen it before, remember, honey? That was the hammer that Breslin, Maelnar, and his father all worked together to take apart. One of the pieces of that hammer was a spiraled ruby, and *that* was what had to be given to Tirgath and Dirgath. This was back when the dragons were cursed and couldn't fly. Or spit fire."

Steve grinned and looked over at Gareth, who was now studying the floor. "Yep. I do recall that. So do you, right, sport?"

Gareth grunted, but said nothing.

"Behave yourself, dear," Sarah scolded. "Gareth has long since apologized for causing that whole mess. And didn't you tell me how much you enjoyed being a dragon?"

"But it was a *girl* dragon," Steve grumped.

"Not just any girl dragon," Sarah corrected, "but Pryllan."

Yes?

Sorry. We were just talking about that time when Gareth switched us all around and I ended up in your body.

And I was in Sarah's. I do remember. Most unpleasant.

Steve snickered, but was unable to throw his face back into neutral before Sarah noticed.

"What? What was *that* for?"

"It wasn't nearly as unpleasant as being in your body, Paco."

Gareth snickered, but sobered the instant Steve fired a dark look at him before he continued. "Wasn't Maelnar's father the one who wrote the spell that located the pieces in the first place?"

Sarah nodded. "Yes, that's him. He was far and away the oldest dwarf I have ever seen. He was able to locate another ruby so the hammer could be reassembled."

"Do you think that's what this is all about?" Steve asked. "Do you think the pirates want the hammer?"

Sarah was nodding. "It makes perfect sense. Think about it. They have the fang, which can offer them protection. They're going after the hammer, which would give them strength. I'd say we need to get that hammer before it can fall into the pirates' hands."

"I agree," Mikal declared. He opened the pewter box, selected a bright yellow crystal key, and held it out for Sarah. "Get it before they do."

"You can count on it," Steve vowed. He ignited his hands for effect and then snuffed them out.

Sarah walked over to the inert portal, inserted the key into the keyhole, and twisted. Pulling the key out, she took a few steps back and waited for the portal to come to life.

"I thought only the dwarves could pick up the hammer," Steve was saying "There's no way the pirates would be able to wield that thing like a normal hammer."

"True," Sarah admitted. "I'm not sure how Flinn plans on using the hammer. Hey, why isn't the portal activating?"

Surprised, everyone turned to the portal, which was strangely quiescent. Sarah stepped up to the frame, inserted the key a second time, and again tried to activate it. As before, it remained dark and quiet.

"That can't be good," Steve commented. "Could the pirates have messed with it?"

Sarah handed the key back to Mikal and then took Steve's hand.

"Okay, I'm done trying to get there the slow way. All those going to Borahgg, give me your hand. Otherwise, Mikal, we'll keep you posted."

"How?" Mikal wanted to know.

"We can send messages back, like what we tried to do with Borahgg," Steve answered, as he placed his hand over his wife's.

"I was thinking we could just ask Pryllan, or maybe Pravara, to relay a message," Sarah suggested. "It would be quicker."

I would be delighted to help.

Sarah nodded. "Excellent. Gareth, do you need a lift?"

Gareth nodded. "I could get myself there, but since I haven't ever been, I could very easily materialize in a stone wall. That'd take too much time to sort out. So, if it's all right with you, I'd like a ride." He reached over to place his hand over Steve's. "Ready."

The castle winked out, replaced almost immediately by a dark, eerily quiet room with hundreds of chairs arranged in rows. Steve whistled as he turned in place. He recognized the Council Chamber from the few times he had been here with his wife, visiting Maelnar and Breslin. It had always been crammed full of people, but not today. In fact, they were the only three people present.

"This is weird," Sarah quietly whispered, as she looked around. "I hate dark places. This room is so big that I can't see the other side."

Four large fireballs flared into existence and then gently rose into the air. Steve nodded. With the added light his jhorun was providing, they could see that a meeting had been underway, since there were overturned chairs, open books on tables, and numerous sheets of paper littering the ground. Steve stopped to retrieve one of the papers. Foreign, exotic runes met his eyes. Shrugging, he set the paper on the closest table.

"Something bad happened here," he decided. "Looks like there's been a fight. Look at all the chairs that have been knocked over."

"Or they were interrupted," Sarah suggested, "and had to leave in a hurry."

Steve shrugged. He ordered the fireballs to pace them as they headed toward the closest exit. Realizing he really didn't know what to expect on the other side of the door, Steve ignited both of his hands.

"You just be careful you don't burn anything down," Sarah cautioned. "These people are our friends. It would be extraordinarily bad if you ended up torching something by mistake."

"The only thing I plan on torching are a few pirates," Steve grumbled. He looked over at Gareth, who was clutching a few figurines in his hands. "Are you ready?"

"I've got two golems and an earth elemental ready to go," Gareth assured him. "Just say the word."

The door creaked open and they all edged cautiously out into the lobby. Sarah automatically headed toward the exterior door, seeing how this part of the structure was also vacant. Together, the three of them stepped out into the streets of Borahgg.

Not a single person could be seen. There was no hustle and bustle of foot traffic. There were no incessant clangs from nearby foundries. In fact, every single building looked as though it had been boarded up.

"There's no one out here, either," Steve exclaimed, looking up and down the various streets. "They've got to be hiding. We can worry about them later. Right now, we need to find those pirates, so ... where to, guys?"

Sarah held a finger to her mouth and then tapped the side of her head, signaling she wanted to try and listen for any signs of disturbance. At the exact same time Steve and Gareth fell silent, a loud clatter sounded directly behind them. All three whipped around, startled to see three figures.

Steve blasted jets of fire straight at one of the intruders and pinned him in place with a net made of pure flames. Sarah ordered her jhorun to pick up the person in the middle and hoist him way above their heads. The third intruder let out a squawk of surprise when he suddenly discovered he had been immobilized in a huge block of stone, leaving only his face visible.

"Where in the Pit of Asdrol did you come from?!" the first dwarf angrily exclaimed, cringing behind Steve's fire net.

Steve blinked a few times. "The Pit of *what*?"

"Asdrol," a voice answered, from above their heads.

"Something I'm wondering right about now, too."

"The Fire Thrower and the Teleporter!" the third dwarf exclaimed. "Ah! That explains so much! Except for my predicament, that is. How is it I've become locked in a slab of stone?"

Gareth guiltily raised a hand. "That'd be me. It's the first spell I thought of. I had to immobilize you without fear of retaliation. You see, I used a locator spell to find a suitable block of granite and then a…"

"That's enough, Gareth," Sarah interrupted. "Free him. The dwarves are our friends. We're sorry."

The fire net extinguished with an audible *poof*, while Sarah gently lowered the dwarf she had been holding up in the air. As for Gareth, he gestured with his hand and the huge block of stone vanished. All three dwarves approached the humans and bowed.

"Nohrin, you are known to us. As for you, underling, you I do not know."

"Maybe not," Steve told the dwarf, "but you've heard of him. Meet Gareth, formerly known as the Renegade Wizard."

"Must you keep telling everyone that?" Gareth complained.

The dwarves, in the meantime, all gasped aloud and jumped back by several feet, as though they had discovered themselves standing on hot coals. Within moments they had pulled out their axes, loaded crossbows, and so on. Sarah moved to step in front of the young wizard, but was pulled out of the way by her husband, who ignited his hands and blasted out heat in all directions.

The dwarves immediately stepped back, away from the heat. Unfortunately, so did Sarah and Gareth.

"Tone that down, honey," Sarah ordered. "You're going to burn us if you're not careful."

"Whoops. Sorry. Better?"

"Yes, thank you. What are your names?"

The first dwarf was holding an axe in one hand and was slowly sliding something out of a holder on one of his bandoliers.

"Milady, I am Darfok. Over there, holding the crossbow,

is Grolim. And holding the orix? That'd be Ferlun."

"What's he holding?" Steve asked, as he studied the third dwarf. This 'orix' looked as though it was made of metal and was meant to be thrown.

"An orix. It's a throwing weapon meant to be used at close ranges. Forget about that for now. What are you three doing here?"

"Belay that," Grolim huffed, as he disarmed his crossbow. "Fire Thrower, are you here to help?"

Steve nodded. "Let me guess. You guys have a pirate problem?"

"As soon as we learned there were intruders in Borahgg," Ferlun began, "every available resource was used to put a stop to these humans. I'm sorry to say, nothing was effective. They slipped by us and used our own damn portal to travel to Foronlir."

"What?" Sarah asked, confused. "The pirates aren't even here? Then why give the order to evacuate?"

"You don't understand, milady," Darfok explained. "These humans made it into our city undetected. They were able to move about in stealth. The Council didn't waste any time and ordered everyone to retreat to the lower caves until allowed to return home."

"That sounds like Captain Windbag all right," Steve groaned. "Whatever he used against us to hide his crew, he's clearly using it here."

"You know these humans?" Grolim asked. "You've dealt with them before? Do you know how we can stop them?"

Steve nodded. "By the only way that has ever been proven effective: direct contact."

All three dwarves were shaking their heads.

"That's a bad idea," Ferlun was saying. "Nothing we have tried has had any effect."

Sarah suddenly snapped her fingers. "The Narian Power Hammer. Where is it? We think the pirates are after it. We need to make certain it doesn't fall into their hands."

Darfok's eyes widened. "The Power Hammer? The invaders are after the Power Hammer? But … but … it's not here. It's in Foronlir!"

Steve's hands ignited and he snapped his fingers a few times. "Then we need to get to Foronlir, on the double!"

"Are the two cities connected via portal?" Sarah wanted to know.

Grolim nodded. "Aye, but…"

"Then let's go," Steve interrupted.

"There's something you need to know," the dwarf interjected, as the other two dwarves turned about and headed toward the council chamber.

"What do we need to know?" Gareth asked.

"The portals," Grolim continued. "You won't be able to use them. Not without authorization."

Sarah turned to Steve and nudged him on the arm. "I'll bet *that* was why we couldn't get the portal to work. It's probably been disabled."

Grolim nodded again. "Aye. After we learned that the humans somehow used our own portal, all access has been restricted."

"So, how are we going to use it?" Steve asked.

Grolim held up a solid gray metallic key. "My key has access. It'll activate the portal when all others have been locked out."

"I didn't even know that was possible," Steve murmured. "And I've never seen a portal key that wasn't made out of crystal."

"That makes two of us," Gareth added.

They had just taken the first step back toward the heart of the city when all six of them came to an immediate stop. Standing before them was a creature that continued to haunt Sarah's dreams, and one that caused Steve to curse violently. His hands ignited and he prepared to blast out jets of fire.

A guur was just emerging out of the shadows.

"Wizard be damned!" Darfok exclaimed. "What the blazes is a guur doing here? We thought they had all been eradicated! Well, that's a problem I plan on rectifying right now."

The heavily armored, ten-legged insect clicked its pincers dangerously, as if it knew they were preparing for battle. Then it did something that caused Steve's eyes to widen with surprise. The guur turned to Gareth and cocked its head, as if it wasn't sure what it was seeing.

Steve glanced over at the young wizard and noticed his eyes were closed and his lips were moving. The wizard was chanting, which could only mean some type of spell was being formulated. Then, a bizarre thought occurred.

Just before the dwarves could launch themselves at the guur, Steve stepped in front of the guur and held out his hands.

"Wait! Just a moment! Don't attack it! At least, not yet."

Gareth's eyes snapped open. "Are you serious? Look at that thing! That has got to be the biggest, ugliest bug I have ever seen!"

"That is a guur drone," Grolim growled. "It made the mistake of coming into the city limits. Well, it'll be the last mistake it ever makes."

"Honey, you've killed hundreds of these bugs," Sarah reminded him. "Why would you want to save this one?"

"Because this one helped us out," Steve cryptically answered. "Guys, I think *that* is Gareth's familiar."

Everyone turned to Gareth, whose mouth dropped open.

"Is that why it's staring at me?" the wizard wanted to know.

Steve nodded. "Yeah, I'd say so. Why isn't it running away? We've fought these things before. They're deathly afraid of fire, yet this one is holding his ground."

"Why?" Gareth demanded. "Why is this one sticking around?"

Sarah nodded. "Of course! Gareth, didn't you say that you offered your familiar a layer of protection? Perhaps it hasn't worn off. Perhaps it feels a connection to you. Whatever the reason, it's looking for help."

"Help with what?" Ferlun was clutching his axe fearfully across his chest and looked ready to bolt in the other direction should the guur so much as give an errant twitch.

"Maybe there are no more guur," Sarah softly answered. "Maybe it's lonely?"

"What are you suggesting?" Steve asked, as he turned to his wife. "Are you thinking you want to take it with us? You're kidding, right? You've seen what these things are capable of doing."

"You're the one who saved it from being killed," Sarah reminded him. "Besides, look at it. If I didn't know any better, then I'd say it was acting like a stray dog who had just been given something to eat. By Gareth."

The guur had approached Gareth and now appeared content to be by his side.

"Oh, this is just swell," the wizard grumped.

"You're the one who cast the spell looking for a familiar," Steve good-naturedly told the teenager. "Perhaps even you don't know your own strength?"

"Go home," Gareth told the huge bug. "Go back to wherever you came from."

The guur paid him no attention.

Still not certain the guur wouldn't attack them, Grolim finally sheathed his weapons and led his two companions, along with the three humans—and one guur—through a series of hallways and doors until they were standing before an inert portal. Its frames were covered with many of those same, mysterious runes Steve had noticed before. Apparently, the portal's frame could be customized to whatever the owner wanted. Their own frame, back home, had been covered with all manner of designs: dragons, swords, griffins, and so on. Personally, Steve thought their portal looked better.

"Come on," Steve heard Gareth's voice say. "You've got to have something better to do than tag along with us. Go home! You're free! I release you from the spell!"

"How's that workin' out for you?" Steve called back to their young companion.

"Not well at all," Gareth complained. "It's not going away. What are we supposed to do?"

Steve shrugged. "Well, I'd feed him, give him plenty of water, and take him out on walks."

That earned him a giggle from Sarah.

"This isn't a dog. There's no way my mother is going to let me keep something like this."

Ignoring the ongoing argument between the humans, Grolim stepped up to the portal, warily eyed the guur, who seemed content to remain by the human wizard's side, and inserted his key into the keyhole. "Not everyone has an override key. Only those who are trusted by the Council can reactivate a disabled portal."

"Looks like you don't seem to be too trustworthy, Grolim," Darfok snickered. "The portal is still dead."

"What? No, that cannot be. Let me try again."

Once more, Grolim tried activating the portal with his special key. As before, with Sarah's attempt at activating the portal, the magical doorway remained dark and quiet. Speechless, Grolim angrily turned to his two companions, as if he believed one of them to be responsible.

"I didn't do it," Darfok said, holding up his hands.

"Nor did I," Ferlun added, before dropping his voice. "I would if I could, you pompous, arrogant…"

Darfok jabbed his elbow into his companion's gut, cutting him off.

"What was that?" Grolim asked, turning to see who had spoken.

"Oh, nothing," Ferlun hastily answered.

"Who has the power to override your override key?" Steve asked.

Grolim shrugged. "I really don't know. The Council, perhaps?"

"They must have thought it was too dangerous for anyone to use it," Sarah decided. She looked helplessly at her husband. "Now what? I can't teleport us if I can't see where I'm going."

Steve scowled at the inert portal. There had to be a way they could make it to this other city. Perhaps there was some 'master key' which could make it work?

Gareth pushed past the dwarves, who gladly backed out of the way as the guur fearlessly strode by them. Gareth gazed up at the portal and placed a hand on the frame. The wizard's eyes closed and he began to chant.

"That portal was commissioned by none other than Maelnar himself," Grolim began. "There's no way you are going to be able to…"

The dwarf trailed off as the frames began to glow. The

door shimmered and was replaced by a small, well-lit chamber that had its only door closed. All three dwarves closed in on Gareth, clearly angry.

"How is it you activated that portal when it had been rendered inert?" Grolim demanded.

"He's a wizard," Steve shrugged, as if those three words were the only explanation that was needed. "Now, are you three coming with us?"

The dwarves shook their heads no.

"We stay to protect the city," Grolim told the three of them. "This is a human affair. We trust that you humans will deal with those humans. And that *thing*."

Steve cracked his flaming knuckles. "Gladly. Grolim, take care. We'll deal with this. Gareth, make sure … make sure … hmm. We need to give that thing a name."

"Diez," Sarah suggested.

Steve nodded. That would work, since the guur had ten segmented legs and 'diez' was 'ten' in Spanish, it should make an adequate name. How in the world did she know that?

Sarah gave him a cryptic smile and looked back at Gareth. "Make sure Diez can keep up, okay?"

Gareth finally smiled as he gave the huge ten-legged insect a cautious pat on the top of its armored head. "Deez, huh? All right. Deez it is."

"Diez," Steve corrected. "Dee-ehz. That's his name."

"Oh, leave it Deez," Sarah decided. "If it's easier for Gareth to say, then let him keep the name."

Steve shrugged and looked at the guur. "Alrighty, Deez, can you keep up? We're not going back for you if you fall behind."

The guur tapped two of its legs on the ground, as if it was impatient to be on the move again. Satisfied, the three dwarves moved off as Steve, Sarah, and Gareth stepped through the activated portal. After a few seconds of hesitation, Deez scurried through.

"So, how *did* you get that portal to work?" Steve asked, as soon as the portal shut itself off.

Gareth frowned. "Everyone always asks me to explain how I can do what I do. When I start to tell them how it's accomplished, I'm told that I don't need to go into detail. Well, I'm telling you, if you want to know, you'll need to be prepared to hear the long side of it. It's quite fascinating, really. What I did was … there. There are those faces again. Too much? Fine. I, uh, waved my hand at it and the portal started working. Would that suffice?"

Steve looked at his wife. Both of them nodded.

They stepped out of Foronlir's portal room directly into a deserted city. They could also tell, unfortunately, that the pirates must have skirmished with the dwarves here, because the street was a mess. Carts were tipped over. Doors were barely hanging onto their hinges. Most windows facing the street had been boarded up, only it looked like the majority of the boards had been ripped down. Several were still hanging precariously by a single nail.

Steve squatted on the ground and ran a hand over the cobbled street's surface. He could feel small rocks, bits of sand, and broken slivers of wood. Exactly as if an unexpected wind storm appeared out of thin air.

Flinn. He had been through here, no doubt about it. However, where was he now? Why couldn't they hear anything? Were they somehow hiding themselves again?

Pryllan? Can you hear me?

Aye. What manner of creature is behind you?

Steve turned to see Gareth and Deez as they quietly looked at the carnage in the streets.

Deez? The creature Gareth used to spy on Borahgg sought us out when we arrived. Now, it looks like Gareth has picked up a new pet.

Again, I ask, what manner of creature is it? I do not recall ever sensing its kind before.

Oh, sorry. It's a guur, a large ten-legged insect that came back from extinction centuries ago by a mistake on the dwarves' part. These BNPs threatened to drive the dwarves from this area, but they managed to beat the bugs back. No one thought there were any more of them, so this is a surprise.

BNP?

Bug of Nightmarish Proportions.

Ah. Can it be trusted?

I honestly have no idea. There are no plans for me to ever turn my back on it, if that's what you were wondering.

Understood.

Hey, here's a thought: can you communicate with it?

Unknown. I've never initiated contact with a creature other than wyverian or human before. Would you like me to try?

Yes, please.

While Pryllan attempted to make telepathic contact with the guur, Steve looked at his two human companions.

"Well? What now? What do we do? This place looks just as empty as Borahgg."

"We need to find this hammer. Gareth? Could you write some type of spell to locate it?"

Gareth nodded and began to chant.

"We need to contact Breslin," Steve decided. "He's the rightful owner of that hammer. He's got to be around here somewhere."

"You need your sword," Sarah decided. "You should be able to contact him with Mythrin."

Mythrin was one of the three Mythra Triad weapons, given to Steve years ago after—oddly enough—the battle against the guur. For his part, Commander Rhenyon had been presented Mythron, a twin to Steve's own sword, but with a blue blade instead of a green one. Breslin had been given Mythryd, the battle-axe with the double red blades. Only when the weapons were held by their owners could contact be made, and it was always telepathic.

Sarah closed her eyes and held out her hands. A few moments later, Steve's green-bladed broadsword made the journey from their world to Lentari in the blink of an eye. Mythrin appeared in Sarah's outstretched hands. She passed the sword over to him and waited for him to buckle the baldric across his back.

Finished.

Steve's eyes widened with surprise.

And? Is it friendly??

We've reached an enemy/non-enemy agreement. It typically doesn't think on its own, not without contacting the rest of its colony first. But, it does recognize that

the three of you are not enemies and, seeing how it desperately wants to rejoin a hive collective, it now believes it has found its new hive: you three. You, Sarah, and especially Gareth, are fellow drones in its eyes.

That means it doesn't have any plans on attacking us, right?

Correct.

I guess that'll have to do. Thank you, my friend. That's a load off my mind.

You're welcome. Contact me if I can be of assistance.

Count on it.

"Get this," Steve excitedly began, as he tapped Sarah on her shoulder. "Pryllan says…"

"Were you able to contact Breslin?"

"Oh. Whoops. I'll do that now."

Sarah sadly shook her head. "Your short-term memory is shot."

"Hey, I was distracted, all right? It's not my fault."

"What were you going to say?" Gareth asked, as he, Sarah, and Deez watched Steve spin his baldric around so that he could unbuckle the safety strap which held the sword in place.

"Just that Pryllan contacted our mascot, Deez, over there," Steve explained, as he pulled his sword free of its scabbard. "Apparently, Deez thinks we're part of its hive now."

Gareth grinned. "How cool!"

Mythrin grew warm and the green blade began to glow.

Sir Steve? Where the bloody hell have you been?

Breslin? Wow, that was quick. I just now got my sword. I'm…

We need your help! Hurry! I do not think we will last much longer!

Breslin, what's going on? Are you fighting the pirates? Tell us where you are. We're here to help! Oh, we also need to be certain that your Power Hammer thingamajig doesn't fall into pirate hands. I wouldn't want to think what would happen if…

They already have the blasted hammer! They have it, and they are using it!

What? That can't be right. I thought only dwarves with Narian blood could…

Trust me on this, Sir Steve. They're using it all right, and they're using it against us! You must hurry!

Chapter 5 — Pirate Parasites

It's not possible, right?" Steve asked, several minutes later, after relaying everything Breslin had just said to Sarah and Gareth. They were also running for the far eastern wall of the cavern. Breslin had told him there was a large stone structure there, and that the pirates were holed up inside.

"There must be some rational explanation," Sarah was saying, as she raced alongside him. "You and I both know that only dwarves can use that hammer. It doesn't make sense that Captain Flinn would be able to use it. Could he have cast a spell to make himself stronger?"

"No clue," Steve admitted. He shot a quick glance over his shoulder to see if Gareth was keeping up, which he was. "Gareth, do you think that's possible?"

"Anything … anything is poss-possible," the teenager wheezed, as he ran alongside the two of them. "It depends … it depends on the sp-spell."

"That must be the answer," Sarah decided.

Steve glanced over at his wife. He was already breathing

hard and they had only been running for a minute or two. Sarah was not only breathing normally, she didn't appear to be winded in the slightest. Steve smiled. At least he was faring better than Gareth.

A loud clattering sounded a few feet behind them. Steve risked another glance backward and saw that the guur was easily keeping pace with them. What was its deal? Why would the guur willingly want to tag along with them? If it only knew how many of those large, armored bugs he had personally dispatched, then he was certain the guur would be making for the deep caves as fast as its ten legs could carry it. As such, everyone seemed to be treating it like it was a pet. Well, he had seen firsthand what type of destruction a guur was capable of, so there was no way he was willing to trust it.

"Where are we headed to again?" Sarah asked, as they sprinted through deserted streets filled with row after row of silent, stone houses.

"East," Steve said, trying his hardest not to wheeze. "Breslin said the pirates were holed up in a large, communal building. He said we couldn't miss it. Apparently Breslin, and several battalions of dwarves, are trying to find a way into this building, but thanks to Flinn and that damn hammer, every doorway has been blocked. Effectively, whatever that means."

"Effectively?" Sarah repeated, confused.

"His words, not mine."

The three of them sprinted through a long, narrow tunnel. Their footsteps echoed noisily as they hurried to reach the other side. Several hundred feet away, they could see the beginnings of a large open plaza through the opposite tunnel opening. There were also, Steve noticed, the first signs of inhabitants he had seen since stepping foot in Foronlir. Several small figures, clutching axes, clubs, and a slew of other weapons, were hurrying to and fro.

"Oh, no," Steve heard Gareth exclaim.

Husband and wife skidded to a stop. Steve's hands ignited while Sarah turned to regard their young companion.

"Gareth? What is it? What's wrong?"

"We lost Deez."

Steve finally turned around to look. Sure enough, the

guur was gone. Perhaps it had finally come to its senses?

"Where is he?" Gareth asked, as he looked back the way they had come. "Deez? Are you there? Where are you?"

It was important to note that the tunnel they had been running through, while narrow and short as far as tunnels are concerned, was designed and constructed by a race of people much smaller than the humans. Steve could easily touch the ceiling, without rising up on his tiptoes. So, when he turned to look back at the bustling activity on the other side of the tunnel, he let out a bellow of fright and inadvertently blasted out a jet of flames.

Deez, it would seem, had elected to race along the ceiling, hanging upside down, as soon as they had entered the tunnel. The friendly guur was hanging down at eye level, watching Steve intently, undoubtedly wondering why they had stopped running. It saw Steve's blast of flames and assumed it was under attack. Thankfully, Deez didn't suspect the attack came from its own hive mates, but from elsewhere, so it deftly scuttled down the side of the tunnel and peered anxiously out at the dwarves, who were now looking straight at them. The guur's two front forelegs, the longest of the ten it possessed, angrily dug at the wall it was clinging to, leaving deep gouges. Steve was reminded of a bull, pawing at the ground, as it prepared to charge the matador.

"If I didn't know any better," Sarah began, as she gave the huge insect an appraising look, "then I'd say Deez there is ready to fight on our behalf."

That's because he is. It is. I apologize. I do not know whether to refer to the creature as 'it' or by its moniker.

Hi, Pryllan. For the sake of argument, let's just call it by its name: Deez.

Deez? Does the creature accept this?

Beats the hell outta me. Could you ask it? Er, him?

"Pryllan just confirmed Deez here is ready to go to battle," Steve relayed.

Gareth was impressed. "Really? Why?"

"Isn't it obvious?" Sarah asked, turning to look at the young wizard. "We're in his hive. He's protecting us."

"From what?" Gareth wanted to know.

Sarah pointed a finger at Steve. "From him. Steve got spooked…"

"Did not," Steve grumped.

"…and shot off a blast of fire. Figuring we'd never try to bring him harm, Deez determined we were in danger. The only other beings he can see are the dwarves. Look at him. Gareth, you need to calm him down. I think he's ready to go after them. The dwarves don't know he's on our side. I don't want them freaking out when they see him."

Gareth hurried around Steve and laid a hand on the guur's armored carapace. Deez finally stopped digging his forelegs into the stone and turned his head to regard Gareth.

"False alarm. All is well. There's no need to attack, okay?"

Deez gave a series of rapid clicks and then slowly retreated down the wall until he was standing alongside Gareth. The guur anxiously tapped the ground with its two elongated front legs. Whether to indicate it wanted to see for itself what the 'creatures' were up ahead of it, or it was anxious to get going, Steve didn't know.

"So, do you trust Deez now?" Gareth asked, as he came up alongside Steve. "He was ready to jump into battle for you, you know."

"Time will tell, kid," Steve told the teenager. "I'm kinda the reason why there aren't more guur around these parts. What do you think Deez is gonna do once he realizes that?"

"You think he'll figure that out?" Sarah asked.

Steve inclined his head toward the end of the tunnel and broke into a light run. "I don't know. I hope not, 'cause if he does, he's liable to attack me, and we both know my jhorun won't like that one bit."

"I'll keep an eye on him for you," Gareth promised. "He won't hurt anyone. Well, he won't hurt anyone we don't want him to hurt."

There was commotion on the other side. Steve groaned. Nearly half a dozen dwarves were now sprinting down the tunnel, straight toward them, brandishing their axes. They had spotted the guur and had assumed the worst.

Steve sighed. If someone had told him he'd ever try to protect a guur from the dwarves, he'd have said they were a few sandwiches short of a picnic. He raised his arms and blasted a brief, but powerful, wall of flames then snuffed it out almost immediately.

It had the desired effect: dwarves skidded to a stop, shouts, exclamations, and demands for explanations all erupted at once. One dwarf, outfitted in the standard dark leather armor of the Kla Guur but embellished with sparkling gold and silver, pushed his way through the increasing crowd of angry onlookers.

"What the blazes is going on here? Sir Steve, are you there? Please tell me that you were the one responsible for that blast of fire."

"I'm here, Breslin," Steve announced, stepping in front of the dwarf. His hands remained lit.

Breslin was rubbing his eyes. "Why did you do that, blast us with bright light? Why would you … wizards be damned! What the ruddy hell is a guur doing here? I thought we had exterminated the last of those monsters! One side, Sir Steve. I'll deal with this."

Steve deliberately stepped in front of his diminutive friend. "Sorry, that's what I was doing when I blasted out the fire. Your companions spotted Deez. I couldn't let them hurt him, so I had to get everyone's attention."

"Deez? You travel with a *friendly* guur? Why in the name of Usol's ungainly ass do you think you could trust a monster like that?"

Steve slapped a hand over his mouth and snickered. "Usol's ungainly ass?"

Breslin's face colored and he gave a sheepish grin. "My apologies. I should have a care with my language." Mythryd was removed from its holder on the dwarf's back and clanged three times against the nearest wall.

The metallic clanging echoed noisily throughout the narrow tunnel.

Steve stuck a finger in his right ear and jostled it about. "Dude, what the hell was that for? That was loud."

"I really shouldn't have said that."

"About Usol's ass?" Steve chuckled.

"Hush, Sir Steve. If you only knew who Usol was, then

you'd be more respectful."

Steve sobered instantly. "I know full well what it's like to be on the receiving end of an Ancient's bad mood."

Breslin stared in shock. "You know Usol is an Ancient? How?"

"That's a story for another time."

"Now, back to the guur. You've given it a name?"

Steve nodded and held a friendly hand out to Deez, who cautiously inched forward until Steve's hand was resting on the top of its armored head. Steve then motioned for Breslin to approach. When the dwarf flat out refused to budge, Sarah used her jhorun to slide him over to the guur.

"Deez, this is our friend, Breslin. He's a dwarf, and can be trusted. Consider him part of the hive. There will be no attacking any dwarves, okay?"

"And you really think that monster can be trusted?" Breslin scoffed.

Steve nodded. "He's making a believer out of me. He was ready to attack you guys on our behalf, plus Pryllan tapped in telepathically to determine the nature of Deez's intentions."

"And?" Breslin dubiously asked.

"Deez just wants to join another hive. And, right now, he thinks we're it. So, here we are, with a guur in tow."

"And you will vouch for this creature?" Breslin asked, looking Steve straight in the eye.

"Yeah, I will. I trust Pryllan, and if she says Deez is harmless, then her word is good enough for me."

"Oh, sure," Gareth grumped. "Believe the dragon, but not the wizard?"

Ignoring Gareth, Steve gestured at the tunnel opening and the plaza beyond it.

"What's going on? Where are the pirates?"

Breslin beckoned for the others to follow him. "Right through there. I hope you can help us flush them out. They've barricaded themselves in Myrm. I can personally guarantee that we won't ever design a structure like that again."

"Myrm?" Sarah repeated, as she followed Breslin out of the tunnel. "What's that?"

"Myrm is a place where we can gather and reflect," Breslin

explained. "We wanted a place where the various clans could pool their resources and share their knowledge with their fellow dwarves."

"It's a school," Steve decided.

"University," Sarah corrected. "Or some type of institution."

"The Ninth Hall of Myrm holds the artifacts we've recovered from Nar," Breslin glumly added. "My hammer was on display there. I can only assume that's what the human pirates wanted."

Steve frowned. "Speaking from experience, I want to know how in the world Captain Windbag could even pick that hammer up. I've felt how heavy that thing is, and it's not something you can effectively use, unless you're part Narian. That's what you guys originally told us, remember? I ... whoa. There's something you don't see every day."

They finally emerged from the tunnel. Steve peered out across the open plaza and whistled with amazement. Encompassing the entire eastern wall of the cavern Foronlir called home was a solid wall of carved stone. There were a number of huge arched doorways, and a multitude of windows peeking out at them, going all the way up to the domed ceiling high above their heads. Although, Steve noticed the number of windows decreased the higher he looked, culminating with only two or three windows near the dome of the cavern.

"Is all that carved from the same stone?" Sarah incredulously asked. "I don't see any seams anywhere. Breslin, that's impressive work!"

"It was specifically designed to give a flawless look," Breslin answered. "It looks like it was carved out of a single stone, but it's not. Most of the space Myrm encompasses was already hollowed out by natural occurrences. We discovered the eastern wall was so riddled with caves that, with minimal effort, we could turn it into an asset the entire dwarf population could be proud of, and I'm not just talking about our clan. Myrm is a collaboration between us, Kla Chanus, Kla Luthur, and Kla Rehn."

Sarah nodded appreciatively. "That's wonderful, Breslin.

You must be proud."

"It was my grandfather's idea," Breslin admitted.

Steve perked up. "Kasnar? Wow. I didn't know he was still alive. That was one old, wrinkled ... ow!!"

Horrified, Sarah had stomped on Steve's foot to shut him up.

Breslin waved off Steve's comment. "I can only hope that, when I reach that age, I'm just as spry as he is. Grandfather has been helping catalog and identify the items recovered from Nar."

A loud clamor echoed noisily throughout the plaza, rattling windows and knocking over chairs, benches, signs, and other things that were not nailed down.

"What was that?" Steve anxiously whispered, as he followed Breslin over to a trench that had been dug in the street.

The four of them hastily hopped into the trench and squatted next to a group of very angry-looking dwarves. But, before introductions could be made, a ten-legged surprise dropped in between Sarah and Gareth, and chittered.

Every dwarf, except Breslin, leapt out of the trench and grabbed his weapon. Steve, fighting valiantly to suppress a laugh, was reminded of what a room full of unsuspecting cats would look like if properly spooked.

"This is going to take some getting used to," Breslin muttered. "A moment, if you please."

Their dwarf friend approached the others and a heated argument ensued. Breslin's voice finally broke through the objections.

"Enough! Do you not recognize the humans who came in with me?"

"No," one voice snapped back. "I was too busy running for my life after *you* led a blasted guur into our midst."

"Come on back and I'll make the introductions."

"I'm not getting back in there as long as that monstrosity is present," another voice declared.

There was another loud explosion. Windows rattled in their frames, several of them breaking apart. Breslin suddenly dropped into the trench. He knelt next to Steve and Sarah, holding Mythryd tightly in his hands.

"Are they coming back?" Steve wanted to know.

Breslin nodded. "Aye, but not before they argue amongst themselves first."

"We don't have time for this," Sarah decided. "I could teleport them all in here."

Breslin shook his head. "No, they need to come back on their own. Give it a moment."

A dwarf suddenly dropped next to Breslin. He was clutching his axe and fearfully staring at Deez, who was regarding him with equal fascination. The newcomer pointed a shaking finger at the guur.

"Wha- what's it doing in here? Can you make it go away?"

"You don't have anything to worry about," Steve told the dwarf. "As long as you don't try to attack us, Deez will leave you alone. Isn't that right, Deez?"

The guur rapped a front leg on the ground, inadvertently digging out a sizeable hole.

Breslin turned to the newcomer and held out a hand to encourage the nervous dwarf to stand up. He introduced Jotuth to Steve, Sarah, and Gareth.

"You're looking at, quite possibly, the strongest wizard you'll ever meet," Steve told the dwarf. "Remember hearing about the Renegade Wizard?"

Jotuth wordlessly nodded.

"He's given up those ways and is now helping us. Don't do anything stupid, okay? You've already met Deez, who is very protective over his new hive. Remember that."

Jotuth's mouth fell open. "You are a powerful wizard, underling, if you can command a guur to do your bidding."

"Here's the thing," Gareth hesitantly admitted, keeping his eyes closed. "I'm really not controlling him with any spell. I did use him as a familiar, but when the spell wore off, he stuck around. I had expected him to flee the city, but he didn't. Now, he stays with us because that is his wish. He wants a new hive, and we seem to be it."

"Incredible," Jotuth breathed. He approached the guur and cautiously held out a hand, as though he was meeting a strange dog for the first time. "Hello. Uh, are you friendly?"

Deez regarded the dwarf for a few moments before climbing out of the trench.

"What's he doing?" Steve hissed, looking back at Gareth. "He's putting himself in danger by being out in the open. We don't know if Flinn is watching, and if he is, he could blast him with some type of air jet. Get him back in here!"

Gareth poked his head out over the rim of the trench and looked for their unusual companion. Deez was a few feet away, poking his long forelegs at a large mound of recently excavated earth. Gareth whistled. When Deez didn't respond, the teenager grabbed the closest stone he could reach and thumped it on the ground. The guur whipped his head around and stared straight at Gareth.

"If you don't get back in that trench, then you're gonna get hurt! Do you understand me? You need to hide!"

DANGER

Steve popped his head up over the lip of the trench and stared at Gareth and his guur. "What did you say?"

Gareth spun in place and shrugged as he looked back at Steve. "I didn't say anything. I heard it, though. Up here," the wizard added, tapping his head.

That was your insectoid companion.

Pryllan? Are you telling me Deez was the one who said, 'danger'? They're capable of coherent thought?

Evidently. I left the mental connection open, in case the creature wanted further communication. I apologize. I will close the connection.

No, wait! Leave it open. If Deez is willing to communicate with us, that can only be a good thing.

As you wish.

"Gareth? You're not gonna believe this. What we heard was Deez, via Pryllan's mental connection. He was warning us of danger, and I'd have to agree. Get your butt back down here. Deez? Can you understand me? You need to get back in here, too."

Deez remained motionless as he silently studied Gareth. His armored head slowly swiveled until he was looking straight at Steve. Then it was back to Gareth.

"What's going on?" Sarah called from within the trench. "Get back in here before either of you get hurt!"

"We're trying!" Steve called back.

A sudden blast of wind sent Steve and Gareth diving—head first—into the trench. The condensed air jet swirled high above their heads before slamming into the cavern roof. Several stalactites fell heavily to the ground. Unfortunately, they fell right where the guur had been standing.

"Deez!" Gareth exclaimed, horrified. "Oh, no!"

Steve immediately heard a chant. Gareth was concocting some type of retaliation.

"Cool your jets, pal," Steve snapped back. "Before you do anything, check out the wall!"

Climbing up the smooth rock face, as easily as if the wall contained handholds everywhere, was Deez. Even from this distance, they could hear the guur clicking angrily as it rapidly scaled the vertical surface, looking for those responsible for attacking its hive.

Gareth cupped his hands to his mouth and shouted as loud as he could, "Deez! What are you doing? Get back down here!"

ELIMINATE THREAT

They watched Deez pause at one of the barricaded window openings at the fourth floor, where something must have attracted its attention. Had the guur discovered one of the pirates?

Deez began digging through the stone as if it were sand. Chunks of broken stone and rock rained down on the cavern floor. Just then, they heard a high-pitched scream of absolute terror, followed by sounds of a scuffle and incoherent shouts. Then, a huge blast of air effectively cleared all remaining pieces of the barricade from the window, as large pieces of stone and timber went flying in all directions. Also flung out the window was Deez, whose ten legs were splayed in all directions.

"He's in for a rough landing!" Steve shouted helplessly.

"Sarah! Can you slow him down?"

"I'm way ahead of you," Sarah informed him.

The guur's rapid freefall slowed until Deez's ten legs gently touched down onto the cavern floor. Wasting no time, Deez immediately oriented himself and prepared to climb up the wall for another attempt.

"No, Deez!" Gareth snapped. "Let them go for now! We'll have to find another way to get past them!"

THREAT NOT ELIMINATED

"Yes, we know they're still up there," Gareth told the guur. "We'll find another way."

Steve suppressed a chuckle. The guur looked as though it was pouting, as it slowly made its way back to them. The armored head kept swiveling to look up at the window he had dug through, as if he was considering another attempt.

There was another loud clang, and the earth shook for nearly ten seconds.

Breslin was scowling. "I do not understand it. How? How is that infernal villain wielding my hammer? No Narian blood runs in his veins!"

"You saw Captain Flinn wielding the hammer?" Sarah asked. "Are you sure?"

"I saw a human collapse several tunnels and severely damage a bridge as they tried to make their escape. It'll take us months to repair all the devastation he has wrought."

"Were there any humans in Nar?" Steve asked, as he crouched next to Sarah and Gareth. "Could he be a legitimate ancestor?"

"No," Breslin stoutly declared. "Nar was peopled by dwarves. Humans have been to Nar, sure, but only to steal its treasures and sell them off to the highest bidder. No, there are no true Narian humans."

"Then how?" Sarah demanded. "How is he making the hammer work?"

"I'd like to know how he can even lift that thing," Steve mumbled to himself.

"That makes two of us," Breslin added.

Gareth cleared his throat and leaned forward. "This hammer. Tell me about it. How does it work?"

Breslin shrugged. "The Narian Power Hammer has four pieces: handle, head, counterweight, and helix."

"Helix?" Gareth repeated, looking over at Steve.

"Spiraled ruby," Steve translated, twirling his finger in a corkscrew pattern.

"Oh."

"The hammer," Breslin continued. "is capable of reducing the largest boulder into gravel with the slightest touch. The wielder could effectively work with the hammer for hours without growing weary. I've used that hammer for more than twelve hours straight and I never once grew fatigued."

"Are all dwarves Narian?" Gareth asked.

Breslin and Jotuth both shook their heads no.

Gareth nodded. "But all Narians were dwarves. Got it. How many dwarves can wield the hammer?"

Jotuth gave Breslin an expectant look.

"Not many," Breslin finally admitted. "My family can, and I suspect a few others can as well, but none have revealed themselves. Why?"

The teenager shrugged. "No reason. I'm just trying to understand as much as I can about this hammer. Now, if one is not Narian, what would happen with the hammer?"

"The hammer becomes inactive," Breslin reported. "Sir Steve can attest to the ineffectiveness of an inert Narian Power Hammer."

"Sucker weighs a ton," Steve reported, eliciting a grunt from Gareth. "Not even Conan could wield that baby."

"Conan?" Gareth repeated, confused. "Who's that?"

"No one you would know," Sarah answered. "Imagine a hammer so heavy that you can't even lift it. Now, how would you be expected to use it?"

Steve raised a hand. "I have a question..."

"Put your hand down, dear," Sarah quietly ordered, as she pushed his hand down. "You're not in school."

"Has anyone used that hammer besides Captain Windbag?"

Breslin was silent as he considered. "No. I only remember

seeing one human wield the hammer, and it was the same one who seemed to be able to control the air."

"That's Flinn," Sarah confirmed.

"Is there a back way out of Myrm?" Steve asked.

Breslin shook his head. "No. We find it puzzling. Why steal the hammer and then barricade yourself inside a facility with no means of leaving? How do they plan to escape? Your human pirate is able to wield the hammer, aye, but what does he plan to do? Bash his way out?"

Right on cue, they heard a distant, loud metallic clang, and the earth shook once more.

"Could be," Steve decided. "How far do those caves go? Is it possible they could find someplace to hide and just wait until the coast is clear, so to speak?"

"Myrm is comprised of four large caverns and several dozen small caves," Breslin informed him. "Those we decided to use were prepared for use, and those we knew we wouldn't use were sealed."

"Could Captain Flinn break into one of the sealed caves with that hammer?" Sarah wanted to know.

Breslin groaned. "Easily. However, he wouldn't know where to find the sealed caves, so it'd be pointless to…"

"Come on, buddy," Steve interrupted. "Think about it. They found the door leading down. They managed to get through your barrier in the first great cave. They've proven they can wield the hammer. Would you put it past them to not know how to find a sealed cave?"

"What else is back there?" Sarah asked. "Could they find a way out?"

At this moment, three more dwarves dropped into the trench and crouched next to Breslin. All three of them warily eyed Deez. Breslin pulled all the dwarves into a huddle.

As the dwarves quietly conversed amongst themselves, Steve turned to look at his wife.

"We know you're great at teleporting people from one locale to another, right?"

Sarah regarded him with a curious look. "Your point being?"

"Do you think you could teleport the pirates out of there?"

Sarah shook her head. "Not without seeing them first. If I knew where they were hiding, then I might be able to get them."

Steve pointed at Deez. "What if we send him in there? Gareth, couldn't you use him as a familiar again? If you can share that vision with Sarah, wouldn't we be able to safely extricate those pirates from their museum?"

"You'd be putting Deez at risk again," Gareth answered. "You saw how easily he was blasted out the window. I don't want anything to happen to him."

"Nor do I," Sarah agreed. "Putting Deez back in harm's way is out of the question."

"Why don't we ask him if he'd be willing to go?" Steve suggested. "Maybe he'd do it for us."

"I know he'd do it for us," Gareth announced. "I'm thinking he'd do it without a second thought. However, I don't *want* him to do that."

Steve felt a tap on his shoulder. Turning, he saw that the dwarf huddle had broken up and Breslin was before him. The dwarves all had frowns on their faces.

"What's with the long faces, guys?" Steve asked. "Let me guess. There's bad news?"

"We don't know what else lies within the caves. The area beyond the Myrm caverns is largely unexplored. There very well *could* be an undiscovered avenue which could return the human invaders Topside."

Just then, there was another blast, much louder and much stronger. Dust filled the air, and when it finally cleared, Steve, Sarah, and the dwarves were shocked to discover a sizeable hole had been punched through Myrm's smooth exterior. Steve narrowed his eyes. It was directly above the farthest arched doorway on the right. Steve silently counted the arches. Nine. Wasn't that the one where the Narian artifacts were being stored?

Several people appeared at the mouth of the hole and quickly flung out coils of rope. In the blink of an eye, three pirates were on the ground, and one was sprinting alarmingly fast straight toward him. Steve groaned. There was only one pirate who could move that fast, and he already had several encounters with this individual in the past. None had ended well.

"Here comes our friend," Sarah remarked. "Don't worry. I have him."

Out of nowhere, a blast of air appeared and threatened to knock Sarah off her feet. Within moments, Steve generated a jet of fire and flung it straight toward the hole, where he could see more pirates waiting to drop down to the street. The air jet instantly reversed course and pushed the fire jet safely out of harm's way.

Steve had expected this. He was ready with a second blast. Steve's jet of fire could have easily torched any human it touched, in just a few seconds. The last thing he had ever wanted to do was to take a life, and Flinn was easily able to deflect his shots, which was what Steve was counting on: a distraction.

"Can anyone see where he is?" Steve asked, between blasts of fire.

"I can't," Sarah called back. His wife had her hands full, picking up pirates and flinging them back into the hole they had crept out of.

"Don't put them back in Myrm!" Breslin shouted, as he and several other dwarves pulled their weapons free of their holders and leapt out of the trench. "We're trying to get them *out* of Myrm, not back *in*!"

"I know that," Sarah crossly informed the dwarf. "Don't you get it? The pirates are coming out on their own. That means they've realized they have been pinned down. The only way for them to escape is to make it past us!"

"Is that Captain Flinn?" Gareth suddenly asked, as he pointed at a window on the fourth floor, the same window Deez had been blasted out of by Flinn.

Steve shot a quick glance up at the fourth level. "Yeah, that's him, all right. Don't worry about him. I've got him a wee bit preoccupied at the moment."

Momentarily distracted by Steve and Gareth's conversation, Sarah let her guard lapse. Several pirates were able to approach the trench and engage with the dwarves. Thankfully, even though the dwarves were nowhere as large as the humans, they were extremely well-trained soldiers. They were easily able to keep the humans from pushing past the trench and into the tunnel leading away from Myrm.

Overhead, blast after blast of super-condensed air swirled about, slamming into stalactites, crashing into buildings, and doing its best to force Steve and Sarah to take cover. Steve was scowling. For every blast of fire he could throw at Flinn, it seemed like the pirate was able to generate two: one to counteract whatever he had thrown, and the second seemed to target either he or his wife. Since when had Flinn become more powerful than him? There had to be something he was missing.

"I can't seem to get any advantage over this guy," Steve growled, as he shot blast after blast of fire up at the fourth floor. No matter how quickly he generated his blasts, Flinn always seemed to be marginally faster.

May I make a suggestion?

By all means, Pryllan. If you have an idea, I would love to hear it.

Retreat.

That's a lousy suggestion, my friend. We can't let those pirates get away. They have the hammer! We have to get it back.

They occupy the high ground. They have the advantage. Give them time to remove themselves from … Look out!

A stalactite dropped noisily to the ground less than a few feet from where he and Gareth had been standing. Small bits of gravel and stone pummeled the two of them, leaving both of their faces bloodied. Steve felt the trickles of blood run down his face and scowled.

"Gareth, are you okay? Your face is covered in blood, dude!"

The teenager wiped a finger down his face and stared in horror at the amount of blood collected on his fingers. His eyes closed, his mouth silently moved, and Steve heard a faint chant. Less than five seconds later, Gareth's face had returned to normal.

"Your face looks just as bad. Allow me."

After his face had been healed by Gareth's spell, Steve angrily turned to look up at Flinn. What he saw had him gasping in shock. Flinn, it would seem, had been busy while the two of them were recovering from their wounds. Nearly a dozen different air jets swirled high above their heads. Then, it began raining huge stone spikes.

Horrified, Steve turned to Sarah, but before he could get out an angry response, he noticed his hands. Both had turned an ugly, mottled red. And, both hands were tingling so bad that it felt like he had shoved them deep into a nest of fire ants. His eyes widened. That only happened when his jhorun was supremely pissed. It meant...

"Get out of here!" Steve shouted at his wife, holding up his hands to show her their color. "Get everyone clear! Hurry!"

Sarah gasped, quickly spun in place and closed her eyes. At the exact moment Sarah teleported everyone to the other side of the narrow tunnel leading away from Myrm, Steve's jhorun detonated.

Shock waves exploded in all directions, shattering the falling stalactites, blowing out every window in the plaza, and crumbling many of the smaller houses. The tunnel shuddered, then collapsed, dropping hundreds of tons of rock to erase any sign the tunnel had ever existed.

"Is everyone all right?" Breslin asked, as he slowly got to his feet.

Sarah's spur-of-the-moment teleportation had literally dropped their group, including the dwarves, into the middle of the plaza, in front of what used to be the Myrm Tunnel. Gareth rose painfully to his feet and waited a few moments for the dust to clear from the air. Once it did, he immediately looked for Deez. The friendly guur was already on his feet and staring at the mass of broken rocks sticking out of their end of the tunnel.

A faint rumbling began and grew progressively louder. Steve painfully pushed himself to his feet and looked over at his wife. They were both eyeing the collapsed tunnel and backing fearfully away.

Breslin hurried over to the collapsed tunnel and laid a hand on one particularly large slab of stone. Jotuth joined him moments later. In less than five seconds, all the dwarves either had laid their hands on some of the recently dislodged stone or else were holding them on the ground.

"It's collapsed," Jotuth said, after the deep rumblings faded away.

"What's collapsed?" Steve hesitantly asked.

"Myrm's cavern," Breslin whispered, as he pulled his hand off the stone. He approached Steve and laid a hand on his shoulder. "It wasn't your fault. You couldn't have known that would happen."

"Are you saying that the whole cavern has collapsed?" Steve sputtered, appalled. "There's been a cave-in over there, is that it? That would mean that ... oh, no. That would mean that the pirates..."

"Aye, lad," Breslin said, after Steve trailed off. "It would seem you have fixed our pirate problem for us."

Chapter 6 — Between a Rock and a Hard Place

When can we panic, Cap'n? Look around you! We're trapped!"

"Someone find Puck and sew his mouth shut," Captain Flinn scowled. "We will be fine, men. Observe." He tapped the hammer, fast becoming his most prized possession after the Alchos Stone, against the nearest boulder. The huge stone broke apart like glass.

"We're pinned, Captain. How will we escape?"

"Is that Puck again?" Flinn demanded, growing angry. "There be an extra ten pieces of gold for the first person to smack the fool upside his head."

The pirates were sprawled on the ground, trying to make themselves as flat as possible. Tons of rocks were less than six inches above their heads, giving barely room to wiggle.

"Captain ... why weren't we squished flat? How is it none of us are harmed?"

Flinn tapped a fourth boulder with the power hammer, giving him room to sit up. "Really? Be that the answer ye be looking for at this present moment in time? Fear not. We have been through worse."

"When?" Rusty's voice asked from somewhere on Flinn's left.

Ignoring him, Flinn took stock of his surroundings. Everywhere he looked, he saw stone. Broken slabs of solid rock and boulders the size of the now defunct *Cadaymas* were the only things he could see. Oddly enough, he couldn't see any reason why he and his men had been able to survive unscathed, either. Those huge slabs of stone should have squished them to jelly, yet here they were, still fighting for their survival.

He automatically tried rising to his feet, only to painfully smack his head on the stone ceiling, which was dismally low. About ready to let out a mighty curse, Flinn hesitated. Did the Lentarians know they had survived? Could they have posted some type of lookout? Perhaps now wasn't the best time to try and blast their way out of here.

"Keep yer voices down, men," Flinn whispered. "In case there be hostile eyes and ears nearby."

"How can you be so calm, Captain?" Flinn heard his quartermaster ask. "We are all but pinned in here!"

"I still have the hammer, men," Flinn reminded them. "The stones seem to have stopped falling, and we are all accounted for, so … are we? Are we all here? Head check."

"Quartermaster here," Rusty's voice said.

"Casimir, check," another voice added.

"Grenden," the ship's doctor said.

"Von here," another voice said.

"Jino," the *Emberbrand*'s best warrior grumped.

"I'm here," a final voice added, after a few moments of silence had passed.

"Puck?" Flinn snapped. "Be that you? That be not how we do 'head check', and ye know it. Now, do it properly."

"I am Alquin," the tremulous voice declared.

"Alquin? What about Puck? Who has eyes on Puck?"
Silence.

"Perhaps he didn't make it?" Rusty hesitantly suggested.

"Spread out," Flinn automatically ordered. "Find him. I want…"

"Cap'n?" Casimir quietly said. "We cannot search if we cannot move!"

Flinn was silent as he strained to hear any outside noise. As far as he could tell, there was nothing moving besides them. More than likely, the blasted fire thrower's explosion collapsed the entire cavern.

The fire thrower. How had he generated such a large explosion? That would put the advantage squarely back with him. That, Flinn gruffly thought, was not a pleasing prospect. He, along with the invaluable advice his Alchos Stone was giving him, *had* to be the one with the advantage.

The Fire Thrower troubled him greatly. He would have to think about how to counteract this ability to generate explosions. For now, they had to find some way out of this mess.

Just then, part of his jacket grew warm. More specifically, the inside pocket where the stone once belonging to an Ancient was sitting. Surreptitiously checking to see if he was being watched, Flinn slipped a hand into his coat pocket and he wrapped it around the stone. Yes, it was warm. Almost too warm to handle. What did it mean? Was the Stone trying to tell him something?

Then, it clicked.

The Stone! That's why they were still alive. The Stone had somehow prevented the rocks from crushing them flat. How, or why, the stone did it, he didn't know. However, considering the circumstances, Flinn wasn't about to argue.

Hefting the hammer in his right hand, he started exploring his immediate surrounding. If a boulder hampered his progress, then it was reduced to gravel. However, unsure of how many boulders he could safely remove without causing the rest of the stones to finish their fall, the captain decided to choose his targets with care.

"I'm tellin' ya, Cap'n," Casimir was saying, "Puck's dead. He's probably under one of these big rocks. He's a goner."

"And if you were the one missing? Rusty countered. "If

you were the one unaccounted for, would you want us to assume you were dead and move on?"

Casimir's eyes fell. "No, Q."

"I didn't think so. And stop calling me 'Q'."

"Sorry, Q."

His back ached terribly. Not wanting to test the strength of his Stone, Flinn had only cleared about four feet of space in which to move around. As much as he wanted to keep smashing boulders, he also didn't know if any Lentarian was nearby. Therefore, they had to be as quiet as possible.

Ten minutes later, an excited shout drew Flinn's attention. He had cleared enough room so that the men were able to explore the area of where the arched doorways had been. Jino's voice had come from way off to the left, near the remnants of the first arch. From the sounds of it, Jino had found Puck. At least, Flinn hoped it was Puck, or whatever was left of him. He was anxious to move on. He was eager to stretch his back. And furthermore, he was anxious to see the open skies again.

Shushing the men, and angrily pushing his way to the front of the group, Flinn confronted Jino. His best warrior turned to point at two large slabs of stone. One was resting flat on the ground, and the other had one end resting up on the other, creating a small, protected enclosure. In that space, Flinn could see an arm.

"Is he alive?" Flinn asked, as he knelt down next to his men, who were frantically trying to leverage the slab off of Puck's still form.

Jino gripped Puck's wrist and nodded. "Aye. He's alive, Captain."

"Good. Stand back. That goes for all of ye."

Two taps of the hammer were all it took to break apart the large slab. The men immediately began scooping the broken gravel away from Puck's body. Grenden pulled the fallen crewman to a sitting position and smacked a hand on the side of Puck's face.

"Oy! Wake up! Come on, Puck. We know you're alive."

Puck groaned and finally opened his eyes. "Am I dead?"

"Ye will be if ye get separated from us again," Flinn

growled. "What the blazes are ye doin' all the way over here?"

"Wha- what do you mean, Captain?"

"All of us were over there," Rusty informed the hapless crewman, pointing south. "You're the only one who must've wandered off."

"The roof was collapsing!" Puck cried. "I was tryin' to find cover! What did you think I was gonna do? Hang around to see if it'd miss me? Absolutely not!"

"Whatever," Flinn grumbled. "Now that we all be here, let's find a way out."

"How?" Jino sullenly asked.

Flinn was silent as he studied their surroundings. As much as he didn't want to believe he was losing hope, he had to admit their present situation was exceedingly dire. He finally sighed and eyed his men.

"I am open for suggestions. Let's hear 'em."

Puck suddenly pointed east, back toward Myrm.

"There. We have no choice but to find a way out through there."

Every single person turned to look back at the destroyed entrance to the dwarf institution.

"Think about it," Puck continued. "It looks like the bulk of the cavern collapsed out here. Chances are, we'll find less damage inside. We might even find something that could help us out."

The men continued to regard Puck as though he had sprouted wings.

"What?" Puck stammered. "What's the matter?"

"I don't think I have ever agreed with Puck before," Rusty began, "but I do have to admit he has a point. We're not going to find much assistance out here. Our odds are better if we go back in there."

"We've already looked in there," Jino pointed out. "We cannot escape that way. We'd be trapped, all over again."

Captain Flinn eyed Puck speculatively before shrugging. He didn't want to admit Puck's idea was sound, either, however, what choice had he? He rose to a crouch and pointed in the direction Puck had indicated.

"We head east. I, for one, be tired of stooping, so be

on the lookout for any place where we can stand normally. I cannot think hunched over like this."

The pirates retraced their steps back to the Ninth Hall of Myrm. What greeted their eyes didn't look promising. The entire archway had collapsed. Standing before an impassable wall of broken stone, the pirates all turned to look at their captain. He pushed wordlessly by the crew and slowly straightened his aching back. The only positive aspect of returning here appeared to be the simple fact that there was a tiny aisle, no more than five feet wide by ten feet long, where the men could finally straighten their backs.

Rusty pointed at the hammer. "Will you do the honors, Captain? We want to go that way, and that hammer is the best way to accomplish that."

Flinn sat heavily down on the closest rock. "In a moment, Q. My back be botherin' me somethin' fierce. I need a moment to rest."

Rusty held out his hand. "Could I have the hammer? You rest, Captain. I'll clear this rubble."

Knowing there was no way for his quartermaster to abscond with his hammer, since there was nowhere to flee, Flinn set the tool down on its head in front of his feet. "Be my guest, Q."

Rusty leaned forward, grabbed the handle with his right hand, but the hammer refused to budge. Embarrassed, he leaned forward to grab the handle with both hands.

Once more, the handle slid through his fingers, as though it was cemented in place. Gritting his teeth, Rusty grunted with effort as he channeled every ounce of strength he had into his arms, willing it, *begging* it, to move. It didn't.

"What's with that hammer?"

Flinn shrugged. "Ye saw me using it, did ye not? I did nothing special. I cast no spells. As far as I am aware, there be no spells on it."

Captain and First Mate then heard several disgusted grunts. Flinn turned to see that Jino had successfully picked the hammer up off the ground, but was holding it with both of his hands. As soon as he tried to heft the hammer with one, it would slide out of his grip and fall noisily to the ground.

"Well, that makes me feel better," Rusty observed.

Not bothering to hide the smirk on his face, Flinn waved his hand at Jino, indicating he was giving his crewman permission to use the hammer to clear the way. With beads of perspiration running down his face, Jino struggled to carry the hammer over to the wall. Determined to use the tool as easily as the captain had, and gripping the handle as though he was clinging to it for dear life, Jino swung the hammer at the rocks.

They heard a muffled metallic clang as the hammer bounced harmlessly off the closest stone. Surprised, the pirates leaned forward to inspect the damage. Not only had the hammer failed to break the huge boulder, but there didn't appear to be any cracks or chips on the stone whatsoever. Jino stifled a curse and swung again.

Once more, the hammer made contact with the wall. As before, a quiet muted clang could be heard, but that was all that happened. The wall remained unblemished.

With his jhorun tiring, and his strength failing, the hammer slid from Jino's grip and thumped onto the ground. Wiping his sweaty palms on his trousers, Jino looked at the captain with a new appreciation in his eyes. Flinn had to stifle a laugh as clearly the sailor was trying to figure out how he had effortlessly wielded that hammer when he could not. Ignoring the sharp pains in his back, Flinn rose to his feet, covered the distance to the hammer in just a few steps, and easily picked it up, as though he was picking up a simple goblet. Maintaining eye contact with Jino, the captain stepped forward and tapped the hammer's head on the stone.

A loud clang erupted, just before the rock shattered like glass and was reduced to hundreds of pea-sized bits of gravel. Captain Flinn moved on to the next and repeated the process. Within moments, he had gained noticeable ground as he worked to clear a path back into the dwarf stronghold they had previously been holed up in. A few more blows cleared the last three boulders and, just like that, he was standing inside the front lobby area. It was badly damaged, sure, but they could all easily walk around without hunching over.

"What now, Captain?" Rusty asked, as he appeared by

Flinn's side. "Why bother coming back in here? Do you really think we can find a way out? I strongly doubt we'll find a back door. What are we supposed to do?"

Flinn was silent as he considered. What he really needed to do was to consult the stone. However, he needed a quiet, secluded spot to do that, with no interruptions. And no witnesses.

"We've been through an ordeal, Q. Let the men rest for a bit. The solution will present itself."

"And if it doesn't, Captain?" Rusty asked.

"My instincts are telling me to wait for a while, and I long ago learned to listen when my instincts were talkin'. We wait here. Tell the men to spread out and look for anything that could help us."

Rusty nodded. "Aye, Captain."

The quartermaster wandered off, taking the majority of the men with him. Flinn eagerly looked up as he noticed how quiet it had become. Certain that a bit of luck had finally fallen into his lap, he started reaching for his stone when he noticed that one man had stayed behind. It was Puck. His crewman was sitting down nearly a dozen feet away, with his back against the wall. He was also, Flinn noticed, facing the other direction.

Should he risk it? Could he consult the stone without Puck noticing? What if Puck noticed the prized Alchos Stone? How would he be able to explain his possession of a large, fist-sized sapphire in his pocket?

Flint grunted irritably. He couldn't. He'd have to wait for the hapless fool to leave, or else find a location far enough away from prying eyes that he could unwrap the large jewel.

Realizing that his luck had, indeed, soured, Flinn rose to his feet, much to the chagrin of his throbbing back. About ready to check the few remaining spells to see if there was anything that might be able to take some of the pain away, Flinn hesitated.

He heard something. He paused as he strained his ears to listen for the faintest of sounds. His own labored breathing made it almost impossible to hear anything else, let alone hear over Puck's snoring. What, then, had he heard?

There it was again! It was a faint, repetitive noise that was reminiscent of a scratching sound. It almost sounded like…

Flinn's eyes shot open, his pain forgotten. It had sounded like digging! Someone was digging, and they were nearby! Were they the Lentarians? Were they the dwarves?

"Puck! On yer feet, man! Somethin' is comin'!"

Puck's eyes shot open as he fearfully turned to look his way.

"What is it, Cap'n? What do you hear?"

"I think someone be diggin'. That can only mean the damn Lentarians know we be still alive. Find the rest of the men. Get them back here, on the double!"

"Aye, Cap'n!"

Puck took off like a shot, disappearing into the same darkened tunnel that the other five crewmembers had used. Apparently, his crew hadn't made it far, because in less than twenty seconds, all six of his men were standing before him. Casimir's mouth opened.

"Belay that!" Flinn angrily hissed. "No unnecessary talkin'! The Lentarians may know we be still alive, but they may not know *where* we be. The only voice I want to hear will be my own, be that understood?"

Every single one of his crew nodded and disobeyed his order, saying, "Aye, Captain," at the same time.

The digging grew louder. Much louder. It had to be the dwarves. They were known miners. They spent their entire lives underground, digging in the earth. Only they could dig this fast. Flinn gritted his teeth. If it was a battle they wanted, then it would be a battle they received.

Several jets of air appeared, and swirled around the seven of them in the lobby. Jino was the first to join him in his readiness to go to battle by drawing both daggers. After a few seconds of hesitation, the rest of the pirates drew their weapons.

"Spread out!" Flinn snapped, as he ducked behind a large boulder. "Hide! We have a better chance if we can attack all at the same time, but we cannot do so if we be seen."

The pirates scattered across the large cavern serving as Myrm's lobby. Two pirates, Grenden and Rusty, darted over to nearby staircases, and crouched low. Casimir chose to duck back into the entryway. Alquin and Jino chose to hide in two separate tunnels on the opposite side of the lobby. Puck, suddenly realizing he was standing by himself out in the open, let out a squeal of fright and scrambled back into the original entryway, joining Casimir, much to his chagrin.

"Let them come," Jino growled, from his tunnel opening.

"They will rue the day they ever encountered pirates from *The Emberbrand*," Rusty vowed. "They…"

The ship's quartermaster trailed off as the sound of digging suddenly stopped, only to be replaced by a series of loud, piercing cracks, as though something impossibly huge was easily breaking through huge slabs of stone. Just then, right on cue, huge jagged cracks appeared on the floor. The cracks rapidly expanded in size, as clearly *something* under the stone wanted *out*.

Captain Flinn's face paled. Mere dwarves wouldn't have the resources to do that. They'd simply tunnel through the rock instead of trying to push their way through. Whatever it was could only spell trouble for them. He pulled the hammer from his belt and whistled to get everyone's attention.

"That be no dwarf! Somethin' be comin' up, through the rocks! Retreat! Follow me!"

The men, detecting fear in Flinn's voice for the first time ever, abandoned their positions and immediately sprinted after their captain. Flinn ran toward the closest closed door in the opposite direction, away from whatever monstrosity was trying to emerge. The door was locked, and refused to open. One swing of the hammer reduced the door to splinters.

Deeper into the heart of Myrm they ran, oftentimes making their own doors as they attempted to put as much distance between themselves and the source of the ever-increasing terra tremors. In fact, as soon as Flinn stopped to gather his bearings, he felt the trembling increase in intensity. If he didn't know any better, then he'd say that whatever was responsible was *following them*!

The room shuddered as the terra tremors increased in strength. Alquin waved his arms at him from across the room, drawing his gaze. His lookout pointed at a tunnel leading further into who knows where. The only thing Flinn cared about was that it was away from the trembling.

"It's not as strong this way, Captain!"

"We head toward Alquin!" Flinn snapped. "Move! Get yer arses out of here!"

Ten minutes later, Flinn thought for sure his lungs were about to burst. Whatever was out there was digging through the ground faster than they could run, and *that* scared him more than he would ever admit. The only thing he would admit, though, was that he knew—without a doubt—that this wasn't dwarfish by design.

Thinking that they might have lost their subterranean tracker, at least for the time being, the men collapsed to the floor, their sides heaving. Jino appeared to be the only one who wasn't out of breath. Flinn sank down against the nearest wall and rested his back.

A soft clattering sounded right next to him. Flinn rested a hand on the ground and noticed a small pebble was rolling away from him, even though the ground—as far as he could tell—was flat. His eyes widened with surprise. The tremors were back and were growing at such a rate that it became clear that whatever had been tailing them had, unfortunately, finally caught up. Before he could say anything, though, Jino suddenly leapt to his feet and cursed.

"What in the name of the Great Kings is that?!"

Flinn scrambled to his feet as fast as he could. He stared in open-mouthed shock. He had been right. There had been something that had been following, and unfortunately, it was *huge*! The wall on their immediate right splintered apart and collapsed noisily to the ground. Something large, gray, and rounded, like the concave shields the king's soldiers used back home, appeared.

Flinn blinked with surprise. What was it? Some type of battering ram?

The domed object pushed its way further into the room, on a direct line north. Whatever was in its way, be it walls, or stone formations, crumbled apart as the domed object increased its size. Flinn suddenly heard an exclamation of surprise and glanced over to see Alquin pointing at the object.

"Scales! I see scales, Captain!"

Shocked, Flinn squinted his eyes as the rocks began to fall away from the domed object. Yes, he could see scales. That meant that whatever this thing was, it was reptilian in nature! What kind of horrors must live in these mountains to become that big?

The bulk of the creature's head appeared. It was large, heavily muscled, and contained numerous scars on the top of its head. Was that because it chose to push its way through the earth rather than digging?

Two long, muscular forelegs appeared. Each arm was tipped with thick, two-foot-long talons. Flinn noted the arms *were* removing obtruding objects which could pose a threat to the creature's eyes.

The creature struggled to pull more of itself into the cavern. The overall shape of the body emerged: that of an enormous reptile, with huge powerful hind legs. It could easily stand well over twenty feet tall, Flinn guessed. Had it tried to step foot on the *Emberbrand*, he was certain it would sink.

Dragon, Flinn decided, but not of any type he'd ever seen. For one thing, there were no wings. There were no back plates. Sure, the creature was heavily scaled, and the talons on its forelegs were very intimidating, but there the similarities ended. It was as if this dragon had become adapted to living underground.

Whatever it was, Flinn angrily thought, it had to be stopped. What if it was a pet belonging to the dwarves, one that did their bidding? Judging by its size, it could easily snap all of them up for breakfast and come looking for seconds. No, this monster had to be dealt with before it came after them.

About ready to signal his crew to attack, Flinn hesitated. The creature had just opened its eyes, stared stupidly around the cavern they were in, and let out a huge blast of air, as though it had been holding its breath. The eye closest to him, the left, looked glazed over; unfocused. Perhaps it didn't know they were there? Why, then, would it stop at the exact spot where the seven of them were hiding?

Flinn saw Jino crouch low, gripping a dagger in each hand, and slowly creep out of the tunnel, staying in the creature's blind spot.

"Belay that," Flinn called out, in the softest tone he could muster while still being able to be heard. "I do not think the creature knows we be here."

"It's distracted, Captain," Jino angrily informed him. "If we do not strike now, then we'll lose the advantage. I can take out the eyes first. It won't be able to see us coming."

"It cannot see us coming as it is," Flinn pointed out. "Stand down, man. That be an order."

Jino sheathed his daggers, while letting out an exasperated huff. Flinn pointed at the giant head.

"See the eyes? They look like they be open, but not seeing anything."

"This eye is the same," Rusty added, appearing next to Jino. "What does that mean? Is it sleep-walking? Do monsters do that?"

The creature had finally pulled itself completely out of the tunnel that it had emerged from, tried to rise to its feet, but cracked its head on the overhead ceiling. Appearing completely unperturbed, the wingless dragon shook itself for a few moments, as though it was trying to figure out what it wanted to do.

After watching the monster scratch itself under its chin for nearly twenty seconds with one of its front forelegs, Flint looked back at the burrow the creature had emerged from. The tunnel was large enough to allow the seven of them to walk—side by side—and was almost twice as tall as Grenden, who was the tallest member of the crew at nearly six and a half feet. It wasn't the size of the tunnel which had attracted the captain's attention, but the direction in which it was going, namely south. South would be away from the dwarf city and away from any possible pursuers. Perhaps they should just simply follow the burrow and see if they could find a way out?

The creature suddenly dropped back to the ground and resumed its crawl north. Directly in front of it, blocking all forward progress, was an impassable wall of stone. Undeterred by the presence of an obstacle, the wingless dragon closed its eyes and thrust forward, easily penetrating the wall, which caused the entire cavern to shudder.

Suddenly, a rumbling could be heard. The ceiling directly over the mouth of the tunnel he had emerged from shuddered and then broke apart. Tons and tons of rocks and stone crashed down, effectively terminating the burrow as a possible escape route. Flinn groaned and silently cursed his bad luck. That tunnel would have been the perfect avenue away from this accursed city.

Movement from his left caught his attention. The creature had already disappeared from view, with only the tip of the tail still visible. They could hear the monster dragging itself along as it burrowed farther away.

"What now, Captain?" Rusty asked.

Flinn shrugged and pointed at the disappearing monster. "We follow him."

That one statement brought everyone up short. Half a dozen protests erupted as everyone turned to look at the captain as though he was the one with scales.

"You can't be serious, Captain!"

"Why would you want t' follow 'im, Cap'n?" Puck all but whined.

Flinn ignored the outbursts and hurried after the creature, careful to avoid tripping on the pieces of broken rock and stone littering the pathway. Not wanting to be left behind, the rest of the men quickly followed suit. Not a word was said as the men hurried to catch up to the captain, who was hurrying to catch up to the monster.

Only when the tail was once more in sight did Flinn allow his pace to slow. He turned to see that everyone was silently following him, which they were. None appeared to be too happy about it, though.

What the blazes was he doing following this strange-looking dragon? He had no idea where it was leading them, nor did he have any idea what to do when they got to wherever they were going. He only knew that wherever they were headed, it was better than the dwarves' collapsed cavern.

For close to an hour, the pirates followed the burrowing

creature. Captain Flinn was scowling. The monster was digging much, much slower than it had been when they were being pursued. The question was, why? If it was capable of digging much faster than this, then why wasn't it? Wouldn't that suggest it had known of their presence after all? Was something—or someone—responsible for spurring it on?

Flinn sighed irritably. He would probably never know. All he knew was that they were still making progress. Slow progress, mind you, but at least it *was* progress. The men had only grumbled for the first twenty minutes. Then they had befallen another terra tremor, and just like before, it collapsed the tunnel. There would be no going back. If they didn't follow the creature, then they would be undoubtedly stranded.

The notion did not sit well with him, but what choice had he?

Ten minutes later, some good luck finally paid them a visit. The creature burrowed on, oblivious to their presence. However, another small terra tremor opened a tiny crack in the tunnel wall. Light seeped through, bringing a loud round of cheers from the men, and a very stern warning from the captain. Everyone thought them to be dead. It was a notion the captain was more than willing to entertain.

As soon as the creature burrowed away, and the ground had stopped trembling, the pirates peered anxiously through the crack. Directly on the other side of the tunnel wall was an open street with rows of buildings on either side. And, most important of all, it didn't look like there was anyone present. In fact, the street looked deserted.

Flinn hefted the hammer and was about to bash his way out when he hesitated.

"Come on, Captain!" Rusty pleaded. "We're so close to being free of this damnable rock! Why stop now?"

"That be part of the city out there," Flinn reported, placing his eye to the narrow crack once more.

"So?" several men prompted.

"So, why be it deserted?" Flinn asked.

"It wasn't when I looked," Rusty argued. "I saw several people walking along the street."

Flinn studied the quiet street for a moment longer. After nearly a full minute had gone by, the captain grunted. A lone figure had just wandered into his field of vision. Then another. And another.

"That be more like it."

"Why would you want people to be there, Captain?"

"Think about it, Q. If there are no people there, then would that not suggest they be in hidin'? That perhaps somethin' has got 'em spooked? Like, perhaps, us?"

Rusty was nodding sagely. "Ah. I understand. Well, it's good that they don't know we're here."

Flinn scowled. "Which makes it harder to slip out of here without being detected. Perhaps we could wait until … Just a moment. We do not have to wait another blasted minute in here!"

"How do you figure, Captain?" Rusty wanted to know.

Flinn spun on his heel and pointed at Casimir.

"Get over here, man. Use yer jhorun. Fear should be able to clear that street. Get to it, understood?"

Casimir nodded and hurriedly replaced Flinn at the crack in the wall. He gritted his teeth and, after a few moments, everyone felt his jhorun at work. High levels of fear blasted at them from all sides, making them all think danger was lurking just around the corner.

Having long been accustomed to this type of weapon, Flinn shook off the nagging sensation to flee. He waited until Casimir waved him over and pointed at the crack.

"It's done, Cap'n. The street looks as empty as a tavern run by monks on sermon day."

Flinn checked for himself. Yes, the street was clear. Not waiting for the people to second guess their emotions, Flinn pulled the hammer from his belt and smacked the wall right on the crack. The wall practically exploded outward.

The pirates hastily dropped out of the newly formed hole and onto the cobbled street. Giving each other hearty slaps on the back, the pirates strode confidently away from the broken opening, eager to put as much distance between the dark, dank hole in the earth as possible.

"Look up there, Captain!" Rusty cried, as they rounded a

corner and found themselves on a side street running along the base of a large mountain. "Is that a sight for sore eyes or what?"

"Freedom," Flinn grunted approvingly, nodding his head. "We be finally leaving this wretched place."

"Not yet you're not," an all-too-familiar voice contradicted.

All seven pirates came to an immediate stop. Standing directly in their path were a familiar man and woman. A small band of dwarves were at their side. The man's hands suddenly burst into flames.

"I *knew* you guys survived that blast," the Fire Thrower smirked. "We'll be taking back that hammer, thank you very much."

Chapter 7 — Out of the Frying Pan

Ye must be jokin'," Steve heard Flinn grumble, which put a huge smile on his face. His hunch had been right. If anyone could survive the collapse, it would most certainly be Flinn. So, when Breslin offered to show them around the city, both husband and wife had jumped at the chance.

"I told you I heard something," Steve insisted, giving his wife a friendly nudge in the ribs. "Maybe next time you'll believe me a little bit quicker?"

"You're old, dear," Sarah replied, patting his arm in a patronizing manner. "So, you got one right for a change. Surely you could understand my skepticism?"

"Ye cannot have possibly known where we were," Flinn was saying. "How in the blazes did ye find us? Ye heard that diggin' monster, did ye not?"

Steve looked puzzled. "The what? I didn't hear any monster. I heard what I thought sounded like an explosion, which I can only assume came from that huge hole in the wall there. What, did you use that hammer to do it? Surely, you're smart enough to realize that sound travels, right?"

"I have had it with his insults," one of the pirates sneered as a dagger appeared in each hand. He took a few menacing steps toward Steve. "Say the word, Captain, and I'll cut that smile off his face."

Steve pumped extra jhorun into his hands, causing them to blaze brighter and hotter. "Unless you have no qualms about seeing what it would feel like to be a French fry, then I'd like to see you try, pal. Jino, isn't it?" He felt a tap on his shoulder and turned to see Sarah giving Jino an unconcerned look.

"Allow me, dear."

One look at Sarah's determined face was all it took to wipe the smug look of confidence off of the pirate. A look of recognition had fallen across Jino's features. The pirate immediately sheathed his daggers and had started backing away.

"That's right, Paco," Sarah calmly told the pirate. "Look around you. There's no water to dump you in. If you take one more step toward me or my husband, then I'll personally drop you right onto an *occupied* dragon nest, is that understood?"

Oh, please do.

Steve suddenly grinned, *Pryllan, did you hear that?*

"Go ahead and do it," Steve urged his wife. "Not only is Pryllan currently there, but so are Kahvel and Pravara. I'm pretty certain they would love to say hello again."

There was a pregnant pause as each group glared at the other. Then, the pirates scattered. Jino kicked in the closest door and promptly dove through, followed closely by Casimir and Von. Grenden and Alquin ran over to a collection of benches on a street corner, tipped them over, and crouched behind them. Rusty hooked an arm through Flinn's and forcefully pulled him to a nearby building. One swift kick made short work of the door. As was the usual, Puck was nowhere to be seen, presumably hiding behind the closest rock he could find.

"I see I have been far too lenient with ye, Fire Thrower,"

Flinn's voice called out. "That will be endin' now. Surrender, and ye might make it through this with yer life. Continue to pester me, and yer journey stops here and now."

"Please," Steve scoffed. "You couldn't stop me before, and you sure as hell can't stop me now. Give up the hammer, Captain Windbag, and maybe we can cut a deal."

"What?" Sarah whispered, as she turned to him. "Since when do you have the authority to make a deal?"

"I don't," Steve quietly confirmed. "However, *they* don't know that."

"No deal, Fire Thrower!" Flinn's voice responded. "I think we be doin' just fine here. Now, we be heading back to the surface. Step aside, and ye won't be hurt. Resist, and ye will experience pain the likes of which have never been dreamt of, is that understood?"

Steve sighed and gazed down at his burning hands. "That's it. I'm done negotiating. Let's put an end to this once and for all." He felt another tap, on his right hip. Breslin was there. Steve hunched over so he and the dwarf could talk. "Yes?"

"What are your plans, Sir Steve?" Breslin inquired. "How may we be of assistance? We wish to be rid of this cumbersome pest just as much as you do, I assure you."

Before Steve could respond, a powerful blast of air spun around the street corner and came straight for him. Steve pushed Breslin and Sarah out of the way and blasted out a huge jet of fire in return. Air met fire, resulting in a violent explosion that shattered windows and doors in all the surrounding buildings.

Almost immediately, a second air jet came spiraling around the corner, followed closely thereafter by a third. Steve was able to deflect the second, but watched helplessly as the third whooshed by him and headed straight for Sarah. His wife nodded knowingly in his direction and then flicked her hand, as though she was shooing away a pesky fly. The jet of air ended up slamming into one of the boarded-up storefronts, causing huge cracks to form as the stone building shuddered under the massive blow.

Steve nodded. "That's my girl."

He fired off several shots of his own, directed where the pirates had fled. He and Sarah watched with grim satisfaction as several of them abandoned their hiding places to run away before the fire jet could arrive. Then both husband and wife felt a wave of fear envelope them. Steve gritted his teeth. His first instinct was to grab Sarah and have her teleport them to safety. However, now he knew better. Both of them did. This was nothing more than one of the pirates trying to scare them away using his jhorun.

Well, it wasn't going to work. They had already fallen for it once, and Steve was determined not to put on a repeat performance. He nudged his wife on the shoulder.

"Feel that? Our friend Mr. Fear Factor is out there somewhere."

"I can feel it," Sarah said, nodding. "It's easier to ignore once you know where it's coming from. And why it's there."

"Where's Gareth?" Steve asked.

Sarah turned to point back at the small group of dwarves, who were busy assembling something. The young wizard, and his guur sidekick, were standing off to the side, watching intently, as two large, bulky foreign devices were assembled.

"Any idea what they're doing?" Steve inquired.

Sarah shook her head. "No. But once the dwarves start using it, you'd better believe Flinn will try and destroy it. We need to protect those things."

"We don't even know what *they* are," Steve reminded her.

"Does it matter?" Sarah countered.

"Not really."

"Good. See if you can get Gareth's attention."

Steve waved an arm at their young wizard friend, but it was Deez who noticed first. The guur tapped its two front legs several times and came scuttling over, followed closely by Gareth. The guur had such a friendly demeanor that, before he could think about what he was doing, Steve reached out to pat the guur on its armored head.

Deez chittered softly, nudged Steve's hand, and then looked over at Gareth.

"What's up?" Gareth inquired.

"Keep your head up," Steve instructed. "I think Captain

Windbag has finally lost his patience with us. Have you noticed the air jets? They haven't stopped yet. I'd say he's trying to drive us away."

Gareth reached into a pocket and pulled out a small stone figurine. He hefted it appraisingly as he grinned at Steve.

"I'd like to see them try."

"What's that?" Steve wanted to know. "Some type of spell?"

"It's an 'Earth Elemental'," Sarah answered. "I've seen one before, back when we were helping the Fae and that flock of griffins."

Steve grinned as he looked at the tiny figurine. "Nice! I'd love to see that thing in action!"

"Today might be your lucky day," Gareth told him. "I think the pirate who controls fear must be nearby. I have a growing sense of urgency that, if I don't act, makes me think something bad will happen."

"We feel it, too," Steve confirmed.

Steve sent off another blast of fire to deflect air jets that were angling straight for them, swirling with bits of gravel and metal—now lethal projectiles. The first jet whooshed by them, and Steve let out a bellow of pain. A jagged cut ripped his bicep.

"That miserable son of a…"

"Watch your language," Sarah scolded. She was already holding out a hand. Within moments, a tarnished, non-descript medallion appeared. She wrapped both of her hands around it, gave it a subtle twist, and caught the tiny vial of burgundy-colored liquid that seemingly appeared out of nowhere. Sarah carefully pulled the stopper out of the vial, wet her finger with a drop of the liquid, and cautiously touched the wound on Steve's arm.

The torn skin sealed itself.

Steve flexed his arm and turned to his wife. "Thanks. Well, it's my turn now."

He spun toward the jets, generated a large chaser, held the fireball aloft for a moment, and then knelt to the ground. He brought up a mental picture of Captain Flinn and ordered the chaser to flush him out. Then he smacked the chaser onto the ground.

The fireball promptly melted into the stone floor, leaving only a burning circle on the surface. Then it took off, leaving a blazing fire trail as it moved. It quickly zipped around the bend and vanished from sight.

"Think it'll work?" Sarah asked.

Steve nodded. "It should. Flinn will probably have a way to put it out, but it won't be easy. Let's just see what..."

They all heard a loud curse, followed by muffled shouts. The two jets of air that were swirling about above their heads suddenly reversed course and sped back around the corner. Then came even louder shouts.

"I think you got their attention," Sarah surmised, with a smile. "How long do you think it'll be before they'll be able to put it out?"

"Well, they're not gonna be able to blow the thing out," Steve chuckled. "Now, while they're distracted, I say we should..."

Right about then, two sets of dwarves hurried past them. Each two-dwarf team was carrying a bulky, clunky-looking metal contraption. Steve studied the identical devices and shook his head. He didn't have a clue.

Each object had a large hexagonal base, a smaller box-like midsection, and what looked like a two-foot section of pipe sticking out of a small, irregular shaped object on top. The devices were made entirely of metal, and the condition of the metal suggested these contraptions hadn't been used for some time. One dwarf opened a hidden panel on the middle box-like section, poured a large canister of water into it, and then sealed it back up. Steve glanced over at the second device and watched as another dwarf performed the same operation, only instead of water, he carefully dropped in what looked like a white pebble, only he was wearing thick, leather gloves.

"I have no idea if this will work or not," a voice suddenly announced from Steve's right. It was Breslin, and he was frowning. "Do you have any idea how long it's been since the Hoarfrost was last used?"

"The *what*?" Steve asked, confused.

Breslin indicated the dual mechanical devices. The dwarves were finished assembling and were ready to push them into the middle of the street, directly in the line of fire with the pirates. Two dwarves approached and bowed low.

"This is Lunko and Ullmor. They'll be the ones running Hoarfrost."

"What the hell is a hoarfrost?" Steve demanded, growing angry. "I have no idea what that means."

"Isn't hoarfrost another name for ice?" Sarah asked.

Breslin eagerly nodded. "Aye! The Hoarfrost can encase objects, any objects, in solid slabs of ice."

"What in the world would you need that for?" Steve wanted to know.

"Dragons," Sarah quietly breathed. "You used this weapon against the dragons, didn't you?"

Aye, they did.

"It's not something we're proud of," Breslin sadly admitted. "Pryllan, I know you're listening. On behalf of my people, you have my sincerest apologies we ever used that thing against any wyverian."

We were not without blame, friend Breslin. There is no need to apologize. Should you insist, then I will be forced to apologize on behalf of all wyverians for all the brutal retaliations we enacted upon you dwarves. The less said of this unpleasant subject, the better.

Steve relayed Pryllan's response. The small group had fallen quiet while the dragon's message was spoken aloud. Breslin solemnly nodded. Then he reached into a leather pouch on his belt and brought out a handful of thin gold cuff bracelets. Breslin handed one to him, and then one to Sarah.

"Put them on. You'll thank me later."

"What's it for?" Steve asked, as he forced the small metal bracelet around his left wrist. "It's not really my style. Do you have anything in silver?"

Sarah fired him a look. "Really?"

"Sorry. I'll shut up now."

"It's for your own protection," Breslin assured them. He passed another bracelet to Gareth, who wordlessly slipped it on his right wrist.

Steve hesitantly cleared his throat and pointed at the two devices.

"So, how's it work? If this thing shoots out ice, why do you need two?"

"The left-hand device envelopes the target in water," Breslin explained. "The right-hand device freezes it solid."

"I saw how much water was dumped in there," Steve reminded the dwarf. "There's no way that would be enough to cover a dragon. What am I missing here?"

"You and your fascination with their weapons," Sarah groaned. "Let it go, okay? Clearly, they have some way to amplify the quantity and then freeze it solid. Just accept it as fact."

"What was that white thing you dropped in the other one?" Steve wanted to know. "Can you at least tell me that?"

Breslin rocked back on the soles of his feet and proudly puffed out his chest. "That, my friends, was a hailstone."

"That can't possibly mean what I think it means," Steve said, as he turned to his wife. "So, what is it? A jewel?"

Breslin shook his head. "No, it's a rare crystal that only forms when diamond quartz is mixed with the proper minerals, and is rapidly melted and then just as rapidly cooled."

Steve ignited both hands and readied himself. Once the unique weapon was visible to the pirates it would become an instant target. Gareth appeared by their side, tightly clutching the tiny figure in his right hand. The young wizard focused on the dwarf weapon and was softly chanting.

Lunko nodded to his companion, flipped a hidden switch, and then pressed two buttons recessed into the device's surface. It began humming. Ullmor mimicked the motions, and when his device was also humming, both dwarves hurriedly pushed the bulky contraptions into the middle of the street. Then they each crouched low, aimed the weapon at a specific point, and nodded their readiness.

Twin air jets immediately formed and slammed into both devices. Lunko and Ullmor ducked down and waited. Once it passed, Lunko pressed a few more buttons and nodded in Ullmor's direction. The nozzle of Lunko's device suddenly rotated a few feet to the left and then lifted nearly twenty degrees.

"Fire!" Breslin bellowed.

Impossibly, a steady stream of water shot out of the device, more than through a fireman's hose.

"Magic," Steve murmured softly to Sarah. "You've gotta love it."

Ullmor's machine had already rotated into position and fired a single white pulse of light. Both machines immediately powered down and each operator enthusiastically pumped their fists into the air. Breslin hurried past the two of them to see the results.

By the time Steve and Sarah had joined their dwarf friend, there was no sign of Captain Windbag, and no air jets swirling overhead.

"Now there's something you don't see every day," Steve quipped, as soon as he was able to look back at the hole the pirates had smashed through the wall during their escape.

The Hoarfrost, it would seem had been very effective. The entire eastern wall of the cavern, from floor to ceiling, was encased in ice nearly a foot thick! The hole in the wall was completely iced over, and of the pirates, there was no sign anywhere.

"How long will the ice last?" Steve asked.

Breslin shrugged. "As long as it takes for it to melt, I would imagine."

Sarah approached and ran her fingertips along the cold, slick surface. She stopped, tapped her fingers on the surface, as if to verify the integrity of the newly formed ice, then turned to Steve and motioned him over.

"What's up?" Steve asked.

Sarah pointed at a section of ice that was several feet thick. There, encased in the ice, looking surprised and scared, was a pirate. Long white ruffled sleeves, wool waistcoat and trousers, and knee-high black boots. The question was, who? Clearly not Captain Flinn.

"Hey, we got one! Look, he's even awake. He can see us!" Steve remarked as he ignited his hands.

The pirate began to tremble.

"Who are you?" Steve asked. When there was no answer, he raised his voice. "What's your name?"

The pirate's mouth perceptibly moved, but not by much. "Grenden."

"Where's Flinn?"

Grenden tried to say something else, but neither of them could make it out.

"Enough of this," Sarah said, with exasperation evident in her voice. "We need to talk to this guy, and we need to do it now."

"Want me to melt him out?" Steve asked.

Sarah stared at the ice then her eyes closed. Just like that, Grenden vanished, only to reappear by her side a heartbeat later. Steve raised an ignited hand as a warning, should the pirate try to use jhorun against her.

Grenden, to his credit, sank down to his knees and held his hands up. "I surrender, Fire Thrower. Please don't hurt me."

Steve pointed at Sarah. "You should be saying that to her, not me. She's the one that can turn you into dragon fodder with a simple wiggle of her nose."

"For the last time, you nitwit, I *don't* wiggle my nose."

Steve grinned at his wife. "Perhaps not. Not usually, that is. I swear I've seen you do it before."

Breslin appeared. He had noticed the exchange and was already holding a set of manacles. He held them up and jingled them in front of the pirate.

"Unless you plan on wearing these for the rest of your natural existence, you had better start cooperating, human."

Before Grenden could respond, the thick slab of ice suddenly shuddered, then edged forward by an inch or two. Huge cracks formed and shot out in all directions.

"That can't be good," Sarah quietly observed. She grabbed her husband by the hand and pulled him away from the ice.

Breslin pulled Grenden to his feet and headed toward the other dwarves. At that moment, the ice broke apart. Air jets pummeled them into retreating. Broken bits of ice flew toward them.

Steve snapped at his wife. "Get behind me, hurry!"

Sarah threw her arms around him. Breslin and the dwarves were taking shelter in the nearest building. Steve ordered his jhorun to increase his flames.

The flames on his hands, already an angry red, blazed brighter, hotter. They started creeping up his arms, toward his chest. He cast a worried look back at Sarah.

"I know what's going to happen. Don't let go of me, babe. No matter what, okay?"

"What's happening?"

"Do you remember what I told you happened to me and Lissa, when we went back in time?"

"You said your flames spread across your body and then across hers."

"Right. That's about to happen here."

"Oh, *hell* no," Sarah stoutly declared. "You told me her clothes were burned off. You will do no such thing to me, Paco."

By this time, the flames had spread across his chest and just made contact with Sarah's skin. Steve saw his wife's arms go up in flames and swallowed nervously. He closed his eyes and sent out a strict order to his jhorun. In fact, it came out more like a chant:

Do not burn her clothes off. I'm begging you. You have no idea how much trouble I'll be in if that happens, got it?

Steve turned his attention to the ice shards whipping through the air, courtesy of Captain Windbag. He raised both hands and waited for the jet to venture close again. As soon as it did, he blasted out a huge wall of flames, ordering it to burn fast and hot.

The air jet practically poofed out of existence. Unfortunately, Steve's blast of fire wiped out all traces of the Hoarfrost. That also applied to the pirates, including Grenden, who had vanished.

"What the hell?" Steve sputtered, as he looked around the open street. "What happened to Grenden? There's no way he could have wandered off."

"He is my fault," Steve heard Breslin say. The dwarf was approaching with a fierce scowl. "One minute I had him, and the next, his arm was yanked out of my grip and he vanished, right in front of my eyes."

May I try to locate them using your senses?

Go ahead, only I should warn you that my senses aren't the greatest. They...

The human invaders are still there. Hold your breath so I can be certain.

What? Are you sure?

I was right. I hear them. They are, indeed, still there.

Steve released his breath. Sarah eyed him speculatively before releasing her own. She met his eyes and raised an eyebrow. Steve solemnly nodded, confirming the pirates were still present.

"That means they're hiding, hoping to sneak by us," Steve scowled. "That really pisses me off. Talk about finding the coward's way out. Did you hear that, Captain Windbag? We know you're still here. You coward! What are you hiding for? Are you afraid of us? Well, you should be!"

Sarah slapped his shoulder. "What did you do that for? Why would you let them know that we know they're still here?"

"It doesn't matter. We need to find them. Draw them out. Got any ideas how we can do that?"

Sarah suddenly smiled and pointed back at the twin guns of Hoarfrost. "Yes! As a matter of fact, I do. I think we can use steam to flush them out."

"Steam? That thing doesn't produce steam, but ice."

Gareth and Deez appeared by their side. Sarah hooked a thumb at the Lunko's machine and then tapped Steve on his chest.

"What happens when fire meets water?"

"The fire is typically extinguished," Steve answered, frowning. "Why?"

"And if the fire is hot enough?" Sarah countered. "What then?"

"Well, I'd say you get ... steam! I'll be damned! Sarah comes up with a winner. Ow! What'd you hit me for?"

"For the insinuation I never have good ideas. Thank you. That'll be a fifteen-minute back rub tonight."

"Damn," Steve breathed. He hurried out into the middle

of the street, waved to get Lunko's attention, and then held his arms out away from his side, forming his body into a 'T'. "Fire away, dude. Let's see if we can find us some pirates."

Lunko, to his credit, looked skeptically over at Breslin. "Is he serious, Master Breslin?"

"He is. Water only, please. Now!"

A super condensed jet of liquid was shot straight at Steve, who flamed up just before the water arrived. A cloud of vapor immediately formed, followed by a loud hissing noise as the water became steam. Breslin then signaled for the water to be shut off.

"Does anyone see anything?" Sarah hopefully asked.

Breslin pointed toward the far corner of the street. There, amidst the swirling vapors of steam, was a long, irregular shape devoid of form and substance.

Steve squinted at the swirling tendrils of vapor. Was something there? Could it be the pirates? Well, there was certainly one way to find out.

Steve ignited both hands and blasted a jet at the strange figure. Just like that, he was staring at a line of pirates, holding hands. The only one missing was Captain Flinn, who had been at the head of the procession.

Apparently, if he was in physical contact with the rest of his crew, he could render all of them invisible.

"Ye are nothin' but a thorn in my side, Fire Thrower," Flinn began, aiming a fist-shaped blast of air at Steve.

The rest of the pirates—including Grenden—looked like deer in the headlights. After a few seconds of indecision, the pirates fled, several of them through the hole Flinn had created earlier with the hammer.

Flinn, it would seem, was tired of running. He raced to the closest building, pulled out the Power Hammer, and promptly smashed the wall to bits. Once there was plenty of rubble on the ground, he used his jhorun to fling the bits of stone and wood into a deadly maelstrom of flying debris.

"Let's see how ye deal with this, Fire Thrower," Flinn challenged.

He flung a jet at Steve, a separate one at Sarah, and two at Breslin and his company of dwarves. Picking up bits of debris, the deadly air jets streaked toward their targets.

What the pirates hadn't counted on was that the Hoarfrost was not the only trick Breslin had up his sleeve.

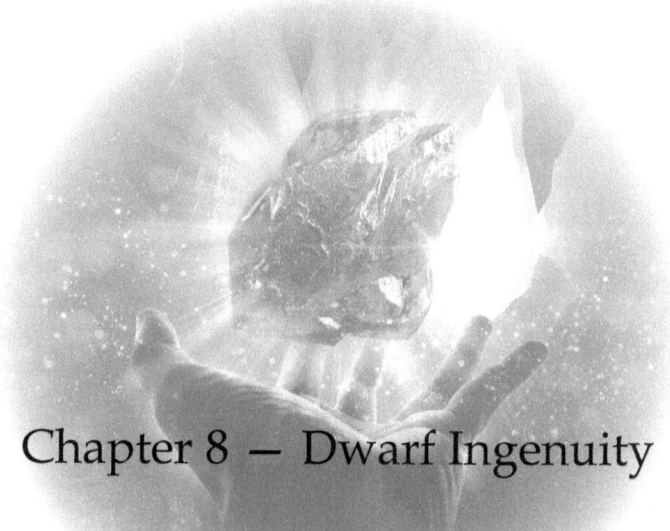

Chapter 8 — Dwarf Ingenuity

Tap your bracelets!" Breslin hurriedly instructed. "Three times!" When Steve eyed the dwarf as though he had lost his mind, Breslin scowled with irritation. "Just do it!"

Steve eyed the flurry of mini projectiles headed his way and followed Breslin's orders. The metal band clicked once, and suddenly doubled in size. Then it clicked again, and again. And again. Steve watched, transfixed, as the metal band expanded up his arm, across his chest, down his legs, and encompassed his head. In less than five seconds, he was wearing a full suit of armor the likes of which he hadn't ever seen before.

For one thing, the suit was lightweight and completely mobile! In fact, the metal was lighter than most of the clothes he typically wore. This was so cool!

The air jet arrived, along with all the debris. Steve felt the rocks and chunks of stone bounce harmlessly off of him, as though they were no more than Styrofoam packing peanuts. Bemused, he turned to see how Sarah was faring. What he saw brought out a snort of laughter. Sarah's suit was golden, with silver adornments woven throughout. His own suit was completely silver in color.

Sarah, also suffering through a veritable windstorm of debris pummeling her, was madly waving her hands around her face, as though she had stumbled into a swarm of flies. The various bits of junk were colliding into their suits and hadn't even *scratched* them.

"What are we wearing?" Sarah's muffled voice asked, as she stared at the silver and gold protective layering.

Half a dozen much shorter versions of Steve's suit appeared. One tapped his chest.

"These are suits of armor made entirely of bryl," Breslin explained. "It's our lightest, strongest metal, and something we have honestly not had to wear in quite some time."

"You're telling me you dwarves used these suits against the dragons?"

Breslin nodded. "Aye. Quite effectively, I might add."

Agreed. Many a dragon has lost teeth while trying to bite one of those suits in half.

Seriously? These things are that strong?

Indeed.

"Pryllan just confirmed what you said," Steve told Breslin. "Apparently, there are a few dragons walking around missing some teeth because of these things. And that's why you guys aren't getting these back. Nuh uh."

Breslin bowed once. "Of course not, Sir Steve. Take them. They haven't been used in years."

"Can I still use my jhorun with this thing on?" Steve cautiously asked. "I can only imagine these suits are fireproof?"

Breslin nodded. "They are, but only to a certain point. Prolonged exposure to dragon fire would eventually melt the bryl, but I would like to think that whomever is being attacked with fire would not try to wait it out."

Steve clenched a fist and ignited his hands. Nothing happened, as far as he could tell. He ignited his other hand and then stared at his two gauntleted hands.

Nothing.

"I think my hands are lit," Steve sullenly reported, "but only on the inside. I'm not sure how that's going to help me."

"You could try taking the gauntlets off," Sarah idly suggested.

Steve sighed and shrugged. That ought to work. Then he caught movement in his peripheral vision. It looked as though the pirates were about ready to launch their retaliation. He looked down at his hands and realized he didn't have any idea how to lose the gloves without removing any other pieces of the armor. He turned to Breslin and held out his hands.

"How do I do this? How do I make them come off?"

Breslin reached over and slid his finger along the area where the cuff originally sat on his arm, and then tapped twice, hesitating several seconds between taps. Then, the gauntlets retracted into the sleeve and just like that, his hands were bare. And lit.

"Ah. That's more like it."

"Just be sure to protect your hands in the event of another air strike," Breslin told him. "Your hands will be unprotected."

Steve pumped more jhorun into his hands and shook his head. "On the contrary, they are very well protected."

Two additional air jets came screaming around the corner, complete with bits of rubble interspersed into the stream of condensed air. Not wanting to take any chances, Steve hurriedly positioned his hands behind his back and faced the attack head on. As before, the debris bounced ineffectively off his protective bryl suit.

Several dwarves appeared, holding unloaded crossbows. Each dwarf placed a foot in the stirrup and locked the string into position. From a leather satchel they withdrew special pewter bolts, with what looked to be small, cylindrical tubes attached to either side of the projectile. Steve pointed at the leather case full of the bolts and turned to Breslin.

"What type of arrows are those?"

Breslin nodded. "We call them whistlers. They seek out and target air disturbances."

Sarah approached and frowned. "Why would you need to … oh. Duh. This is just another weapon you used against the dragons, isn't it?"

Breslin sadly nodded. "Aye. Pryllan, if you are listening, rest assured we have not fired any of these against your fellow dragons for well over a century."

Let the past stay in the past.

"She said, 'Let the past stay in the past'," Steve relayed.

"Good. Now, those holding the crossbows, target the end of the street. Wait for the next attack. As soon as those blasted air jets appear, then open fire. Understand?"

Both dwarves nodded.

It only took a few moments before the next attack came. An air jet came rushing around the street corner, and angled straight for them. The two crossbows were immediately aimed and, after a moment's hesitation, as each looked at Breslin, the weapons were fired.

The two bolts practically vanished as they raced toward the end of the street. However, before either of them could make contact with any of the buildings that were there, both arrows suddenly veered off course and immediately disappeared to the right. Steve could also hear a slight whistling noise as the arrows traveled.

Then they heard bellows of rage. Flinn was cursing, and he was using every conceivable combination of expletives imaginable. The arrows, it would seem, had sunk deep into a wooden door a scant two inches away from where the pirate captain had been crouching.

"Do ye have any idea how close them arrows were?" Flinn raged aloud. He angrily shook a fist in the air. "Ye will rue the day we met, Fire Thrower!"

"I'm already there!" Steve called back. "And besides, those arrows didn't come from me. Why would I shoot you when I could torch you instead?"

"If ye weren't responsible for them arrows, then who was?" Flinn raged.

"We were," Breslin answered, raising his voice in an effort to be heard. "You stole my hammer, thief. You will return it or suffer the consequences."

"Come and get it!" a different voice exclaimed.

Steve recognized that voice, all right. It belonged to none

other than Mr. Steroids himself, Jino. About ready to fire off his own insult, Flinn's voice suddenly rose above all others.

"If ye want a fight, Fire Thrower, I'll be more than happy to be the one to give it to ye! If ye value yer life, then ye best be lettin' us leave! I don't want to have to kill ye, but if ye force me to, I will! I swear!"

"All bets are off, pal," Steve returned. "You want to leave? Drop the hammer, and drop the fang. Only then will you be allowed to leave this place."

A series of metallic clangs echoed noisily throughout the street. The ground started to tremble and the wind increased to hurricane force. Steve and his wife nervously eyed each other. Now what were those blasted pirates up to?

Visibility dropped significantly. Not only were small bits of rubble now flying through the air, but so were great quantities of dust. Strangely enough, the wind didn't seem to be attacking anyone, only swirling about above their heads.

"The blasted cretin is trying to escape!" Breslin angrily exclaimed. "If we can't see five feet in front of our faces…"

"…then how would we tell if they snuck by us?" Steve finished for his dwarf friend. "Damn! We can't lose them! Not now!"

Steve pumped more jhorun into his hands and ran out into the street, as if tempting the pirates to reveal themselves. Breslin and both Hoarfrost gunners, Lunko and Ullmor, quickly appeared by his side. Axes were drawn, crossbows were loaded, and all appeared ready to fight. However, there was no one to receive them.

The pirates had disappeared.

"Oh, hell no," Steve scowled. "They're here somewhere. Everyone, spread out! Look around! They're hiding somewhere close. The only way they're going to be able to … wait." He closed his eyes and tried to quell the thoughts bouncing around his mind.

"What are you doing?" Breslin asked, concerned. "Were you struck on the head?"

Sarah and Gareth poked their heads around the corner. Deez was approaching, too, walking along the walls of a building as easily as walking along the street.

"I think he's trying to contact Pryllan," Sarah decided, after studying Steve's face, which he immediately gave her a thumbs up.

Pryllan, are you there? I could really use your help right about now.

I am here, although I am not sure how much help I can give you from a remote distance.

Can you use my senses and tell me if the pirates are still in the area?

I will try. A moment of silence, if you please.

"She can hear the pirates all the way from Topside?" Breslin asked, amazed.

Steve shook his head and tapped an ear. "No. She's using my own senses."

No, I am sorry, Steve. For some inexplicable reason, I am unable to access your senses.

What? Why not? You were able to do so earlier, weren't you?

Aye. It feels like I am being blocked, but if I were, then I'd be unable to communicate with you. I have no further explanation.

"Damn," Steve softly swore.

"No luck?" Sarah guessed. "She couldn't hear anything?"

"Not a thing," Steve confirmed, "and that's because Pryllan couldn't access my senses like she normally can."

"That seems a bit suspicious," Sarah said. She looked at Breslin and Gareth, who both shrugged in unison. "How is she able to talk to you if she can't...?"

Steve held up both hands in surrender. "She's already said she didn't know. Damn! I was really counting on her to be able to find them."

"What about Deez?" Gareth asked.

Steve and Sarah looked up. Their young wizard companion was looking affectionately at the friendly guur, who—from his perch on a nearby building—was returning the frank stare. After a few moments, the guur scuttled down the side of the wall, like a spider, and approached Gareth. Deez's two front forelegs tapped the ground impatiently.

"Do you think Deez could find them?" Sarah hopefully asked. "I don't know, Gareth. It looks like the pirates up and disappeared again. They're probably using that Alchos Stone again."

Gareth looked straight at Steve. "Is Pryllan still listening?"

Are you?

Yes.

"She's listening," Steve confirmed.

"Pryllan," Gareth began, in a louder voice than was necessary, "could you make sure Deez understands me? We need him to find the pirates. They're around here somewhere, only we don't know where."

State your instructions. Just be warned: the creature's communication skills are rudimentary. Complete comprehension might not be possible.

"Go ahead and tell him what you want him to do," Steve relayed. "You just have to remember that Deez's level of communication is not the same as ours. He might not be able to understand everything you say."

"Can't Pryllan make sure he understands?"

"She's the one who just gave me the warning about Deez's ability to understand your request."

"Oh. All right. Deez? I need you to listen to me. Somewhere out there are pirates. I'm going to help look for them, but I also need you to look for them, too, okay?"

The guur's heavily armored head turned until he was staring at Gareth.

"Do you understand?"

THREAT NOT DETECTED

"I know you don't see them, Deez, but they're still out there. We need to find them."

A few seconds of silence passed before the guur's next thought came through:

THREAT CONCEALED?

"Yes!" Gareth exclaimed excitedly, happy and proud that his new pet understood him. "The threat is still present. Do you think that you could find them?"

The guur's long front legs stopped digging small gouges into the ground. Several small, short vibrissae, which Steve had never noticed before near the guur's mouth, started quivering and swaying from side to side. Deez's head turned to regard the surroundings. The short white vibrissae were now whipping about so much that Steve briefly thought Captain Flinn was back and had generated a stiff breeze. However, the air was still, the surroundings quiet.

Thirty seconds of silence passed, with Deez slowly rotating in place, when the guur chittered excitedly and sprang forward.

"Do you think he found something?" Steve asked, as he turned to Sarah.

"How in the world would I know that?" Sarah demanded. "Do you think I suddenly speak guur?"

MOVEMENT DETECTED. THREAT?

Steve's hopes deflated as he gave his immediate surroundings a cursory glance. There were a few dwarves still milling about. The guur must've been alerted to their own movement.

"Everyone be still," Breslin ordered, as if he had picked up on Steve's thought. "Now, lad," Breslin added, addressing Gareth, "would you ask him to see if the threat is still there?"

Gareth nodded. "Deez, we're all standing still now. Do you still detect movement? Can you tell me where you detect them?"

BIPEDAL MOVEMENT DETECTED.

"Bipedal?" Gareth asked, confused.

"Creatures who walk on two legs," Steve translated.

A look of understanding passed over the young wizard's face. "Oh. Hey, wait. That could mean us, right?"

Sarah nodded. "Exactly. Deez, are you detecting human or dwarf?"

Breslin grunted an approval. "Excellent question, Lady Sarah."

"Deez," Gareth began, "are you sensing dwarves or humans?"

The guur stared at Gareth uncomprehendingly.

"He doesn't understand you," Sarah said. "Try again, using words he'd understand."

Gareth pondered for a moment before tapping himself on the chest. "Are the threats human? Human like me?" He then pointed at Steve and Sarah. "Like them? Or are they dwarf?" Gareth then swung his finger over to Breslin. "Short? Uh, smaller bipeds? Big or small bipeds?"

Deez looked at Breslin first before turning his head to look directly at Steve.

"That works for me," Steve decided, igniting his hands. "Where are they, Deez? Come on, boy. Show me where they are!"

"He's a guur, not a dog," Sarah scolded, smacking him on the arm.

Deez turned until he was looking at one of the buildings on the far side of the street. Without preamble, the guur scuttled straight for the building. With Steve, Sarah, Gareth, Breslin, and several more dwarves in hot pursuit, Deez angled straight for the closest wall and, without missing a beat, started digging through.

Once more, Steve was amazed at the ease with which the guur could dig through stone. He was also certain that, were he to try digging through the softest dirt imaginable, the guur would still out dig him while digging through solid rock. Perhaps the guur had jhorun-hardened/enhanced legs that could easily break down the rock? Whatever the case may be, in less than ten seconds there was a three-foot diameter circular opening in the side of the building.

"I'll go first," Breslin decided, as he attempted to push his way past Steve.

"Oh, no you don't," Steve countered, as he pulled the dwarf back by grabbing Mythryd's handle. The special red dual-bladed battle axe was swinging freely in its holder on the dwarf's back. "I'm first. I'll light the way. Then Breslin, then Gareth."

"And me?" Sarah asked.

"I don't suppose you'd be willing to wait here, would you?"

Sarah fired him a scathing look. "What do you think?"

"Fine. I had a feeling you'd say that. Stick close to us. Be ready to jump us out in case they're gonna try to ambush us in there."

"I've got quite a few safe zones to choose from," Sarah advised. "I think I'll go with our cabin in the woods. Say the word and everyone here will find themselves there."

Just as Steve was about to crouch down to step into the hole, he turned to Sarah and grinned. "Actually, you know what? If you don't mind, change your safe zone to Pryllan's nest. That way we'd have several dragons to back us up if the need arises."

An excellent idea.

"Pryllan is ready," Steve reported. He ducked into the hole, waited a few moments, and then signaled the coast was clear. "Come on in. I already see another hole in the wall, and this time, it wasn't made by Deez."

Once they were all inside the street side building, Breslin whistled admirably. The greater portion of the west perimeter wall was missing. And, since this building and the next shared a wall, it was easy to determine where the pirates had fled. They were simply punching holes through any wall that presented itself as an obstacle.

"How long is this street?" Steve asked, turning to Breslin. "And why the hell didn't we hear anything when Flinn smashed his way through? Wouldn't we have heard him smash that?"

Breslin was silent as he studied the destruction. With a sigh, he turned to face his human companions. The other three dwarves fell silent.

"I do not know what to tell you. There are too many impossibilities to comprehend. Your pirate captain should not be able to wield the hammer, but he can. He should not have inside knowledge of our city, but apparently, he does. And, he should not be able to wield the hammer with the ferocity necessary to destroy that wall without a sound. I am at a loss here."

"What about that Alchos thingamajig?" Steve asked. "Could he be somehow using it to disguise his actions?"

Both Breslin and Sarah shrugged.

"Hey, where's Deez?" Gareth asked.

He hurried over to the broken wall and peered into the next building, which turned out to be a butcher's shop. A plethora of nauseating smells was wafting and making Steve's stomach grow queasy. Gareth fanned the air in an attempt to rid his nose of the foul smells. Then he began to chant.

A light breeze formed, which, unfortunately, started blowing *more* of the sickly smells their way. Gareth smiled sheepishly. He drew a few imaginary symbols in the air and just like that, the breeze reversed itself.

"Sorry about that. I think we can all agree that we don't want to smell any more of *that* than we absolutely have to."

"What's wrong with it?" Breslin inquired. "Can you not smell it? Ripe meat that's practically falling off the bone. Chops the size of your head, aging naturally, in the open air. Makes me hungry, it does."

A commotion sounded from within the darkened butcher shop. Steve increased the amount of jhorun flowing into his hands, resulting in brighter flames, and carefully stepped over the broken stones littering the floor. He cast a quick look behind him to verify Sarah was able to safely follow along, which she was.

A form jumped out of the shadows, eliciting a cry of alarm from Steve. Breslin hastily pulled Mythryd from its holder and dropped into a battle stance. Sarah, having already selected several large stones for this very purpose, used her jhorun to lift the heavy rocks off the ground. They waited, eerily floating by her side, to be of use.

The only reaction that could have caused serious repercussions was Steve's. He had blasted out a jet of fire at the small form the instant he clapped eyes on it. Thankfully, the small form turned out to be Deez, and had already jumped to the side, as though he knew his life was in peril.

"Sorry," Steve apologized to the large insect. "Dude, you gotta stop jumping out at me like that. Be thankful I'm getting older. In my prime, I would have been able to torch you with my eyes closed.

"In your prime," Sarah repeated, giggling.

"Hey, I had a prime," Steve insisted. "One might say that

I'm still in it."

Sarah laughed harder "In your dreams."

"Thanks. Snot."

DANGER.

"We know, Deez," Steve told the guur.

"We're trying to find the pirates," Sarah added.

DANGER.

"Why does he keep saying that?" Steve asked, as he turned to Gareth. "Can he tell us what the danger is?"

"What's the danger?" Gareth asked the guur. "Tell me what the problem is, okay?"

Small stones clattered on the ground, as if something heavy was sneaking up on them. Everyone leapt to attention, clutching their weapons.

"I have a bad feeling about this," Steve muttered.

He strode to the closest wall and laid a hand on its surface. Breslin mimicked him. The dwarf's eyes shot open.

"He has set the building to collapse!" Breslin cried, turning to his companions. "We must flee! Hurry!"

Steve turned to his wife, who nodded. In the blink of an eye, they'd exited to the street, watching the building shudder violently before collapsing to the ground. The next building over began trembling, and the next.

"Gee, I wonder which way they're going," Steve joked. "They certainly aren't the sharpest tools in the shed, are they?"

Breslin began snapping out orders. "Two full legions are to report here at once! Seal off this street and the street to the south. Pleider's Square is nearby. Seal that off as well."

The three dwarves turned to go when Breslin called them back.

"No, wait. One of you stays. You. I want you to fetch the dragon pens."

Two dwarves rounded the corner a few moments later, completely winded, carrying a large, wooden trunk. The trunk was placed at Breslin's feet and then the two deliverymen disappeared up the street.

Steve squatted next to Breslin, who was busy unlatching the many fasteners holding the trunk closed. "Are these those dragon pen things?"

The trunk's lid was lifted, revealing six squat cubes the size of basketballs. Breslin gingerly pulled one free of its padding and presented it to Steve who grunted with surprise. The cube was far heavier than it looked, at least seventy pounds.

"What do I do with it?" Steve asked.

"Once you spot the pirates, press that button. Then, you have five seconds to place it within ten feet of the intended target."

Steve looked back at the shuddering buildings. In the time it had taken to retrieve the trunk, three more buildings had collapsed. Sarah appeared at his side, looked at the cube, and then at the next shop to fall.

"I'll take it from here."

Steve moved to block his wife's outstretched hands. "It's heavy. Use your jhorun, okay? And while you're at it, send it into that building there."

Sarah, Breslin, and Gareth all turned to look where Steve was pointing. It wasn't at the next house to be demolished, but at the next house after that.

"Why that one?" Sarah whispered.

"Because that's where they are," Steve whispered back. "Just a gut feeling, that whatever they're doing to make the buildings fall takes a little time. By then, they've already moved to the next. So, will you send it into that one, please?"

Breslin pushed his way between husband and wife. "Let me activate it. There. It's ready. Hurry lass! Get it out of here!"

Sarah whisked the cube out of Steve's hand and propelled it through the window of the shop in question. A series of rapid clicks and metallic clangs followed, and the second building literally broke apart as a large metal box took its place. By the time the dragon pen reached full size, the entire building was leveled, as well as the next two shops.

"I think we got 'em!" Steve shouted. "Listen! You can hear them yelling in there. Hey, Captain Windbag! How are ya doing, pal?"

An eardrum-piercing clang suddenly rent the air, followed by another, and another. Unfortunately, the pens were designed to confine dragons, not pirates who had access to fully functional Narian Power Hammers. Dents appeared. They could all hear the groan of metal as the hammering continued.

"I have a feeling that isn't going to hold them forever," Sarah observed. "What's your Plan B?"

Breslin pointed behind them. Nearly half a dozen dwarves were scrambling to set up several devices with tripod legs. What Steve saw looked promising.

"They look like some type of guns," he decided.

"Anchors," Breslin proudly proclaimed.

"Is this another weapon used on dragons?" Sarah asked. When Breslin nodded, Sarah let out a sigh. "And just how many different weapons were used against the dragons?"

Quite a few.

Sarah looked up, as Pryllan now shared her wyverian senses.

Those 'anchors', as the dwarves call them, were brutally effective. The weapon fires a projectile. One end latches onto the dragon, be it by leg, wing, or tail, and the other end anchors itself to an immovable object. Would you care to guess what would happen to the dragon?

Steve flinched. *Good God, no. That's terrible! Holy cow.*

Sarah's mouth formed an 'O' of horror.

"These guys aren't flying," Steve added, looking toward the captive pirates, "so they won't have body parts ripping off. All it needs to do is incapacitate them."

"Get back here!" Breslin ordered. "They're about to break free of the dragon pen!"

Steve, Sarah, Gareth, and Deez hurried away from the line of demolished houses. The three anchor guns were pointed straight at the badly mangled pen. Just as the four of them were safely behind the guns, the dragon pen shuddered a final time under a massive blow, and fell apart.

Captain Flinn stood there, wielding the hammer, a fierce look of determination in his eyes. He caught sight of Steve and shook the hammer at him.

"There be no prison that can hold the likes of us, Fire Thrower! Now suffer the wrath of ... what? What the blazes be this? Get this off me, Q! Now!"

Steve grinned. Flinn was cut off, mid-sentence, as the first anchor gun fired. The projectile—two small, metallic weights connected by a thin silver chain--had instantly wrapped itself around Flinn's left leg and what was left of the dragon pen. The weights spun around each target, ensuring there'd be no escape.

"I'll cut this off, Captain," one of the pirates was saying. He pulled his cutlass from his belt and started sawing at the thin silver chain. When it became apparent no progress had been made, the pirate looked at his sword: the blade was ruined. To Steve, it looked as though the sword had an unfortunate encounter with a grinder.

Another of the anchor guns fired. This time, Rusty found himself tethered to Captain Flinn. The dwarves cheered as captain and quartermaster gave each other a disgusted look.

"This will not hold the likes of me," Flinn vowed. He hefted the hammer and sneered at the dwarves. "Would ye like to see what I think of these pathetic attempts to stop us?"

"You're not going anywhere," Breslin told the restrained captain. "Give back the hammer and I'll see to it you are returned to your ship. Then you can be on your merry way, never to darken the shores of our kingdom again. What say you?"

In response, Flinn hefted the hammer with his right hand, slipped his left hand into his long overcoat, and then tapped the hammer against the chain anchoring him to the dragon pen. The chain fell apart, as if it had been nothing more than a string clipped by a sharp pair of scissors. Grinning, the captain then tapped the chain holding his first mate in place. It, too, fell away.

"How the ruddy hell is he able to break a chain using a hammer?" Breslin demanded.

"Maybe if he smacked the hell out of it," Steve conjectured, "but he's barely touching it. What are we missing here?"

Sarah's eyes narrowed. "He's got the stone. Did you see how he slipped his hand into his jacket pocket? Physical contact with that stone must be how."

"Then we need to get that thing away from him as soon as possible," Steve decided.

"Good luck with that," Sarah observed. "I can't teleport it, the hammer, or the fang, and sadly, I'm willing to wager he has all three of them."

"Then let's take them back. Right now. What do you say? Are you with me?"

In response, the guur suddenly rushed by Steve's leg and headed straight toward Flinn, chittering angrily.

Gareth was by his side in a flash. "No, Deez! Stop! Quick. What will stop an attacking guur?"

"Fire." Steve tore out after their insectoid companion.

"Steve!" Sarah exclaimed. "Get back here! Don't be stupid! Don't … forget them. I'll just … Gareth, what are you doing?"

The young wizard's eyes had closed, and he was furiously chanting. However, all Gareth had to do now was open his eyes and observe the simple fact that Steve had managed to stop Deez. Yes, a thrown chaser exploding only a few feet in front of the guur might have been a bit extreme, but quite frankly, he was tired of running. The guur turned to look accusingly at him.

"Nuh-uh. Get your ten-legged butt back there, to Gareth. Now. You need to…"

Steve trailed off as he noticed a very familiar pirate start to make his way over to Sarah. The grim, determined look Jino had on his face spoke volumes; the pirate was out for blood. Indeed, Jino was holding a dagger in each hand. Without missing a beat, the pirate threw both daggers at his wife.

Sarah, thankfully, had spotted the pirate. Both daggers slowed to a snail's pace, until Sarah was easily able to pluck them from the air and drop them on the ground. With a scowl on his face, Jino scooped several large strips of wood from the ground and, seeing how each sliver of wood already tapered to a sharp point, broke into a run.

Steve generated a chaser and flung it at Jino. Flinn, who must have been watching, easily redirected it at the last moment, so that it detonated against the side of the badly damaged dragon pen. The loud explosion was enough to momentarily attract everyone's attention, including Sarah's.

"Watch out!" Steve called out as he generated three more chasers. "Mr. Steroids is…"

Steve trailed off as, in a blur of motion, Jino briefly reappeared. He slashed viciously at Sarah, who had ducked out of the way. Steve's chasers were hot on his tail, and he made one last lunge toward his intended target.

"Look out!" Steve cried, both arms raised, as if he was preparing to brace for an impact. He quickly looked at his hands and saw that they were an ugly, mottled red. "Uh-oh."

Intent on protecting Sarah, Steve's jhorun detonated. The explosion ripped through the street, which destroyed the remaining buildings. The shock wave expanded upward and slammed into the cavern ceiling.

Hundreds of tons of rocks came crashing down, flattening everything in its path. And unfortunately, that included Steve.

Chapter 9 — Turning Up the Heat

This one next, Lady Sarah. Hurry! Move that to the side, quickly now. Aye. Now these two. Slowly, slowly. We cannot run the risk of causing any more damage by removing the wrong stones."

Sarah sniffed loudly and wiped the corners of her eyes. Her stomach was in knots and she knew, without a doubt, that there was no way Steve could've survived under such an onslaught. What was she going to do? How was she expected to go on without him?

Sarah felt a light tap on her elbow. Breslin was there. He gently guided her away from the site of the roof collapse and gently pulled her down until she was sitting on the ground.

"Stay here, milady. Let us do our work."

The call must have gone out to every dwarf in the area. Dwarves were everywhere. Most had formed chains and were hurriedly passing rocks and stones from one set of hands to another. No one spoke as the rock was painstakingly removed from the street.

Ten minutes later, Breslin was back by her side.

"I am so sorry to disturb you, Lady Sarah, but…"

"But what?" Sarah quietly asked. "Did you find him?"

"We have encountered several boulders we are unable to move. We could always tunnel through them, or set up machinery to move them, but that would take time. Do you think you would be able to help us?"

Sarah eyed her shaking hands. "Steve is under there. Of course, I'll help."

Gareth appeared. Solemn-faced, he placed a hand on Sarah's shoulder.

"Stay here. Rest. I've got this one covered."

"Thank you, Gareth."

The wizard looked down at the carved figurine in his hand. Gareth muttered a soft incantation and then flung the small carving toward the destroyed street. Then, making sure Deez was at his side, he quickly stepped back to watch his spell activate.

The instant the figure made contact with the street, it disintegrated into a small puff of dark smoke. Large boulders, including several which Breslin had hoped Sarah could move, and small rocks alike converged together.

A rudimentary humanoid shape began to emerge. Huge, massive legs, an elongated torso, long bulky arms, and a misshapen chunk of granite for a head completed the figure. The golem took a hesitant step, looked down at the wreckage on the street, and then the body rotated until it was facing its creator.

"Help them," Gareth instructed, as he pointed at the dwarves. "Move only the rocks they ask you to. Do not take it upon yourself to do anything without proper instruction, is that clear?"

The golem grunted, a sound like two slabs of rock grating together. It lumbered over to the dwarves and began following their instructions. Satisfied the golem was doing exactly what it should be doing, Gareth returned to Sarah's side.

"I am so sorry all this happened," Gareth began. "I should have been able to stop it. I could have ... maybe I should have…"

Sarah laid a friendly hand on the teenager's shoulder. "There's nothing you could have done, Gareth. No one knew this was going to happen."

"Do you think we'll find him?" Gareth hopefully asked.

Sarah's face fell. After a few moments, she took a deep breath. "I think they'll find him. I just don't want to be here when they finally do. I don't want to see him like that. Oh, God. I think I'm going to be sick."

"Well, I think he's still alive," Gareth insisted. "If ever there was a person who could survive that collapse, it'd be him."

* * *

For what felt like eons, he rested, content to revel in utter silence. The peaceful solitude was the only thing to keep him company. With nothing else to do, he explored his surroundings.

It was dark. He couldn't make out any distinguishable features, which should have struck him as odd, but it didn't. With nothing recognizable to look at, his mind wandered again and promptly refocused on the quiet. There, faintly audible in the background, was something different.

Faint noises, light murmuring, growing progressively louder. They appeared to be harmless, soothing sounds, which began to fade away.

Relaxing, he returned his attention to his surroundings. He still couldn't see anything besides the darkness.

He strained his ears, hoping to hear something tangible. There. Random sounds—chains? A monster?

Steve tried opening his eyes and hesitated. So dark. He couldn't see or feel his hands. Where was he, anyway?

Why couldn't he remember?

Loud shouts sounded nearby. Then an excruciating noise, like fingernails running along a chalkboard. He decided to turn away from it, but his head remained stationary. At least, he thought it did.

Come to think of it, he couldn't feel his head, either. That must be why he couldn't tell if his eyes were open or closed, blinking or still. Was he even breathing? Wait. He'd have to be breathing, or else he'd be dead.

Oh, no. Was he dead? Was this what death felt like? No, that couldn't be it. He still had full control of his thoughts, only he couldn't feel any parts of his body. Was this an out-of-body experience, then? Was he experiencing some type of astral projection? If so, how the heck was he supposed to stop it? He wanted to get back to his body now.

He heard the loud, grating sound again and concentrated on the noise. It was familiar.

Stones, dragging …

Memories of a cavern collapsing. Something about his jhorun causing an explosion to save Sarah?

Sarah.

Where was she? Was she safe? And the big question: how was he still conscious after all those rocks had fallen on top of him? His mind began to imagine his surroundings. There were stones and a large pile of rubble to the left, and then half a dozen large flat slabs —part of the paved cavern room? After a few moments, those first stones passed by again. He felt as if he were spinning to view the scene, but why wasn't he getting dizzy?

The scene shifted and the rocks disappeared. Steve got the impression that he just dropped into a large, cavernous room. He momentarily panicked and paused, wondering how he was going to make it back up. The cavern wasn't a cavern, but a tunnel. It had to be the largest tunnel he had ever seen. Perhaps a dwarf highway?

Steve focused on shifting his gaze, and was rewarded with a sensation of drifting upward. In his mind, the rocks reappeared, but then dropped away as he continued to rise. And there, he realized with a start, was the source of all the voices he had been hearing: dwarves.

He envisioned the dwarves, outfitted in full digging gear: protective leather padding, picks and shovels strapped to their bodies, and candles attached to the sides of their helmets.

There must have been at least four dozen, all of them digging fervently.

Steve tried calling out to the closest dwarf, a robust fellow with a streaked silver and black beard, wielding a pick in each hand, but he couldn't hear his own voice.

He tried again, taking a deep breath shouting at the top of his lungs. No response from the dwarves

Alarmed, Steve surveyed the floor of the destroyed street. Everywhere he looked, the scene repeated itself over and over as dwarves with tools dug at the stones littering the plaza.

"Keep digging, lads," a somber, but firm, voice said from behind him.

Steve spun his view around until he was looking at the speaker. Breslin! He'd recognize his pugnacious friend anywhere!

"He's under there somewhere," Breslin was quietly saying, to a dwarf Steve didn't recognize, obviously a high-ranking elder, judging from the number of pins, badges, and decorations on his robes. "There's no doubt in my mind that Sir Steve is under there."

"Could he still be alive under all of that?"

Breslin shook his head. "No. No human could have survived that. This is not a rescue mission, but one of recovery. We must retrieve his remains. He deserves to be laid to rest."

Breslin! I'm right here, pal! I'm standing in front of you! Can't you see me?

"Use whatever resources you must," the elderly dwarf said, with a sigh. He placed a fatherly hand on Breslin's shoulder. "See to your friend. Show him the honor he deserves."

Damn it! Why can't you hear me? How can I … wait. Pryllan! Can you hear me? Are you there?

Silence.

Pryllan, come on, my friend. If anyone can pick up my thoughts, it'd be you. Please say something.

More silence.

Damn! What the hell am I supposed to do now?

"What was that?" a dwarf's voice suddenly asked.

"What was *what?*" the digging dwarf asked.

"All three of our candles just flickered," the first dwarf answered, tapping the side of the helmet with the candle attached.

"So?"

"Have you felt any breeze?" Digging Dwarf asked.

"Probably just picked up a draft from somewhere," the second dwarf suggested. "It happens."

Steve kept his vision centered on the three dwarves and the three candles attached to the left horn of the dwarf helmets. The flames had flickered?

My jhorun! I haven't tried using it since the collapse. Perhaps those candles were reacting to me?

Focusing on Digging Dwarf's burning candle, Steve sent a command to his jhorun: snuff the candle out.

The candle poofed out. The two rock-removal dwarves pointed wordlessly at the helmet. Digging Dwarf grunted irritably, removed his helmet, and inspected his extinguished candle.

"What put it out?" the first dwarf asked. "I didn't feel anything. My candle is still lit."

"So is mine," the second dwarf added.

Digging Dwarf stared at his candle for another few seconds before shrugging. He held his helmet up to another one, lit the candle, and then plopped the helmet back on his head. He retrieved his picks, ready to resume work.

I can still affect fire. Can I use this? Okay, all three candles, poof out. Now.

All three candles obediently winked out. *Ha! Just like a birthday cake.* All three dwarves removed their helmets and stared suspiciously at each other.

"You're responsible for this," Digging Dwarf accused. "Admit it."

Both of the other two dwarves raised their hands in mock surrender.

"It wasn't us," the first dwarf said.

"No other candles have gone out," the second added, as he looked around the street.

Not yet, they haven't.

Steve glanced around at the activity in the street. An idea

formed. Maybe he could alert the others that he was still alive.

Every single candle on every dwarf helmet suddenly poofed out. Torches, which had been placed in holders all along the street, also puffed out. Several nearby cook fires were also extinguished.

The street was plunged into absolute blackness.

"Still think there's nothing going on?" came Digging Dwarf's voice.

Steve waited a few moments before ordering his jhorun to restore every fire it had just extinguished. Gasps of astonishment erupted throughout the street as candles, torches and cook fires relit.

Breslin appeared next to Digging Dwarf in a flash.

"Let me see your helmet." Digging Dwarf passed it over to Breslin, who rotated the helmet in his hands, careful to keep the candle lit. "Did you feel anything just then? Perhaps an errant draft?"

"That affected everybody?" Digging Dwarf asked. "No, Master Breslin, I did not. While I am comfortable working in the darkness, it does make it difficult to see what I'm doing. Could we have more candles brought up? I wouldn't want to be caught out here without fire and light."

"Fire," Breslin softly murmured. "By the Benevolent Hand of Usol! Sir Steve? Is that you? Did you do that?"

Yes! Breslin, that was me! I'm here! Can you hear me?

Digging Dwarf gave a mighty sigh and briefly looked at his two companions before turning to Breslin. "My apologies, Master Breslin. I know I have no business saying this to you, since you and the fire thrower were friends. However, no amount of wishing will bring him back. No one survived that. I am sorry for your loss."

"Don't give up on him that easily," Breslin cried. He snatched Digging Dwarf's helmet off his head and tapped the candle on the left horn. "Sir Steve? If that's you, put this out. Only this one, mind you."

More than happy to comply, Steve snuffed out the flame. Breslin was ecstatic.

"I knew it! Sir Steve, you're alive! Send for Lady Sarah at once!"

"If he's alive, where is he?" Digging Dwarf asked.

Breslin looked left, then right, as if he expected to see Steve rising out of the rocks, like water bubbling up from a spring.

"Sir Steve? Are you able to speak? Can you tell me where you are?"

I wish I could, dude. I have no idea what the hell is going on.

"He must still be trapped, under the stone. Come, lads! Hurry! We must dig him out! Young Master Gareth, have your rock creature come over here. Hurry!"

"What's going on?" a familiar voice asked.

Sarah! Oh, thank God you're safe. You're a sight for sore eyes. You're not going to believe what happened to ... this is pointless. You can't even hear me.

"Lady Sarah!" Breslin was saying. "It's Sir Steve! Somehow, and I don't know how, he still lives!"

Sarah turned her tear-streaked face to Breslin. "How can you be so sure? What's going on?"

Breslin held up the helmet with the lit candle. "Watch, milady. Sir Steve? Please extinguish this candle."

Steve complied. Sarah gave a tiny gasp, but even he could see that his wife wasn't entirely convinced. Breslin waggled the helmet.

"Now, relight it, please."

Steve ordered the candle relit. Sarah gingerly took the proffered helmet and stared dubiously at it. She slowly looked around, noting that all activity had ceased and everyone was staring at her, including Gareth's golem.

"Steve? Is it really you? If it is, then please snuff out every fire in this place."

Steve was only more than happy to comply. He waited a few moments before he restored the flames. That was all it took to convince her.

"Steve! Thank God! Where are you? Why can't you speak to me?"

Breslin pointed at the rubble filling the square. "It is my belief that he is still under there, trapped. Perhaps his chest is constricted? He can clearly hear us, only he cannot respond."

Steve, however, had stopped paying attention to either of

them. He was staring at the two hearths on the opposite wall. More logs had been added to both fires, and his jhorun had felt the added energy the fire was giving off. What if ... what if that was the answer? What if the reason he had been able to survive the cavern collapse was because his jhorun had turned his body into pure fire?

Amazement flooded through him, but was quickly replaced by skepticism. He couldn't possibly be pure fire. If he had, then wouldn't the dwarves have noticed flames trickling up through the rocks?

But, he also knew that his jhorun handled both flames and heat. You can't have one without the other. So, could he currently exist as nothing but pure heat? If he wanted to, could he turn himself to flames?

Fire, guys. I need something everyone can see. Give me some flames!

"Whoa!" Digging Dwarf cried, dancing back several feet. "Look at that! The stones are on fire!"

"Get back, everyone!" Breslin snapped. "Cease what you're doing. Get off the rocks, now!"

The dwarves in both crews, holding stones they were passing from one set of hands to the next, promptly dropped the rocks where they were and hurried away from the street. Digging teams collected their tools and hastily joined the large group of onlookers as they seemingly stared straight at Steve. The rock golem dropped the massive boulder it was holding and lumbered after Gareth.

It's working! They're looking at me! I mean, I think they are. Keep it up!

Right about then, Steve heard shouts of surprise come from the crowd of onlookers to his right. He shifted his vision accordingly and was rewarded with a strange scene: both fires appeared to have jumped off their hearths. What he could see were two large balls of burning fire speeding straight toward him. He also watched Sarah and Breslin jump out of the way as the fireballs sped by.

Steve watched the flames moving toward him. What was he supposed to do? Absorb them? How? With what?

Before he could ponder that, the flames arrived. He felt a sudden increase of energy. His mind sharpened and a flicker of his former self emerged.

He knew what he had to do next.

Concentrating on the space directly in front of him, directly in front of Sarah and Breslin, Steve ordered his jhorun to draw some letters into the air. What Sarah, Breslin, Gareth, and the rest of the dwarves saw, was:

EROM

"Erom?" Breslin quizzically repeated. "Why would Sir Steve say that?"

"That's 'more' spelled backward," Sarah excitedly told him. "He drew it from his perspective. More? More what, fire? Of course! He can regain his strength by absorbing the energy from fires! Breslin, we need more fire in here!"

"Oy! You lot! You, you, and you. You heard her. Gather everyone you can. Bring tinder kits, kindling, wood, and stones. We need to set up additional hearths. Hurry!"

While the dwarves ran for their tinder kits, Steve surreptitiously spun the MORE around so that it would read correctly to the rest of the group. There was no point in coming across as a moron, was there?

Ten minutes later, a total of six fire rings had been added. Not caring about appearance, wood was hastily dumped into the stone rings, ignited, and stoked. Once all six had fires blazing brightly, Breslin turned to address the open air.

"Sir Steve? You wanted more. Will this do?"

Steve was there, waiting. In response to Breslin's question, he directed his jhorun at the burning fires. Reaching out with his mind, he felt the crackling energy each of them provided. He felt his jhorun tingling like crazy. Apparently, his jhorun was hungry!

There you go. Have at it, boys.

His jhorun detected the presence of the additional fire and immediately called out to each. As a result, the roaring fire in each fire pit was pulled off the wood, leaving red-hot coals in its place. The half dozen balls of fire coalesced into one gigantic, twisting ball of flames, hovering over the broken rubble. Then, as if it was being pulled from below, the burning ball of fire dropped until it made contact with the broken stones.

The immense fireball melted into the ground, as though a huge drop of water touched the world's largest paper towel. For a few pregnant seconds, nothing happened. Then the energy from the fires mixed with Steve's own.

Feeling more alive by the second, Steve started concentrating on his body. If his jhorun had turned his physical body to flames, well, then it could reverse it. He wanted his body back. Perhaps if he tried to remember what it felt like to stand? Sit? Walk? Run?

Steve concentrated as he had never concentrated before. He brought up memory after memory, hoping to show his jhorun what it was like to be in a physical body. Memories of walking, hiking, scuba diving, and walking through Disneyland with Sarah all flashed through his mind.

His perspective shifted. It suddenly felt as if he was rising, only he hadn't given the order to view the proceedings from a higher angle. He tried to swing his vision around to the right to see what Sarah and Breslin were doing, only he found he couldn't. In fact, everything had become a muted red.

This was new. Whether good or bad, he didn't know.

Come on, guys. I need to be able to see. Why did you take away my sight? Give it back!

Steve?

Pryllan? Is that you?? You can hear me now?

Were you calling before?

Yes! You have no idea about the ordeal I just went through. Am still going through, for that matter. I thought I was dead.

Figuratively or literally?

Literally, my friend.

Are you still in Foronlir? Have you apprehended the human invaders?

One problem at a time. I need to recover my human body first.

I do not know what that means.

It means several thousand pounds of rocks and stones fell on top of me. I should be dead, but I'm not. The only thing I can think of is that, in order to protect me, my jhorun turned me into fire.

I am not sure how to respond to that. You are serious?

Yeah, I am. I've never been more serious about anything in my life. I ... hey! I just opened my eyes! I can see! It's about damn time! I never want to go through that again for as long as I live. I ... hmm. That can't be good.

What is it?

I seem to be missing an arm.

You are? Does it hurt?

Umm, no. As a matter of fact, my right arm looks as though it's made out of pure fire.

If your physical body is comprised of flames at the moment, then you should be certain that all body parts are restored to their previous condition. You do not want ... what is it? I sense your mirth. Did I say something funny?

Restore all body parts. Yeah, that is funny. Oh, I get it now. If I concentrate, I can direct these flames wherever I want. So, if I want my left arm back, then I can just imagine my left arm flexing and ... yes! Look! My arm is growing back!

Is your body whole?

Umm, I think so? Seriously, how would I know that? I can look down at myself and see a humanoid shape, but that's it. Everything is lit on fire.

Then extinguish yourself and make sure you are whole.

Steve looked down at his arms, grateful he was now looking at *two*. He experimentally poked a finger into his chest. Thankfully, his finger was met with resistance. His body was back! Pryllan was right. He just needed to extinguish his flames.

Taking a deep breath, Steve ordered his jhorun to pull all available flames inward. His jhorun complied. The flames on his arms and chest shrank until he could see bare skin.

However, a new problem manifested: his clothing was nowhere to be seen. He was now as naked as the day he was born. He turned to his right and discovered problem number two staring right at him. Well, he thought it was looking at him. Exactly how had he missed seeing *that* before?

A towering figure comprised solely of rock and stone was standing — motionless — less than a dozen feet away. It had a large boulder tucked under each arm and was preparing to set the stones down into a considerable pile just off to the creature's left. The rock monster regarded Steve for a few moments longer before it returned its attention to the rubble pile and moved a few more stones.

"Steve!" Sarah cried out, from somewhere on his right. "You're alive! Thank heavens! You... you... you're naked. Where are your clothes?"

Steve looked right and cringed. There was his wife. And Breslin. And nearly a hundred sets of dwarfish eyes. He took a step in their direction and then recoiled in pain. It was as if he had just taken a step on a gravel road without wearing shoes or socks. Those rocks hurt!

Realizing he was showing all of Foronlir that which hadn't seen the light of day since, well, forever, Steve hastily conjured two chasers, one in each hand. Holding them in place so as to be considered 'decent', he painstakingly hobbled over to his wife. Steve also noticed Sarah's red eyes and tear-streaked face.

They truly thought he had died. Although, to be fair, he himself had thought he was dead, too. Not even Pryllan had been able to sense him.

Sarah came rushing over, intent to throw her arms around him, when she hesitated. She opened her arms and closed her eyes. Steve could only hope that she was conjuring some clothes for him.

She was.

Shirt, pants, shoes, and everything else he needed appeared in her outstretched arms. She held them out to him, but then remembered his hands were 'full'. With a mischievous smile forming on her face, her eyes closed again. The clothes disappeared, only to reappear on Steve.

"How long have you been able to do... oof!"

Sarah launched herself into his arms "I thought you had died. How did you ever survive that?"

"It wasn't easy," Steve admitted, as he smoothed out the wrinkles in his shirt. "I think ... I think my jhorun turned me into fire. When I came to, I couldn't open my eyes, or move my arms, or even turn my head. It was the weirdest damn experience of my life. I … hey, Breslin. It's good to see you, buddy."

The dwarf approached, and then reverently dropped to one knee. "Sir Steve. I do not know how you continue to be so lucky, my friend. I, too, would like to know how a human survived that ordeal."

"Any other human would have been turned into hamburger," Steve agreed. He repeated what he'd just told Sarah.

Gareth finally appeared. Where had he been? Come to think of it, he hadn't seen the young wizard since prior to the cave collapse.

Steve's eyes automatically dropped to Gareth's hand. The acolyte wizard was clutching something tightly to his chest. Gareth stared at him, wide-eyed, for a few moments before lunging forward to throw his arms around him.

"You're alive! Wizards be damned! And, coming from me, that's saying something. How are you still alive?"

"Weren't you the one who told me you believed he was still alive?" Sarah accused as she turned to Gareth. Thankfully, she was smiling. "You didn't give up hope, did you?"

Gareth's eyebrows shot up. "Give up hope? *You* are the one who said there was no way he could have lived through that!"

Steve chuckled. "Reports of my demise have been greatly exaggerated. Whatcha got there, Gareth?"

Gareth opened his hand to reveal three small figurines.

"More of those rock creatures?" Sarah asked, pointing back at the huge figure standing motionless several feet away.

Gareth nodded. "Aye. I only had the one on me, but in case we needed more, I went back to R'Tal for these. I guess I was wrong."

Sarah pulled Gareth into a hug. "But not about giving up hope on Steve. You called it, from the beginning. He was still alive."

"What about those pirates?" Steve wanted to know. "Where are they? Does anyone know?"

"We just assumed they were with you," Breslin said. "And by that, I mean … well, that is to say…"

"…flatter than a pancake?" Steve finished for the dwarf.

Breslin nodded. "Aye. But, if you escaped, could the pirates?"

Steve turned to Gareth. "Is there any way to tell if they're still here?"

Gareth was silent for a few moments as he considered. Then he nodded his head, closed his eyes, and began to chant. Accustomed to the young wizard's method of spellcasting, Steve and Sarah fell silent and were content to wait. Breslin waited as well. Sensing movement from behind, husband and wife turned to see the throng of dwarves crowding close. Steve chuckled. If he didn't know any better, he'd say the dwarves were anxious to see a wizard at work.

"I thought dwarves hated all things jhorun," Steve whispered to his dwarf friend.

"They do," Breslin confirmed. "However, that only goes for us dwarves. The chance to see a spell cast by an authentic wizard? Irresistible."

Gareth smiled. "Appreciated, I'm sure. I have an answer."

All eyes turned to the wizard.

"No."

"No, *what?*" Steve asked. "No, there aren't any pirates nearby, or no, you can't tell if there are any pirates nearby?"

"Is he always this literal?" Gareth asked, as he turned to Sarah.

"Tip of the iceberg," Sarah softly muttered.

Confused, Gareth shrugged it off. He shook his head for the second time. "No. There are no pirates nearby."

"Then where are they?" Breslin demanded.

"They couldn't have slipped by us again, could they?" Sarah asked, with a sigh.

Breslin was shaking his head. "No. I won't say it would be impossible, only highly unlikely."

"That means they found another way out of this cavern," Sarah decided.

"Impossible," Breslin argued. "No other exits exist. No exits, no tunnels, no nothing."

"What's directly below us?" Steve suddenly asked, as he remembered the vast, open space he had seen earlier.

Breslin shook his head. "Nothing but solid granite, I'm afraid. Why do you ask?"

"Because I know that's not quite correct. I saw it. It was either another cavern or a big tunnel."

"Under here?" Breslin asked, incredulous. "You saw this just now?"

"No, it was about … you know what? I don't know how long ago it was. It was part of my out-of-body experience, okay?"

"And you're sure you saw something down there?" Sarah asked. "Can you tell me specifically where it was?"

Steve walked back to the section of rocks he had risen from and stopped. He double-checked his surroundings to make sure he was remembering correctly. Yes, he was sure of it.

"Right here. Why? Do you think you could teleport there?"

Sarah shrugged. "I'm taking a lot of what you said on faith. If you're wrong, I could teleport into solid stone. I don't even know what would happen if I did."

"Then let's not find out," Steve decided.

Sarah shook her head. "No, you were right about everything else. I want to know what's down there, if anything."

"Then take me with you," Steve said, holding up an arm in an open invitation.

Breslin pushed him away. "I will be the one going, thank you very much. This is our home. If there's something hidden inside these stones, then I'd like to see for myself what it is."

"You be careful," Steve quietly told Sarah, as he pulled her in for a hug. "I don't want you risking yourself."

"You did earlier," Sarah accused.

"Not willingly," Steve reminded her.

"I'll be careful."

"Will you come back for me once the coast is clear?"

Sarah nodded. "I will. We'll be right back. Breslin? Are you ready? Deep breath. Here we go."

The two of them vanished from sight. To Steve, it felt like an eternity before she reappeared—alone—but in reality, it couldn't have been more than ten seconds. The positive side of this was, Sarah was smiling!

"You need to see this," his wife told him as she took his hand. "Breslin is speechless."

"What is it?" Steve asked.

"See for yourself."

The cavern and all the devastation he had created winked out, replaced by the same scene he had observed before. No wonder Breslin wanted to see for himself. It wasn't a cavern but a tunnel! A very big tunnel! A pair of semi-trucks could've driven through it side-by-side without touching the walls.

"You didn't know this was here?" Steve incredulously asked.

"No, Sir Steve. There was nothing below us before."

"Then what do you call this?" Steve asked, as he spread his arms wide to encompass the enormity of the empty space they were standing in.

"This wasn't made by volcanic activity," Breslin told him, "nor was it made by dwarf hands. This, my friends, was made by a Creeg!"

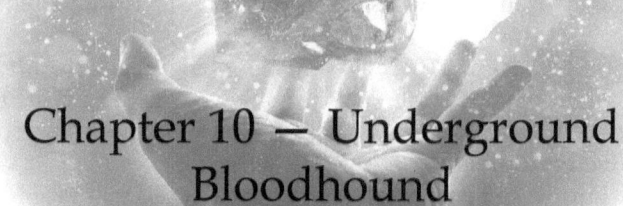

Chapter 10 — Underground
Bloodhound

"Where have I heard that term before?" Steve wondered aloud. He looked over at Sarah, who had a smile on her face. Great. Just great. She knew the answer.

"You and that lousy memory of yours," Sarah muttered, shaking her head. "A Creeg is a land dragon. They can be just as large as their winged cousins and they walk around on their two hind legs."

Steve snapped his fingers. "That's right. They reminded me of dinosaurs."

"No they didn't," Sarah argued.

Steve crossed his hands over his chest. "Did so. The only difference was the front arms. Dinosaurs have tiny vestigial arms, where the Creegs had fully proportioned arms."

"You're thinking of the Tyrannosaurus Rex," Sarah told him. "It has vestigial arms. Do all dinosaurs?"

Steve stared at his wife in shock. How in the world did

she know that? He noticed a look of disgust on Sarah's face and burst out laughing.

"Proof positive I have way too much useless crap in my head," Sarah ruefully informed him. "And I blame you. For all of it."

Steve held a hand over his heart. "Guilty as charged. So, a Creeg made this? That's impressive. This has to be the cleanest-looking tunnel I have ever seen."

Sarah approached one of the walls of the tunnel and ran a hand across the surface. "Too clean. A dragon dug this? There are no claw marks, no blemishes, nothing! It's like someone cut this out of the ground with a ... a ..."

"Laser sword?" Steve helpfully supplied.

Sarah elbowed him in the gut. "Zip it. I wasn't going to say that."

"How do they do it?" Steve asked, as he turned back to his dwarf friend. "They can't possibly create a tunnel this smooth, can they?"

Breslin nodded. "They can and they *do*. The Creeg are some of the most efficient diggers I have ever seen. We have tried approaching them numerous times to work out an arrangement, but alas, they were not interested in digging any tunnels for us."

"Efficient *how*?" Sarah asked.

"Did you know," Breslin continued, companionably, "that a Creeg can dig faster than a horse can run?"

Steve's eyebrows shot up. No way!

"That's something I'd like to see," Sarah commented.

There was a sudden flash of light. By the time the light faded, two more had been added to the group: Gareth and Deez. Gareth noted the size of the tunnel, and the simple fact that it stretched endlessly away in either direction, and whistled with amazement.

"Now *that's* a tunnel."

Steve rapped his knuckles on the side of the tunnel and looked down at the friendly guur. "Not even you would be able to climb up this surface, amigo."

Deez immediately scuttled over to the closest wall and proved Steve wrong. The guur was walking along the tunnel wall as effortlessly as the four of them walked along the ground. They hadn't made it more than a few steps when Breslin pulled them to a stop.

"Wait. Is it your intention to track your pirate friends along this tunnel?"

Husband and wife both nodded.

"Yep," Steve confirmed. "They somehow slipped past you guys, and it looks as though they used this tunnel to do it. So yeah, we're going after them. Come with us. Someone with Narian blood will need to pick up the hammer once we recover it."

"In that case, wait here. Lady Sarah, could you take me to the Council Chamber? I need to report in before I can depart."

Sarah nodded. "Of course. Hon, don't go anywhere. We'll be right back."

"We'll be here," Steve assured her.

After Sarah and Breslin vanished, he turned to Gareth, who was staring up at Deez. The guur had continued exploring the tunnel, and now stood upside-down on the ceiling. The guur was chittering softly and stared straight at the wizard.

"He sure has taken to you," Steve commented. "I never thought I'd be this close to one of them without blasting it to smithereens."

"You said you fought hundreds of these?" Gareth asked, amazed. "I cannot even begin to imagine what that must have been like."

"That battle is not something I'm ever going to forget," Steve recalled.

"How long do guur live?" Gareth wanted to know.

"I have no idea," Steve answered, looking thoughtfully over at the wizard's ten-legged friend. "While I don't think it's too long, I do know the time is measured in years."

Gareth looked affectionately at his new pet. "That's okay. I'll take care of him as long as I can."

"I know you will, sport."

Sarah and Breslin materialized, along with a second dwarf who looked vaguely familiar. Sarah was beaming her approval. She pulled Steve over to the newest addition and smiled.

"Steve, you remember Athos, don't you?"

"One of the dwarf brothers," Steve recalled.

Athos held up a hand. "I am eager to be of service again and am fortunate I was talking with Master Maelnar when Master Breslin came calling."

Steve shrugged. "I'm glad you're here."

Athos nodded once and then looked at Gareth. Then his eyes widened as he saw Deez. In the blink of an eye, Athos had pulled his axe free and hurled it at the guur. Thankfully, Sarah noticed. Her jhorun caught the axe a mere three feet from the guur. Deez recoiled in surprise and immediately scuttled to the top of the tunnel, chittering angrily.

"What the bloody hell is a guur doing here?" Athos demanded. "And why did you stop my axe? I had it in my sights."

"Deez is a member of our group," Sarah explained as her jhorun deposited the axe softly at his feet. "I cannot allow you to hurt him."

"He's legit," Steve said. "Deez answers to Gareth, so try to avoid attacking either one of them."

"If you say so," Athos reluctantly agreed.

"How much do any of you know about the Creeg?" Breslin asked, once they were all underway.

"Only what you've told us," Steve answered. "I mean, we encountered one once. It was big, lacked wings, and wasn't something I wanted to tangle with, if you want me to be honest."

"And it was intelligent," Sarah added. "Very intelligent, if memory serves."

"How does it make these tunnels so smooth?" Gareth asked.

Breslin grinned. "Essentially, the Creeg swim through the ground."

"Swim?" Gareth repeated, puzzled.

"Impossible," Sarah said, at the same time.

Steve whistled, but refrained from saying anything.

Breslin was nodding. "It's true. The Creeg can out dig any living creature in Lentari. They dig so fast that the ground essentially flows around them, like water. Their tunnels are

The Creeg turned its massive head so it could study the tunnel they were in. "No. One much larger than me accomplished this."

"Are you friendly?" Sarah asked.

"Are you?" the Creeg countered.

"Yes, we are," Steve assured the large creature. "Why are you here? Are you here to help us?"

"I am…"

The Creeg trailed off as a second set of tremors shook the tunnel and its occupants once more. As before, another snout appeared, followed immediately by the loss of a huge chunk of tunnel floor. This one was light gray with pale blue blemishes all over its body. The front forelegs were just as muscular as the first, and it, too, had huge talons on each of its claws and was just as heavily scaled as its counterpart.

Once the second Creeg had pulled itself from the ground, Steve could see that, from the angle of its tunnel, it had arrived from a different direction. Humans and dwarves alike turned to look at the first Creeg, as if expecting the newly arrived land dragon to introduce his companion. However, Steve noticed the first Creeg was staring at the second with a look of confusion on his reptilian face. Was the arrival of the second Creeg unexpected?

Sarah flashed them a million-dollar smile. "Why are you here? What are you here to accomplish?"

"I am here to assist you," the first Creeg stated, matter-of-factly. "I am here at the behest of Kahvel, Aerial Dragon Lord."

"Kahvel sent you?" Sarah asked, amazed. She turned to look at Steve.

"Pryllan sent one Creeg. She didn't realize two would be dispatched."

The first Creeg nodded, introducing himself as Vutt. The second Creeg was Hedro, a youngster of only four hundred years.

Steve smiled as he looked up at the large creature. "I like your sense of humor, Vutt.

"You are Steve, you are the Fire Thrower?"

"As evidenced by my hands currently being engulfed in

flames?" Steve held up both ignited hands.

Sarah elbowed him in the gut. "Don't be rude. I'm sorry about my husband, Vutt. He can be a sarcastic twit sometimes."

Vutt chuckled, which sounded like a low series of growls. "Right now, we have lost humans to retrieve."

"Well, they're not exactly lost," Steve clarified. "They, uh, are bad humans who need to be found as soon as possible. You guys say you can smell them? That's great! Lead the way, amigo."

"My name is Vutt," the Creeg clarified, as it stared - unblinking - at Steve.

"No, I mean... forget it. Let's go."

Vutt, who was facing the tunnel in the direction Steve, Sarah, and Gareth had originally come from, did the impossible--seemingly tucked parts of his body away, making himself smaller, shrinking enough to easily turn around in the tunnel. Then, instead of using his back legs to move, lowered himself to the ground and actually *slithered* ahead, like a snake.

"How are you doing that?" Steve asked, amazed, as he walked alongside and stared at the Creeg's body. "Your physiology must be amazing!"

"We were told that Creegs dig so fast that you practically swim through the ground. Is that true?" Sarah asked.

"Humans walk, you run, and you swim," Vutt answered from the front of the line. "If you encounter a different species who has a slower method of locomotion, will they not be amazed by that which you consider trivial?"

They proceeded, exchanging polite conversation about each species' habits, until Vutt came to an abrupt halt. "Problem detected," he announced.

"What is it?" Steve asked. He pumped more jhorun into his hands, increasing their supply of light.

"Aside from you three, I no longer detect any humans."

"What?" Sarah asked, incredulous. "We lost the trail? How is that possible? We've been following the same tunnel they've been using."

"I still detect their scent back here," Hedro announced.

Vutt turned to stare at his Creeg companion. "Indeed?

May I verify?"

"How?" Breslin asked.

"Are you suggesting you don't believe me?" Hedro demanded, growing annoyed.

"That's exactly what I'm saying," Vutt haughtily informed him. "I know not your scent, Hedro, and I can recognize practically every Creeg I've ever encountered. We are not a prolific species, as you may have guessed. So, if it's all the same to you, I would like to verify for myself that the human scent is, indeed, still back there."

"Then may I suggest we simply backtrack for a few paces?" Breslin said. "That way, Master Creeg, you won't have to turn around in here."

"Agreed."

Humans and dwarves were small enough to turn around, unencumbered. Both Creeg, however, simply walked backward for nearly a hundred feet until Vutt lowered his head, sniffed twice, and eventually nodded.

"Hedro is correct. I detect the human scent here, whereas I could not up front."

"Told you," Hedro muttered.

Steve gave the second Creeg a speculative look before turning back to Breslin and the others. "So what does that tell us? The pirates disappeared right about here? How? How would they have done that? I know for a fact that they don't have a teleporter handy. They would have used him by now."

"I am uncertain," Vutt admitted. "I will investigate. Please wait here. Hedro, stay here as well. I will get to the bottom of this."

Vutt slithered forward at quadruple the speed they had been traveling. Nearly two hundred feet away, the huge land dragon veered off course and disappeared through the tunnel wall, as though he'd simply melted into the stone itself.

"There's something you don't see every day," Steve idly commented. "How did he do that?"

"By jhorun," Sarah answered. She started to sigh and stretch her back when she stiffened with surprise. She pointed at the spot Vutt had vanished and looked back at Hedro. "How come we don't see the beginnings of a tunnel right there?"

Hedro gave Sarah a disconcerted stare. "I don't follow."

"Vutt took off and disappeared into the wall. I don't see any tunnel. He was digging, wasn't he?"

"He *was* digging and he *did* create a tunnel," Hedro clarified.

As far as any of the others could tell, the tunnel ran straight as an arrow, with no discernible side tunnels anywhere. Sarah turned back to Hedro.

"You're telling me Vutt dug a tunnel and you can see it?"

"I can see it," Breslin added, trying valiantly to suppress a huge grin. "Quite remarkable, actually. If I didn't know any better, I would say you picked up on the idea to blend the tunnel into the surroundings from us dwarves."

Hedro grunted, but didn't say anything.

Husband and wife wandered over to examine the spot. After a few moments, Steve stumbled, but managed to catch himself before he fell face first into the newly discovered *concealed* tunnel.

"Man alive, that's impressive. The striations in the rock, the colors, and the shapes all blend flawlessly together. So, be honest. Who came up with this idea first? Dwarves or Creeg?"

"Dwarves," Breslin and Athos replied, in unison.

"Creeg," Hedro insisted, at the same time.

Before anyone could say anything else, distinctive footfalls sounded, growing louder and making the ground tremble.

"What do you think it is?" Sarah asked, as she came up behind Steve and clutched his shoulder.

"I'll be optimistic and say it's Vutt."

It was, but he didn't emerge from the side tunnel he had dug, as everyone expected. Instead, the Creeg's large reddish-brown snout and head appeared directly above theirs. They moved aside so the Creeg could safely climb down out of the ceiling.

"What news do you bring?" Breslin asked, as soon as Vutt was standing before them.

"Your humans keep getting more and more curious," Vutt declared. "As to what I found, you'll have to see for yourselves."

"I just hope he found the pirates," Gareth said. "The sooner we deal with them, the sooner we can get out of here."

Steve caught Breslin's eye and nodded his readiness. Breslin gave Athos a friendly slap on the back, and both dwarves pulled weapons from their holders.

"Lead the way, Master Creeg." Breslin waved toward the open tunnel.

Vutt nodded, lowered his head, and slithered off. This time, the humans and dwarves had to jog in order to keep up. Deez chose to run along the tunnel wall's side.

Vutt quickly slithered into the tunnel he had dug earlier. After about five hundred feet Vutt slowed, sniffed the air, and then veered again, this time angling left. As the Creeg's snout touched the wall, the stone seemed to turn to liquid. Steve had to blink to make sure he wasn't hallucinating.

Sure enough, the stone was flowing around Vutt, like a canoe in water. The wall of solid granite rippled as Vutt passed, and then, once the land dragon's long, thick tail moved on, the ripples smoothed out and became as still as glass.

Impressed beyond words, Steve ran his hands along the wall, feeling nothing but the rock's smooth, polished surface. He turned to see Sarah standing beside him.

As they hurried to catch up with Vutt, Steve said, "That is far and away the coolest damn thing I think I have ever seen. It's like the rock and the Creeg are mortal enemies, and the rock is trying to get as far away from Vutt as it can."

"An apt description," Vutt called from ahead. "We Creeg have long believed that, since we are such efficient diggers, the earth has become afraid of us, and that is what enables us to move with such ease."

"How far ahead did you search?" Breslin asked.

"Probably the equivalent of a two-day walk."

"Rubbish," Athos snorted angrily. "You were gone for no more than half an hour."

Vutt nodded. "Exactly."

Ignoring comments by the two dwarves, Vutt spoke up: "While I was searching, I came across something that I wanted to show you. And, as luck would have it, that's where I picked up the humans' trail once more. But, how they knew about this place is beyond me."

"What place are you talking about? And what has this to do with getting the Narian Hammer back?" Breslin asked, impatient.

"You will see, dwarf. At our current pace, we will arrive in just over an hour."

True to his word, after some time, Vutt stopped digging and waited for his companions to catch up.

"We are here. And so, I believe, are the other humans."

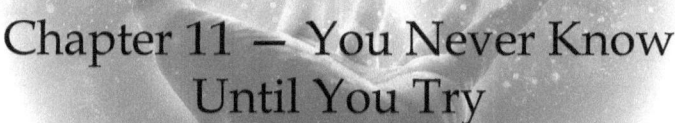

Chapter 11 — You Never Know Until You Try

Steve tried to lean around Vutt to see what he was looking at, but since the Creeg was the one responsible for creating the tunnel, he had to wait until the land dragon moved out of the way. And, when he did, Steve literally became speechless. Sarah appeared on his left, while Gareth appeared on his right. Neither spoke a word as they all gazed at the sight before them.

Directly ahead were the remains of the largest foundry Steve had ever seen. Three gigantic smelting pots were situated in the middle of the cavern. Ropes and pulleys stretched this way and that, from one side of the great cavern to the other. Tunnels, some still intact and others mostly blocked from cave-ins, dotted the cavern walls in all directions.

Anvils of such a great scale that they were impossible to believe lined one wall. Gigantic hammers hung, motionless, from their tethers, awaiting a time when they could possibly be of use again. From their vantage point, they could even tell that one smelting pot still had something in it. What it was, Steve couldn't tell.

"What is this place?" Sarah asked, amazed. "It looks like a big forge."

Breslin nodded. "Aye, that's exactly what it is. To be truthful, milady, I had completely forgotten this was here. These smelters haven't been lit for centuries."

"Why were they abandoned?" Gareth asked.

"The vein of gold we had been mining dried up. We have since located other veins, much larger and, unfortunately, much farther away. So, this one was simply abandoned and we built a new set of forges."

"I remember hearing about this one closing up," Athos said, as he looked around the remains of the once-thriving foundry. "Many a dwarf spent long, hard hours working these forges."

Breslin nodded. "True. But, we go where the gold is, and right now, it isn't here."

Steve felt a slight nudge on his ribs and looked over at his wife. Sarah was pointing at something in the distance. The ledge they were all standing on was perhaps fifty feet wide, and extended at least a quarter mile in either direction. However, Sarah was pointing north. There was something laying, discarded, on the ground.

"What's that?" Sarah whispered. "It looks cleaner than the rest of the stuff around here. It stands out like a sore thumb."

Steve squinted at the distant object. It looked like a piece of clothing. He tapped Gareth on the shoulder and pointed it out.

"Do you think you could send Deez out to get whatever that is?"

Gareth studied the distant object for a few moments and then nodded. "Sure. Do you think there might be a pirate or two trying to ambush us? I don't want to send Deez into a dangerous situation."

"I doubt they'd be stupid enough to hang around here and allow us to catch up, but then again, you never know."

Gareth squatted next to Deez and pointed at the small piece of dark clothing. "Deez, would you get that for us, please?"

Deez's armored head swiveled until he was staring at the fallen object.

YOU DESIRE ITEM?

Gareth nodded enthusiastically. "Aye! I do. Would you fetch it for me?"

COMPLIANCE

Deez scuttled off, making great time across the open ledge. The guur arrived at the object's location, plucked it off the ground, and promptly scuttled back. Deez transferred the item from one of his smaller inner legs to one of the two much larger front legs and offered it to Gareth, like a dog would with a tennis ball.

The teenager patted the guur on his head. "Thanks, Deez. Well, let's see what we've got here. Hmm. It's just a hat." Gareth turned the headwear over and over in his hands. "That's all. There's nothing remarkable about it that I can tell."

Breslin plucked the hat from Gareth's hands. "On the contrary, lad, look at the style of hat. It's a tri-cornered hat, much like I've seen on one of those accursed pirates. And the condition? While nowhere near being pristine, it's much too clean to have been in here long."

Athos took the hat from Breslin's hands and studied it. "Why leave it here for us to find? Is it to throw us off their trail?"

Steve looked at Gareth and nodded in the direction the pirate hat had been found. "Is there anything you can do to identify whose hat this belongs to, and maybe tell us how it came to be left behind? I think Athos is right. I think they left it behind on purpose, but what that purpose is, I don't know."

"I have another possibility," Sarah offered, raising a hand. "What if they didn't know they lost it? What if they were fleeing for their lives and the last thing on their minds was whether or not one of their hats was missing?"

Breslin gave Sarah an appreciative look and immediately squatted to inspect the ground. While thick with dust, they could see no footprints besides their own and that of the guur's. Steve pointed down at the ground.

"Look, all we have to do is follow Deez's footprints. Er, legprints, or whatever they're called. If a pirate dropped this, then there should be footprints to follow. Let's see where they lead."

While the two Creegs waited at the base of the ledge, the three humans and two dwarves hurriedly inspected the area, looking for some signs of the pirates' trail.

"Here," Athos called. He was standing up against the cavern wall that looked no different than the rest of the stone wall they had been studying. "There are footprints here, and they look as though they walked right out of the wall."

"That can't be right," Steve grumped, as he squatted to look at the tracks that were clearly visible in the thick dust. "I … nope, you're right. That's exactly what it looks like. I don't get it."

Sarah turned to look back at the two Creegs, who looked as though they were quietly conversing with one another.

"Vutt? Hedro? Could you come over here for a second?"

Both Creegs swung their heads up and made eye contact. Vutt nodded, and seeing how they were no longer in a tunnel but a much larger cavern, immediately rose up on his hind legs. After a few moments of hesitation, Hedro did the same.

As Steve eyed the approaching Creegs, he couldn't help but think how closely they resembled dinosaurs from his own world. There they were, walking upright on their massive hind legs. Wasn't that the exact definition of one of those giant extinct reptiles?

"What do you make of that?" Breslin asked, as soon as the two Creegs arrived. He was pointing at the footprints. "These prints look like they just walked right out of that wall. I've felt the surface, as has everyone else. There's no tunnel here. Can you explain how that would even be possible?"

Vutt stepped up close to the wall and sniffed. His eyes

widened. The Creeg looked briefly at Hedro, leaned forward to sniff again, and then finally straightened

"I can smell a third Creeg," Vutt reported. "However, yet again, I am unable to identify the scent. Hedro, can you identify it?"

Hedro lowered his head and sniffed. After a few moments, the pale blue and gray Creeg shook his head. "I cannot."

"You're telling me that a Creeg came through here?" Steve asked, looking back at the impassable stone wall. "What happened to the tunnel?"

"While highly unlikely," Vutt hesitantly began, "it is not unheard of for a Creeg to forego leaving behind a tunnel."

"Do you mean to tell us that a Creeg could pass through solid granite without ever leaving a trace they were there?" Breslin incredulously asked. "I cannot even begin to tell you how disturbing that is. What will the Council think of…?"

"Rest assured, friend dwarf," Vutt smoothly interrupted, "that, by mandate of the Great Lord himself, we are never to move about in stealth."

"Yet, someone did," Steve reminded the Creeg. "And, if I didn't know any better, that Creeg is working with the pirates to sneak them out of here. Can you tell how long ago they were here?"

"Approximately two hours," Vutt reported.

"Two hours?" Steve sputtered. He turned to Sarah, who shrugged. "How can that possibly be? Wait. How long was I under that rock?"

"Nearly three hours, Sir Steve," Breslin answered. "Three of the most miserable hours I have had the misfortune of experiencing in my entire life."

"It took us a while to get to you," Sarah gently reminded him. "There were a lot of stones to move out of the way."

"Actually, now that I think about it, I could've sworn it was a lot longer than that," Steve observed. "At least, it certainly felt like it. All right. We know the pirates came through here. Come on! We've got to pick up the pace!"

"Where will this ledge take us?" Sarah asked, as she raced alongside Gareth and Breslin.

"I'm trying to think, milady. We're heading toward the

northern wall, which means … Wizards be damned! They couldn't possibly know about that tunnel, could they?"

"What tunnel?" Steve and Athos both asked, at the same time.

"The one leading to the Gate Cavern."

"The big one with the two unfinished tunnels?" Steve asked. "The one where Sarah originally teleported us across your protective barrier?"

"That's the one," Breslin confirmed. "It's been sealed for nearly two centuries."

"Then I can guaran-damn-tee you those pirates will know about it," Steve grumbled.

"How?" Athos demanded. "How would they have acquired this information?"

"The same way they knew which boulder up on the surface was a dwarf door, leading down here," Sarah answered. "The same way they knew which dragon nest held the oskorlisk fang."

"And the same way they knew where to find the Power Hammer," Steve added. "They've got someone, or something, helping them, giving them advice. I'd like to find out whoever that is and personally pop them one on the nose."

Sarah nodded. "Seconded."

They arrived at the far side of the cavern and saw that the pirates had, indeed, been headed toward the sealed tunnel. However, the tunnel was no longer sealed. There was a great circular hole in the wall, and it was no mystery how it got there. Plus, numerous sets of human footprints led right up to the hole.

"Gee, I wonder which way they went," Steve chuckled. He sighed, stretched his back, and looked at his companions. "How are we going to do this? They have a sizeable head start on us. Sarah, do you think you could catch them?"

Sarah peered into the darkened tunnel and shook her head. "It's too dark to teleport any great distances. I would have to do a lot of little jumps, which would tire my jhorun out. Why don't I just teleport all of us to the cavern? We could catch them by surprise just when they think they've lost us."

"But we have the element of surprise," Steve was quick to point out. "Do you really want to fight those pirates out in the open? I'm not thinking that's a great idea."

"It's no more dangerous than trying to face them in a limited environment," Sarah argued. "For all we know, Flinn could use his jhorun and shoot you out of that tunnel like an oversized cannon."

Steve cringed. "That sounds … painful."

"Which is why it's a smarter idea to surprise him in the cavern," Sarah was saying. "So, who's ready for another jump?"

"If we catch them by surprise," Athos slowly began, "then we have a better chance of getting the hammer from that blasted human before he has a chance to use it." Athos looked over at Steve and colored slightly. "Uh, no offense, human."

"None taken, dwarf," Steve jovially returned. "Well, we can always split up."

"We haven't had the best of luck with that," Sarah dryly commented, as she fixed him with a stare. "Do you remember what happened last time?"

"You were kidnapped in Idaho, and I was stranded on Lentari. Yeah, I remember."

Sarah pointed at the tunnel opening. "You just said it yourself: you hate climbing stairs. How do you plan on getting to them before they'd get to me?"

Steve shuffled a bit, not really having an answer. Sarah summoned Gareth over.

"Steve wants to catch up to the pirates, and it's about a thousand stairsteps up. Or I can simply teleport us all."

Steve looked less than enthusiastic with either option. "So, Gareth, do you have anything in your bag of tricks that would work?"

Athos tapped Breslin on the shoulder, leaned forward, and whispered something in his ear. Breslin snorted with laughter, was silent for a few moments, and then faced the young wizard.

"You could always make him a kritada."

"A what?" Steve asked. Both Sarah and Gareth echoed the reaction.

"I'm not sure I can change you into something I've never heard of," Gareth admitted.

"Hah!" Steve exclaimed, relieved.

"Although," Gareth continued, "there certainly isn't any harm in trying."

"Experiment on your own time, pal," Steve told the teenager. "I'm not your guinea pig."

Sarah looked at Breslin and motioned him over. "Okay, what *is* a kritada? Will you at least tell us that?"

"A kritada is an earth dweller," Breslin explained. "They're diggers, too, and they can get fairly large, not to mention incredibly ugly. Thankfully, there's not many, so they aren't a threat."

"Then why were you laughing?" Steve wanted to know. "What's the catch?"

"The catch, Master Fire Thrower," Athos began, "is that the kritada has got to be the ugliest bug I have ever seen."

"Then why would you suggest such a creature?" Gareth asked, perplexed.

"Because of the nature of the creature," Breslin explained. "Let's see. How can I best describe one of these ... ah! Master Gareth, would you have your guur friend come over here? I believe I can demonstrate my point with him."

"You called Deez a 'him'," Gareth observed. "Thanks for that. Deez? Would you stand next to Breslin, please?"

The guur obediently moved to Breslin's side. After a few moments, the large insect looked up at the dwarf and cocked his head, as if he wasn't sure what he was supposed to be doing. Breslin turned and tapped Deez's abdomen.

"Imagine a large insect, with a trunk that could have as many as twenty segments twice as large as Deez's," Breslin began. "Now, imagine two sets of legs per segment. What do you get?"

"A centipede," Steve groaned. "From the sounds of it, you'd get the world's biggest centipede."

"Kritadas come in all sizes," Athos explained. "While ugly and repulsive, the big specimens can easily carry a few riders. And, with that many legs, they are capable of tremendous speed."

"Meaning I could zip up those stairs," Steve realized. A grin formed on his face. "Hmmm."

"If you're going to do it, then you'd better do it quick," Sarah urged. "We need to be certain we're there before the pirates arrive."

"All right. Gareth, go for it. Do what you have to do."

"I have never even *heard* of these kritada things," Gareth muttered, as he sat down on the ground. "Don't get too mad at me if I mess something up."

"It's taken a while, sport, but you've made a believer out of me. I trust you."

Gareth opened his eyes to look up at Steve. After a few moments, the young wizard nodded appreciatively. His eyes closed once more and he began to chant.

"You'd better kiss me goodbye now before you turn into an ugly mutant centipede," Sarah giggled.

Steve pulled her in for a kiss, smiled at his wife, and then watched her step back.

"Whoever is going with me to the Gate Cavern come with me. Otherwise, you're riding the Centipede Express up the stairs."

Breslin stepped forward and laid his hand over Sarah's. He cast a quick look at Athos, who had a dark look on his face.

"Oh, come, Athos. It's not that bad. You've been teleported by Lady Sarah before, have you not?"

Athos nodded weakly as he stepped forward. "Aye, and it was most unpleasant."

Sarah looked at the two Creegs. "Did you want to go? We could use all the help we can get."

"It's not in our nature to involve ourselves in other species' affairs," Vutt began, shaking his massive head. "Unless we're ordered to by the Great Lord, that is."

"I'll go," Hedro said. "As I said before, I am not beholden to your Great Lord. I will lend my aid."

Vutt eyed them all. "I believe this is where we part ways. Good luck to you in the recovery of your missing item."

"Thank you for your help getting us this far," Breslin formally returned. Both he and Athos bowed. "You have our thanks."

Once Vutt had disappeared back into the tunnel, Sarah, the dwarves, and Hedro all vanished.

"I thought she had to be in physical contact with a person in order to use her teleporting jhorun," Gareth commented. "I didn't see her touching Hedro."

"I think it's easier for her," Steve admitted, "but it's not required. She can teleport something just by looking at it, just like I can make something burn without touching it."

"And if you do touch whatever it is you want to burn? What then?"

Steve shrugged. "Look at it this way. If I'm looking at the bars of a dungeon, I can make the bars so hot that they'll glow red. Do you follow me?"

The teenager nodded.

"Are you ready? I think I know what I have to do to change you to a kritada." Gareth grinned at him and closed his eyes once more.

"Is this gonna hurt?" Steve asked.

He was grimacing as he braced for an onslaught of unfamiliar sensations. He screwed his eyes shut, certain that something unpleasant was in his immediate future. When nothing was forthcoming, Steve opened his eyes and stared.

What the Sam Hill is this? Everything is blurry!

You are no longer in your human form. I have seen that form before. It is insectoid and is elongated.

Hi, Pryllan. You mean Gareth has already changed me? Wow. The kid's getting better, there's no doubt about it. I was expecting something worse than this.

But I can't talk like a human either, can I? Damn. I really didn't think this through.

The human wizard is still present. I could link with his mind, if you'd like.

Absolutely. I need to be able to talk to him.

What am I going to do? Is that what he's supposed to look like? Damn the dwarves and their crazy monsters. How am I going to fix this? He'll torch me for sure if I made some type of mistake.

Gareth. This is Steve.

You're a telepath now?

Pryllan linked your mind to ours, since I don't seem to be able to speak at the moment. For that matter, I can't really see too well, either.

Your insectoid body will have a different manner of seeing your surroundings. You just have to familiarize yourself with it.

Come, come. Time is wasting. You two must be on your way.

Easier said than done, pal. I'm no longer human. I'm not even sure how to move. Maybe I should ask you to send a message to Sarah and have her just teleport me there.

No, we can do this, Gareth's voice interjected.

Do you remember when you were in my body?
He did.

Remember, you don't need to tell your new body exactly which appendage to move. Just communicate your desires and let it do the rest.

But I can't see where I'm going! Apparently, centipedes can't see worth a damn.

Hmm. That is most assuredly a dilemma. Very well. Young Gareth?

I'm here.

You will be Steve's eyes.

What? I've never written a spell to share senses like that before. I mean, I'm sure I could do it, but it'll take some time to figure out all the nuances. I have to be sure I get it right.

What about my eyesight?

Time is what we don't have. Young Gareth, with your permission, I will share your eyes. My sight, in turn, is shared automatically with Steve. Therefore, whatever you look at, he will see.

That's clever, Steve commented. *Will that work?*

It's time to find out. Gareth, say nothing. Do nothing. Allow me to see through your eyes.

Gareth? Turn to look at me, would you? I need to see what I look like.

Steve's 'eyes' slowly shifted to the left and took in the sight, a ten-foot section of a long, segmented body. Each segment was probably around five feet in diameter, lifting him four feet off the ground on scores of short, black legs. The scene shifted again as Gareth turned to stare at his head, which was a rounded, flattened object with several antennae waving wildly through the air.

Suddenly, he was looking at Deez. The guur was petrified with fear. Apparently guur and kritada were mortal enemies, and it wasn't hard to see why. Centipedes were carnivorous, so the kritada must have preyed on the guur.

Gareth, tell Deez that I'm not going to hurt him.

"Deez? It's okay. That's Steve. He's not going to hurt you. He's going to help us get to the surface, okay?"

THREAT DETECTED

"Yeah, I know he looks like a threat, but he isn't. He's a friend."

ENEMY IS FRIEND?

"Yes. Do you remember the Fire Thrower? Well, that's him. Temporarily, of course."

FIRE IS THREAT

Ordinarily, aye, it is. However, the fire thrower is our friend, as is this creature. You don't need to fear him.

The guur was silent as it digested this information.

Do you think I'm big enough to ride? Steve suddenly asked. *Is that why the dwarves suggested this form?*

Gareth nodded. *Easily. It looks like you could not only carry my weight, but the weight of every person in Verdayn, too. Bugs are usually really strong.*

Good. That means this body can fight. Do you think I can use my jhorun in this form?

I would think you should.

Watch me, guys. I'm going to try to light my hands on fire, like I typically do.

Hang on. Let me get Deez out of there. He's already frightened enough of you. We don't need to make it worse.

Roger that. Let me know when he's clear.

He's on the other side of you now. Give it a try.

Steve gave the order for his jhorun to light his hands.

All right, what happened? I can feel something is happening, only I can't see what. I'm still looking at Deez, so try looking back at me so I can … holy crap! Do you see that? The tip of each and every single leg I've got is burning! How about that! I'm now the Centipede from Hell!

If you weren't scary enough before, then you are petrifying now. I know I'm expected to ride you, but I'm not sure I can get Deez on your back if your hands are lit.

I just extinguished them. I gotta make sure I don't do that too much.

Why?

I think I remember reading somewhere that centipedes don't like light. This one may be a thousand times bigger, and from a different world, but it's still a centipede. Looking at those flames was starting to give me a migraine. Gareth? Any luck? We need to get going.

I think I have him convinced you won't hurt him.

Let me try talking to him. Deez? Remember me? I'm a friend. I'm the big bug right now. Don't worry. I'm not going to hurt you.

NO THREAT DETECTED

Does that mean he trusts me? We really need to get going.

It took a minute, but at last Gareth and Deez were aboard, riding on Steve's fifth and sixth segments. They assured him they were ready.

Perfect. Let's go catch us some pirates! Gareth, don't forget. You're my eyes. Keep looking forward.

I will.

Steve looked at the forbidding hole in the wall, imagined himself gritting his teeth, and expressed a desire to move through the hole. What happened next was like riding a roller coaster in an amusement park, the kind that were designed to go from 0 to 60 mph in as little time as possible.

He practically flew through the hole, and before he could wonder how to make his many legs climb stairs, he was well past the first and climbing fast.

His body had responded accordingly.

Steve stopped trying to figure out how to make the legs work in tandem. Instead, he concentrated on keeping himself centered on the stairs and to cover as many of them as he could as quickly as possible.

How are you doing back there?

His 'eyes' automatically shifted to look behind him, where Deez clung to one of his many segments. However, the instant the image shifted off the stairs in front of him, he momentarily panicked, and caused his kritada body to come to an immediate and abrupt stop.

Ow! Ow! Ow! Ow!

Gareth? Are you okay? Sorry. I shouldn't have stopped, but I couldn't help it.

That was my fault. I should have asked if it was all right to check on Deez. Don't start moving yet. I have to get back to my seat.

Hurry.

My rear slid forward, really close to your head now. Hang on, I'm climbing back to Deez.

Steve couldn't sense any movement on his new body. Whether this body lacked nerve endings or whether this insectoid body was so strong that the teenager's weight was miniscule, he couldn't tell.

Once they were back on the move, Steve decided to see how much faster he could push his kritada form. Could he run sideways up the wall, like Deez could?

It's a good thing I used a spell to make sure I wouldn't fall off your back again.

What's that?

Pryllan has our minds linked together, remember? You were just wondering if you could run along the walls, like Deez. Then you did just that. If I hadn't spelled myself to my seat here, you would have flung me off. At high velocity, I might add. That definitely would have left a mark.

Do you see how fast we're going up these stairs? I feel like I'm on a speeding horse, only way faster than a horse ever could. On top of that, you're climbing uphill! Are you feeling tired at all?

Was he?

No, not at all. I don't feel any physical drain on any of my senses. In fact, I think this is kinda fun. Who would've known being a bug would be so cool?

We should have a plan ready for when we catch up to the pirates.

Good one, Gareth. Umm, okay. Well, I'm really fast in this form. I'm hoping we can get the fang and hammer away from Flinn before he even realizes what's happening.

How do you know where they'd be?

Flinn will be holding them. He doesn't strike me as the type of person who'd trust those valuables to someone else.

That makes sense. I might be able to write a spell to help locate those objects.

I thought the fang and the hammer were immune to spells and jhorun?

Steve felt Gareth's pride swell. *And that was where we were going wrong. All I have to do is to use that to our advantage.*

Okay, you've lost me.

The pirate captain has the oskorlisk fang and the hammer, right?

Right.

Lady Sarah can't teleport it, and I can't summon it, no matter how hard I try.

Correct. As I said, those things seem to be immune to jhorun.

Then all I have to do is modify a standard locator spell to look for the items. Look, but don't touch. I might even throw in a second layer and have it look for jhorun-infused objects. That way we'll know for sure we have the right items.

You can do that?

Of course. All I have to do is … again, you don't care, do you?

Steve mentally laughed. What that was doing to his physical body, he had no idea.

Sorry, pal. I don't want to come across as rude, but no, I don't really care how you do it. I'm more impressed by the simple fact that you can.

Thanks. I'll get working on it. I just have to be careful. I usually close my eyes when I'm working on a spell.

Well, you definitely don't want to do that.

Ten minutes later, Steve was fighting valiantly to stay awake. The constant motion of running up the stairs felt an awful lot like being on a boat on the swell of the waves. His brain wanted to give the order to close his eyes and allow himself to fall asleep, but he also knew that Sarah and the dwarves were depending on him to get to the Gate Cavern as quickly—and safely—as possible.

"Look out!" Gareth shouted.

The wizard's voice snapped him out of his daydream and brought him crashing back to the present. He had picked up Gareth's sudden burst of fear and probably given the centipede equivalent of a full-body spastic jerk.

Steve felt his body slow and allowed it to come to a stop.

What is it? What's the matter?

You were falling asleep and I was running out of ways to keep you awake. So, I tried to pretend there was danger in the area.

Steve, would you get back on the ground, please?

Huh?

Look down. Or up, I guess. Wait. You're using my eyes. Look at this.

Steve's 'eyes' shifted up, so that he was looking what should have been straight up. What he saw was a staircase running along the roof of the tunnel. What the hell?

We're currently upside down. It happened after I yelled. So, this is pretty much my fault.

Oh. Give me a second. I'll get back on the ground.

Once they were safely back on the ground, and wide awake, thank you very much, they were on their way.

You are gaining on the thieves.

We are? Where are they, Pryllan?

I do not know for certain, but I can smell them.

How can you possibly smell them? Gareth wanted to know.

I'm sharing your senses, young wizard. You can smell them, so I can smell them, too.

I don't smell any pirates.

You smell them, but are not able to identify their scents. I can. They are close.

Fantastic. Gareth, are your spells ready?

Aye. I'm ready. Once we see the pirate captain, I'll activate my spell. That should locate the fang and the hammer.

Good. There will be no faking us out with phonies this time.

Steve? I have bad news.

What? What's happened?

The invaders have reached the cavern. Your mate and the two dwarves…

Pryllan?

There was no answer. And, to make matters worse, his

vision faded, leaving him with nothing more than wavy lines and blurry images.

Gareth? Can you still hear me? I think we're in trouble. I can't see!

No, Pryllan meant no shared senses, and if there were no shared senses, then Steve became as blind as a…well, as blind as a really big centipede. There had to be something he could do!

He felt a light tapping somewhere on his body. Was that Gareth? It had to be. What was he trying to do?

Suddenly, his vision was restored. He could even see in the dark! How was this possible?

Steve thought about twisting around to ensure the teenager and his pet were still on his back. He felt his body shifting, and suddenly, he was staring straight at Gareth. The wizard was tapping the side of his head.

"You might not be able to speak, but at least you can hear me. I'm sorry, I should have done this sooner. I wrote a spell and modified it for a bug. You're now essentially looking through human eyes."

Steve nodded. But there were more pressing matters—Pryllan had said the pirates had made it to Gate Cavern. That meant they had to double their efforts and get to Sarah.

Steve urged his body to move forward, and his kritada body was only too happy to oblige. Up and up he raced, ascending dozens of steps. While he was watching the stairs zip by him at an amazing velocity, he saw something that drew him up short.

The stairs were going to end in less than fifty feet. He had less than three seconds to respond. There was no way he'd stop in time.

Gareth, you'd better hang on tight!

Chapter 12 — Let's Get Ready to Rumble!

Steve cringed and could only hope his insectoid body would be able to withstand a crash through solid stone. Hopefully the wall wouldn't be that thick. As luck would have it, he barely felt a bump and just like that, he was through and scrambling down the short tunnel he had first visited all those years ago.

The moment he emerged into the main cavern, he sought out Sarah. While he couldn't see her, he spotted several pirates, advancing on the northeastern cavern wall, toward the stairs leading Topside.

"Slow down a little!" Gareth called from his back. "Deez and I need to get off!"

His kritada body slowed enough for both to jump off. Where was Sarah? Then he noticed several pirates flying through the air. That had to be his wife's doing!

But wait—the pirates were flying *toward* the stairs leading up, not away. Were they propelling themselves? No, this had to be Sarah's doing. He fervently hoped it was, but he couldn't see her.

He sped up so that he was practically skimming along the ground. Anger at the pirates had his jhorun tingling like crazy. In a reflexive move, Steve automatically ordered his jhorun to ignite his hands. In his insectoid body, all sixty plus of his legs ignited.

As he sprinted as fast as he could toward where he presumed Sarah was holed up, movement on his left distracted him from the pirates. A fireball, much larger than he could typically generate, was careening straight toward him, on an intercept course. He headed for the closest wall and *up* it.

Okay. I'll admit it. This is pretty cool. And ... here I am. Talking to myself.

He ran along the surface of the wall, sideways, headed toward the cavern's roof. Another fireball appeared, aimed right at him! Where in the world were they coming from?

Steve executed an abrupt ninety-degree turn to the left and increased his speed. He kept maneuvering until he was facing the direction from which the fireballs appeared to be emanating. What he saw surprised him so much that he almost came to an abrupt stop.

A brown winged dragon was circling Hedro in the middle of the cavern, and apparently felt it had enough time to throw an occasional fireball his way. Thankfully, there wasn't enough room in the cavern for the winged dragon to take flight, but that still didn't change the fact that it was probably the last thing he had expected to see down below the ground.

Pryllan? There's a dragon here and it's not a Creeg! Are you there? Come on, Pryllan. Where are you??

Steve allowed himself to slow, unfortunately, attracting the wyverian's attention. It briefly looked over at him, opened its jaws, and spat several blasts of fire his way. Steve barely had enough time to scuttle out of the way.

He kept his jhorun flowing into his kritada legs, and resumed his trek toward the stairs. A large stone went flying past him, headed in the opposite direction. He paused to see what the intended target was, and saw a pirate leap out from behind a large boulder just before it was smashed apart. However, the pirate's jump took him nearly thirty feet away, where the figure landed harmlessly, crouched again, and then jumped up. The second jump was just as long as the first.

How in the world are they jumping so far? They didn't do that before, did they? Come on, Pryllan. Where are you?

Twin roars sounded, drawing his attention back to the center of the cavern. Hedro lowered his head and rammed the wyverian so hard that it landed off its feet. It roared its frustration and helplessly flapped its wings as it tried to right itself. While it was distracted, Steve finally located Sarah. She, Breslin, and Athos were hunkered down behind a ridge of stones directly in front of the stairs. Thus far, they were doing an admirable job of keeping the pirates from escaping.

Steve noticed two pirates, ones he'd had previous skirmishes with, were about ready to rush the ridge at the same time. Alquin and Grenden. He recalled that neither exhibited any special physical prowess. Unique jhorun, sure, but that was it. How, then, were each of them able to leap over tall rocks, hurl huge stones, and run faster than a gazelle?

Tabling that thought for now, Steve returned his attention to Sarah. She was in the midst of a hushed conversation with the dwarves. Well, it was time to let them know he had finally arrived.

Alquin suddenly squatted and came up with a boulder easily the same weight as himself. He hurled it straight toward Sarah. None of them were paying attention!

Steve's body seemed to move on its own accord. He zoomed down the wall, on a direct intercept course with his wife, when he found himself sailing through the air.

Not even aware that this form was capable of jumping, Steve noticed he now had a direct line with the large stone. He assumed he would simply head butt the thing, as he must have done to punch through the stone wall in the tunnel. On second thought, smashing his head into a rock might not be the brightest idea. He imagined his human body swatting aside the stone, as if it were a fly.

His kritada body had other plans.

Two hinged pincers unfolded themselves from somewhere

near his chin, and snapped at the rock. The boulder shattered, raining a shower of gravel to the ground, less than five feet from his wife. He felt a bone-rattling blow, which jumbled his senses for a moment. A quick check confirmed he was now safely back on the ground. His five dozen legs snuffed out when he contacted the ground, but after a few moments, they ignited once more.

Steve took a few menacing steps toward the pirates and clicked his pincers hungrily. That ought to strike some fear in their hearts. They took one look at him and screamed bloody murder.

"Steve? Omigod, is that you?"

Getting more and more familiar with making this new body do what he wanted, he turned and looked at his wife. He tried to nod, but noticed his legs were completely aflame, so he instructed his jhorun to put them out.

"You're right, Breslin," Sarah was saying. "That has got to be one of the ugliest, nastiest looking bugs I have ever seen in my life. Aside from the guur, that is. Honey, can you hear me? Do you understand me?"

Steve stared. Could he hear her? Yes. Understand her? Yes. But speak? Obviously not.

"Look out!"

The shout came from Athos. Steve whipped his head around. Another huge stone—worthy of a trebuchet—was sailing toward them, with a second not far behind. *How* did mere humans have that much strength?

A split second before either rock could strike their target, both were swatted aside like harmless flies. Two huge figures, easily ten feet tall and weighing a thousand pounds each, had appeared out of nowhere. Now, the golems lumbered over to the ridge, turned to face outward, and became inert. Steve stared at their benefactors, hoping the pirates would rethink their current strategies.

"Way to go, Gareth!" Sarah called out. "Where are you, anyway?"

There was no answer.

"I am sure he's safe, Lady Sarah," Steve heard Breslin say. Twin roars sounded again. The wyverian had righted itself and was now going after the Creeg. The land dragon, to its credit, was not backing down. In fact, here in this subterranean environment, the Creeg and the wyverian were evenly matched. The tables would be turned if this battle was happening on the surface, where the winged dragon could attack from the air. Here, however, there was nowhere for the winged dragon to escape to, and Hedro was using that to his advantage.

Where *had* the wyverian come from, anyway? Steve swung his gaze around the cavern, half expecting to see a large open tunnel, but there was none. Perhaps Sarah knew. Maybe she and the dwarves were already here when the winged dragon had arrived?

An ear-splitting roar split the air. It looked as though Hedro might have landed a bite, since the winged dragon was now favoring its left wing and keeping it as far away from the Creeg as possible. Hedro roared another challenge, lowered his head, and then lunged forward, intent on ramming into the wyverian's chest. The wyverian side-stepped out of the way, bringing his long, thick tail up and whipping it in the Creeg's direction.

Steve tried to shout a warning, but he was still mute. Perhaps he could generate a chaser while in kritada form?

Hedro brought his two forearms up and neatly caught the tail before it hit him. Gripping the tail in his talons, Hedro's mouth opened, ready to bite. Would the Creeg bite clean through the wyverian's tail?

But the winged dragon whipped his tail out of Hedro's grip, yanking him off balance, smacking Hedro's chest. The slap echoed throughout the cavern, and Hedro crashed against some stalagmites, snapping them off at the base like toothpicks.

Steve got an idea. He turned to see that the trunk of his kritada body stretched at least twenty feet behind him. Could he use that to his advantage?

Only one way to find out.

Directly ahead, Steve saw Mr. Steroids himself, Jino, crouching behind a boulder. He checked that his flames were still extinguished and crept down the wall directly behind the pirate, hoping Jino would not look up. Luckily, the best warrior aboard the *Emberbrand* was too focused on watching Sarah, clearly nursing his long-held grudge.

The moment the first segment of his elongated trunk touched the ground, Jino's head snapped up, and he was now staring, face-to-face, with the world's largest centipede.

Steve's two mandibles reappeared and clicked loudly together. It had the desired effect.

Jino bolted from his hiding place and sprinted, with superhuman speed, to the safety of another rock. Unfortunately for the pirate, Steve, in kritada form, was faster. Significantly faster.

By the time Jino had broken from his cover and had covered a dozen feet, Steve was already on the ground, his body responding. He felt his legs anchor in place and he lunged forward, his body pivoting. Six or seven segments whipped violently to the right, catching Jino squarely in the chest. There was a loud crack the moment their two bodies met. He barely felt the impact, while Jino flew end-over-end, into the closest hard object. Jino collided with a stalagmite and fell to the ground, unconscious.

Steve's attention darted to the winged dragon who always seemed to know the instant he slowed down.

Dodging the latest fireball spit in his direction, Steve's eyes locked on the dragon. In less time that it took to utter a choice swear word, the winged wyverian's wings snapped open.

A veritable hurricane exploded in all directions as the dragon slammed its wings together, threatening to rip Steve off the ground, sixty legs and all. A sense of self-preservation kicked in and five dozen legs gripped the rock tightly, anchoring him.

The blast of air passed harmlessly over. Would this mean Flinn's aerial assaults would be ineffective against him?

He had no time to ponder this, as the winged dragon noticed he was still alive and growled angrily at him. Hedro had regained his feet and charged again, ramming the dragon in the abdomen so hard that it was flung backward, frantically clawing at everything within reach. Four stalagmites and two stalactites snapped off at the base as the winged dragon flailed about, but in the end, all was for naught as the wyverian flopped helplessly onto its back.

Hedro made it to the other side of the crushed stalagmites, but the winged dragon hooked its tail around a large stone pillar and pulled itself to its feet. It whipped its own body and sent the Creeg crashing backward, snapping off his own fair share of the stony icicles littering the ground.

Steve remembered Flinn, who still possessed both the oskorlisk fang and the hammer.

Where was he hiding? Well, Steve knew how to bring the crafty pirate captain out into the open: go after the crew.

Steve singled out the first pirate he could see, who was hiding behind a stone pillar. Each stalagmite-stalactite pillar looked as though it could easily support his weight.

He zipped across the ground, arrived at the base of one of the pillars in less than five seconds, and spiraled up the stone column. In seconds, he was thirty feet off the ground and less than five feet from the pillar where the pirate was hiding.

Growing angry as he stretched across to the second pillar, Steve allowed his kritada legs to ignite. Shouts erupted. He'd been spotted.

The pirate looked up. Less than five feet from the pirate's face, Steve stretched out one of his front legs and plucked the hat off the pirate's head. His huge primary pincers promptly sliced it into two pieces.

"Aaaauuuggghh!!"

Much to Steve's delight, the pirate scrambled away. In fact, it looked as though, in his haste, the pirate had voided his bladder. There, at the base of the pillar where the pirate had been standing, was a small pool of saturated yellow liquid.

Steve extinguished his flames and slipped behind, to follow the man. He scuttled around the diameter of a huge boulder and came to an abrupt stop. His hunch had been right. This pirate guided him right to Flinn himself. However, the clever captain was clearly waiting for him.

Twin blasts of air pummeled him mercilessly. One was trying to push him backward, and the other was hammering at him from above, almost like the ornery captain was trying to squish him. Steve merely dug in with his many insectoid legs and waited for the air jet to pass.

"See, Cap'n? I told you that thing isn't goin' away! What can we do?"

"Just give it whatever it wants, Captain!" another pirate said, appearing by Flinn's side. "They have two dragons and a huge fire bug! We don't stand a chance against that!"

Flinn regarded Steve and finally nodded. "I gotta hand it to ye, Fire Thrower. Ye are full of surprises. I thought ye were dead! How could ye … Ye know what? It matters not. And I did not think ye could change forms, too. Or … of course! Ye aren't changing form, are ye? Not without help. So, who be here, aidin' ye? Men, spread out! We have a new target! There be someone here with the Fire Thrower and Teleporter. Eliminate them!"

Steve clicked his pincers angrily. They were going after Gareth? Not if he could help it. Why, if he had to, he'd … wait.

They were going to go after the strongest wizard he had ever met? Scratch that. They were going after the strongest wizard he had ever *heard about*?

Gareth could take care of himself. At least, if they went after him, they would probably leave Sarah alone.

Suddenly, something one of the pirates said filtered through to him. They thought he had two dragons and a fire bug helping them. *Two* dragons? That meant they were also surprised at the winged dragon's appearance. Either there had to be a large, concealed tunnel that allowed the dragon in or, more alarmingly, other forces were at play. Neither option sat well with him.

Speaking of those dragons…

Steve turned to look. There they were, still in the center of the cavern, and still circling one another. Oddly enough, neither was roaring or growling at one another. What was going on? Was it merely an argument?

An air jet blasted his head again, which to his kritada body, felt like someone had turned on a desk fan. It felt good.

"This be not workin', Q. We need to … make that, *you*

need to stand downwind. Ye smell like pee, ye daft fool. Did ye wet yerself?"

"N-no, Captain. Not that I know of."

"Hmm. Find Alquin and Grenden and the others. I'm headin' to them stairs there. I'm tired of this. We be leavin', now."

"Understood, Captain."

Steve wasted no time in returning to the stairs. Sarah and the dwarves were still there, and now a newly constructed wall, ten feet high and two feet thick, was also visible. Steve arrived just in time to see the wall's last couple of pieces lift off the ground and settle neatly into place. Where had they found the stones for that?

In answer to his question, he saw Athos point at a nearby stalactite and tap Sarah's arm. A huge boulder silently levitated off the ground, rose to the same height as the stalactite, and then promptly knocked it from the ceiling. The stone icicle fell straight down, coming to a stop nearly a dozen feet from the ground. The first boulder was lowered, while the new building material was put into place, completing the southern corner of the new wall.

"There," Sarah said. "That ought to do it. Thank you, Athos."

"My pleasure, milady. Behold. I see the boy wizard." Athos turned to point at a location across the cavern. Gareth was casually sitting atop of one of the largest rock formations, watching the proceedings below. His mouth was moving, so Steve figured he was chanting. Hadn't he created two earth elementals? Where were they, anyway?

Steve scuttled up and over the wall without either dwarf noticing. Sarah looked up at him, smiled, and waved him over. Being too large to fit in the space she occupied with the dwarves, Steve clung to the new wall and nodded.

"Wizards be damned!" Breslin hollered, turning around. "Sir Steve, is that you? Make some noise, would you? Being surprised by a form like that is not something I want to experience again, rest assured."

"I knew he was there," Athos insisted.

"No, you didn't," Breslin argued. "I saw you. You jumped

just as much as I did. If that had been someone other than Sir Steve, we'd all be dead."

A crackling ball of energy appeared and rapidly expanded. Sarah and the dwarves moved away, and a few moments later, the sparking ball of energy poofed out, leaving Gareth in its place. He quickly glanced over at Steve, opened his mouth to start chanting, when he started looking around.

"Wait, where's Deez? Has anyone seen him?"

Steve crawled back up to the top of the wall. From his vantage point, he could see the pirates arguing amongst themselves, with Captain Flinn looking as though he was going to blow a gasket. Steve could also see the dragons, who were back to rolling about on the ground, flattening stalagmites, and smashing through the same two stone pillars he himself had climbed on earlier.

There was something about the fight between those two dragons. It was almost as if the presence of those two had nothing to do with the fight they had with the pirates. But, if that were the case, then what were they fighting about? And, more importantly, how the freakin' hell did that winged dragon get down here?

One problem at a time. Right now, they had to find Deez. Yesterday, if someone would have told him that he'd be personally trying to find and protect a guur drone, he'd have laughed. However, he now knew the guur was friendly and wasn't about to let anything happen to the little guy.

Little guy? Steve shook his head. Whether or not his kritada body shook its head, too, was unknown. Whatever. It looked like the only one capable of finding the guur was him. A phrase suddenly sprang to mind and he wished he could have said it aloud: it takes a bug to find a bug.

Corny, he knew, but he also knew, without knowing why, he could find their guur companion whereas they could not.

Steve climbed to the top of the wall and fell silent, opening all his insect senses. His attention was pulled toward the unfinished tunnels and the stairs heading back down. Movement caught his eye.

There he was. Deez was scrambling over rocks, up stone formations, and across stalagmites with three pirates hot on his trail. They were all throwing huge stones at the guur. If any of those rocks landed, poor Deez would be squished flat.

Steve scowled with irritation; his pincers appeared and clicked angrily. Sarah was by his side in a flash.

"What is it?"

I know you're not able to understand me right now, but know this: I'll get him. They're not gonna touch him, not while I'm around. That's a promise.

He tried to give Sarah a reassuring look, but his wife could only look blankly back at him. Shrugging again, and giving a mental sigh, Steve climbed to the top of the wall and ran nimbly along its perimeter. Once he reached the cavern wall, he changed angles and promptly ran up. Once he was at a height to avoid most of the stalagmites, he changed course again and headed straight toward his guur friend.

Hang on, pal. I'm almost there.

GRATITUDE

What? What was that? Deez, are you talking to me? Does that mean Pryllan is back? Pryllan, are you there?

There was no answer. Pryllan's comforting presence had not reappeared, sadly. Without her telepathic connection, how had he picked up on Deez's thought?

Steve shook his head. Whatever. He'd have to worry about that later. Right now, one of his companions was in trouble and he had to come to his aid.

Deez, if you can hear me, I'm coming up alongside you, on the wall. Keep the pirates busy. You're doing a great job dodging those rocks. Keep it up. I'm almost there.

COMPLIANCE

Deez zipped by him at top speed. Their ten-legged companion darted around pillars, jumped over small crevasses, and even had to resort to scaling a stalagmite to reach a low-hanging stalactite. In the meantime, large rocks continued to fall around the guur. The pirates were throwing anything they could get their hands on, including stalagmites and stalactites broken during the dragon battle.

Steve extinguished his flames and waited, motionless, as the pirates ran by, hot on Deez's trail. As soon as the last one passed, Steve dropped down to the floor and reignited all of his legs. He even let the flames rise up his legs to encompass his many segmented abdomens. If he didn't look like the Bug from Hell before, then he most certainly did now.

Steve increased his pace and watched the nearest pirate reach for one of the smaller, broken stalagmites. Hoisting the long, skinny stone icicle like a javelin, the pirate sighted Deez, cocked his arm, and prepared to throw. Before he could let the projectile fly, Steve leaned forward and, using his front pincers, bit the stalactite in half.

The two pieces of stone fell harmlessly to the ground. Curious as to what had happened, the pirate turned and came face-to-face with the biggest centipede the Kingdom of Lentari had ever seen. Or the *Seven Kingdoms*, for that matter.

"Aaaiiieeee!!!!!"

The other two pirates whipped around, frozen in fear. Steve grabbed the first pirate with his pincers, and careful not to cut the screaming man in half, tossed him head first into the closest rock formation. The pirate crumpled to the ground and didn't move. After confirming the man was still breathing, Steve turned to the other two.

Both had promptly disappeared into the shadows. Satisfied that the immediate threat had been neutralized, with no fatalities, Steve turned to look for Deez. After scanning the immediate surroundings, he stifled a curse.

The guur had vanished.

Damn it, Deez. Where are you? How am I supposed to…?

A large rock fell dangerously close to him, spraying bits of gravel in all directions. None were strong enough to penetrate the kritada's tough endoskeleton, but had the aim been two feet to the right, then it would have been another story. Steve tilted his head up to see what had been responsible.

Deez.

The guur was frantically jumping from one stalactite to another, like Tarzan in the jungle. Deez was fleeing from something, but Steve couldn't tell what. He watched Deez jump from one particularly large stalactite to a much smaller one, and then, much to his chagrin, the stalactite snapped right off, plummeting both straight to the ground.

Deez! Holy crap! You need to … you should grab…

The guur was several steps ahead of him. As the stalactite fell, Deez nimbly jumped into a dark opening in the wall and vanished.

A blur of motion caught his attention. It was Jino, at the base of the cavern wall, holding a sword in one hand and a wicked-looking club in the other. Steve watched the pirate bunch his legs and leap straight up, more than thirty feet.

Steve groaned. He was really getting tired of all these superhuman powers the pirates suddenly seemed to possess. Jino was understandable, as he was pretty sure his jhorun was responsible for his remarkable physical prowess. As for the others, there was still something that didn't add up, but he'd have to deal with it later. Right now, Jino had just jumped up into the same hole Deez had, and disappeared from sight.

Deez, be careful. You have company! Don't worry; I'm coming in after you!

Steve hurried across the wall, ascended, and discovered it wasn't a cave. Deez had found himself a tunnel!

Vowing to protect the guur at whatever cost, Steve gathered himself and entered the tunnel. While this form was considerably larger than the guur, he still managed to squeeze inside. Gareth's gift of vision wasn't contingent on the presence of light, so he snuffed out all his flames. In mere minutes, he caught up to Jino.

The pirate had his back to him and was slowly creeping forward on all fours, presumably to sneak up on Deez. Figuring turnabout was fair play, Steve approached Jino as quietly as he could. Then, standing less than two feet from the pirate, Steve unfolded his pincers and clicked them angrily.

Jino stiffened with surprise and slowly turned around. At the exact same time Jino made eye contact with him, Steve gave the order for his jhorun to ignite his appendages. A look of recognition passed across Jino's face.

"You! You are the fire thrower! Have you been resurrected in bug form? How?"

Steve advanced, clicking his pincers. His flames grew brighter--hotter. A look of fear spread across the pirate's face.

"Now, just take it easy. I wasn't gonna hurt your little friend. See? He's right over there. He's fine. Now, just let me be on my way and I'll…"

Jino took a few steps away from Steve and paused. There, blocking any potential progress through the tunnel, was Deez. His two elongated front legs were angrily gouging chunks out of the tunnel floor as he stared at the pirate.

Let him go, Deez. In fact, keep digging. Lead us back to the cavern. We'll give him the chance to escape.

ELIMINATE THREAT

Not this time, pal.

ELIMINATE THREAT, SERENITY WILL BE RESTORED

Serenity? Nice word, pal. And I think that's the longest sentence I've heard from you yet. As much as these guys deserve to be eliminated, we're better than that. We're not cold-blooded killers.

ENEMIES ARE

Enemies are? Enemies are what?

ENEMIES ARE KILLERS

Umm, do I want to know how you know? Did you witness something?

ENEMIES DESTROYED TWO MEMBERS OF HIVE

What?! Are you sure? How do you know?

STONE MEN. STONE MEN DESTROYED

This may be hard for you to understand, buddy, but the rock men weren't real. They were, uh, artificial beings Gareth created to help us fight. They were destroyed? Really? Do you know how?

ENEMIES PULLED BROTHERS APART. THREW PARTS OF BODY IN ALL DIRECTIONS

That sounds really gross when you put it that way. Okay, let's do this. Keep digging. Lead us back to the cavern, okay? We'll let Jino here run back to daddy. Then we'll go find Sarah and the dwarves, all right?

COMPLIANCE

Deez resumed his tunneling. With Jino following cautiously behind, and Steve keeping pace directly behind him, they returned to the cavern. As soon as Deez broke through to the open space, he scuttled out of the way, opening up an escape route for the pirate. Jino, not one to question his good luck, bolted through the hole as soon as he was certain neither guur nor Steve was going to attack him.

Nice work, Deez. Okay, let's get back to Sarah.

THREAT DETECTED

The pirates? I know. They're still in the area.

TSAK THREAT DETECTED

Alrighty. Thank you for the clarification. However, I still don't know why a sack would be considered a threat? That doesn't make any sense.

ROCK BITERS DANGEROUS

Rock biters?

A flapping noise could suddenly be heard. Steve scanned the cavern. He didn't see anything flying around, but he sure could hear something. There! Coming out of the tunnel that he had personally broken through earlier was a series of small, black, flapping creatures. Steve was suddenly reminded of a time, almost two years ago, when he and Sarah had been transported back to the late nineteenth century. They had to acquire an athe crystal from the dwarves, and on the way out, they had encountered some type of creature which lived on the ceiling. They, if memory served, were called rock biters and were capable of pulling chunks of stone right out of the wall or ceiling and dropping it on their heads.

This wasn't good.

Come on, Deez! We need to get to Sarah! Hurry!

Kritada and guur made fantastic time through the cavern, darting around impassable rock formations, fallen stalagmites, and so on. They only encountered one pirate, who took one look at them and ran in the other direction. Catching sight of Sarah's newly constructed wall, Steve changed course and veered straight toward it.

Movement in the opposite corner of the cavern caught his attention. The two dragons had ceased fighting and were now circling each other. Whatever their problem was, Steve wanted nothing to do with it and gave both dragons a wide berth.

"You found him!" Sarah happily exclaimed. "Nice job! Deez, are you okay?"

OPERATING AT FULL CAPACITY

Sarah laughed. "Well, that's one way to put it. Good for you. Gareth, do you see this? Steve found Deez, and he's okay. I think it might be time to change my husband back to his human form, okay?"

I second that.

Gareth appeared, gave Deez an affectionate pat on the head, and turned to Steve. "Thanks for finding him. Now, hold still. I'll have you back to normal in no time."

Ten seconds later, Steve shakily rose to his feet. His *human* feet.

"Wow, am I ever glad to be back. So, where's Captain Windbag?"

"He's down there," Sarah said, as she pointed at a group

of rocks about thirty feet away. "He's not using his jhorun or anything. Maybe he's exhausted all of it?"

"I doubt we'd be that lucky," Steve grumbled.

"Then why isn't he going on the offensive?" Sarah asked.

Steve remembered Deez's final warning and snapped his fingers. "Oh, there's something I should mention. Deez says there are…"

"Tsak!" Breslin bellowed, as he pointed up at the cavern roof. "Wizards be damned! They are only active following a strong terra tremor."

Athos pointed at the two dragons, who were still circling one another. "What about those two? They're making quite a racket. Could they have woken them up?"

MULTIPLE THREATS DETECTED

"What now?" Steve groaned aloud.

The guur turned to Sarah.

MULTIPLE THREATS DETECTED

Sarah nodded. "What threats are you talking about?"

INCOMING ROCK BITERS AND CARRION EATERS DETECTED

"Oh, that doesn't sound good," Sarah whispered. She clutched Steve's hand tightly in her own. "Dare I ask what rock biters and carrion eaters are?"

"Remember when we had to get that transporter crystal to help out my ancestor, Luther? We had to go underground, and on the way out, our dwarf guide got us lost. He led us right into a nest of tsak. Nasty little flying things that ate rock."

"Ooo, I remember them," Sarah recalled, with a look of horror in her eyes. "What are they doing here? I'm about ready to just jump us out of here."

"I want to know about these carrion eaters," Steve added. "Deez, what are they?"

SMALL. GREAT NUMBERS. EAT CARRION

"There!" Athos shouted, pointing back at the same tunnel the tsak were using to enter the cavern. "It's a swarm of chra! We must flee!"

"Krah?" Steve repeated, confused. "Where are you looking? I only see those damn tsak thingies. Wait. Why is the floor turning black there?"

"Those are bugs!" Sarah cried. "Hundreds of thousands of little bugs! Steve, they're coming this way! We have to get out of here!"

"What about the pirates?" Steve asked.

"Forget about the pirates!" Athos exclaimed. "Lady Sarah is right. The time to go is now! We'll have to get the hammer away from them another time!"

"Isn't it a little suspicious that the tsak and the chra converge on the same location at the same time?" Breslin asked.

"Would you like to stay and ask them?" Steve snapped. "Okay, let's do a head count. Do we have everyone? Me, Sarah, Gareth, Breslin, Athos, and Deez. Good. We're all accounted for. Are we all agreed? We regroup and try this again later? There are some things here that aren't adding up."

Sarah was nodding. "You've got my vote." She held out a hand. "We're heading to the surface. Everyone who's planning on going needs to give me their hand."

The companions crowded close as they all slapped their hands over Sarah's. Then, much to everyone's surprise, Deez lifted one of his front forelegs and gently rested it on the top. Sarah rewarded the friendly guur with a nod of her head.

"Good job, Deez. Okay, on the count of three. One, two, thr…"

No one moved. No one teleported, either. Confused, Steve turned to his wife and gave her a gentle nudge on her shoulder.

"You forgot 'three', dear."

Sarah didn't say anything. She was staring back at the cavern at the sight before them. Wordlessly, Steve turned to see what had caught her attention. There, in the middle of the cavern, was only one dragon: Hedro. The Creeg was on the ground, with one of his massive hind legs bent at a grotesque angle. The wyverian was nowhere in sight.

Steve? Are you there? Can you hear me?

Pryllan? Is that you? Where have you been?

I have been trying to reach you for nearly two hours! I was blocked.

We have another, more pressing problem.

I can feel your alarm. What is it? Are you in danger?

Steve looked over at his wife and saw her look of determination. He sighed, pulled his hand free from his companions, and turned to regard Hedro in the distance. The land dragon was struggling to regain his feet, but with an injured leg, it was impossible. The tsak and the chra were now headed straight for the injured Creeg.

Steve turned to his friends. "Looks like we have a decision to make. Turn tail and run for our lives, or go help Hedro."

"We'd be leaving these stairs unprotected," Gareth reminded him. "The pirates will get away. I mean, we could always split up."

Breslin shook his head. "Bad idea, lad. We stay together. And that is final."

Sarah nodded. "I think that was their plan all along. Somehow, that winged dragon and the pirates were working together. There's no other explanation."

Steve turned back to the fallen Creeg and eyed the approaching horde of tiny black bugs. Then he looked up and saw that the tsak were alighting on the cavern's ceiling, directly above Hedro.

Steve ignited his hands. "Well? Might as well get this over with."

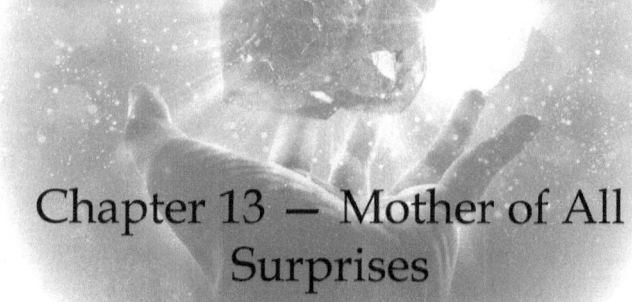

Chapter 13 — Mother of All Surprises

In a chorus of cries and shouts, three humans and two dwarves abandoned their positions at the base of the stairs and descended upon the injured Creeg with weapons drawn. Athos and Breslin, brandishing their axes, took up position on either side of Hedro. The tsak were flying lower and lower, and both dwarves started swinging at the dark, smelly creatures. Neither of them had managed to hit anything until Athos reattached his axe to its holder on his back and pulled out two thin strips of metal from crisscrossing bandoliers across his chest. He flicked both of them open and dangerously eyed the flying pests.

"What are those things?" Steve asked, as he came up beside the dwarf. "They look like modified boomerangs."

"These are orixes," Athos explained. "I modeled them after two dragons you may or may not be familiar with." The dwarf indicated the dark green weapon in his right hand. "This one was designed to honor a female dragon by the name of Pryllan."

There was a history between the two families, but reminiscing would have to wait. Steve shouted, "Look out!"

A line of tsak had broken off from the rest and dropped straight toward them. Steve raised both hands and blasted a huge wall of flames into the air. Three of the four tsak flew through the flames and were instantly reduced to ash. The fourth hesitated.

Steve gave the descending creature a derisive glare. "Dude, really? You just saw what happened to your friends, pal, and you're still coming down here? Very well. Adios, amigo."

The tsak opened its mouth, shrieked a few times, and then tucked into a dive. Steve was ready. One well-timed fire jet brought it down.

"What do you want?"

The utter calmness of Hedro's voice surprised them all, the normalcy after his battle with the other dragon. Gareth started toward the head when Steve shook his head no and pointed back at the approaching horde of chra. The wizard nodded, renewed his chanting, and started drawing invisible designs in the air. Steve and Sarah hesitantly approached the Creeg's head.

"You must want something," Hedro continued. He stifled a groan as he shifted weight off his injured leg. "Otherwise, you would have disappeared along with the rest of the miserable humans."

"News flash, pal," Steve returned, "we're not like the other humans."

"Why did you stay?" the Creeg softly asked.

"You're in pain," Sarah answered, laying a soft hand on Hedro's massive head. "Anyone can see that. You can't stand or escape. Deez called them 'carrion eaters'."

"Nothing," Hedro sighed. "You're telling me you're here because you care?"

Steve eyed his wife. This certainly didn't sound like a Creeg talking anymore. What was going on?

"Sir Steve," Breslin called, "have you noticed? Since you incinerated those four tsak, the others are looking for ways to escape."

"There's a nice change," Sarah softly muttered. "Something is trying to get away from us instead of trying to kill us? How'd we get so lucky?"

"What about those bugs?" Steve asked.

"Still coming," Gareth reported, from the tip of Hedro's tail. "Don't worry. I can hold them off, for now. There are a lot of them."

"Let me know when they get close," Steve called back.

"They *are* getting close!" Gareth informed him. "I've got them blocked for now, but it's only a matter of time before they overrun my shield spell. Unless they have some ability I don't know about, we should be fine for a few minutes."

"Lady Sarah, I have a favor." Breslin held up a slip of paper. "Could you get this to my father? It's to let him know what happened here today, plus to let him know they'll need to repair the Gate."

Sarah nodded and took the paper. A few seconds later, the paper vanished.

Steve turned back to the downed dragon. "Okay, then. How about you tell us what's going on, Hedro? How and why did a winged dragon appear in an underground cavern? And where the hell *did* he go?"

"Let's fix his leg first," Sarah said, placing her hand on his shoulder. "I need my medallion for this. Do you want your sword?"

Steve nodded. "Mythrin's scabbard has all those charged mimets. We may need them, so yes, please get my sword."

Sarah closed her eyes and held out her hands. A few moments later, a two-handed broadsword, in a dark brown leather scabbard appeared. Sewn into the scabbard were small pouches. Each pouch held one of the nine-sided crystal disks, called mimets, which could temporarily hold (and release) jhorun, allowing someone to recharge their magical abilities.

He strapped his unique green-bladed sword to his back while Sarah placed her medallion around her neck. From the hidden compartment inside it, she pulled a tiny vial of kaormac juice. The juice could cure most known injuries.

Sarah applied several drops to Hedro's leg. The Creeg's eyes widened with surprise, but unfortunately, his leg remained bent at a grotesque angle. Hedro raised one of his forelegs up and pointed at the vial.

"The essence of a kaormac orchid? Distilled under the light of a full moon?"

Steve watched his wife return the vial to the medallion. "I'm sorry it didn't fix your leg."

"That's because my femur has become dislocated," Hedro patiently explained, as though receiving a debilitating injury was a common occurrence. "There are no broken bones to fix."

"Who the hell are you?" Steve suddenly demanded. "There's no way you're a Creeg."

"Steve, be nice," Sarah scolded. "Of course, he's a Creeg."

The Creeg sighed, and took a deep breath. "Actually, I'm not. I took this form to explore the area beneath Foronlir."

Breslin and Athos appeared by Steve's side almost immediately. Breslin nudged Athos on the shoulder. "That's why Vutt couldn't identify him."

"Is Hedro your real name?" Athos inquired.

The Creeg weakly shook his head. "No."

"Then what is it?" Steve asked. "You say you took this form. So, does that make you a wizard, like Gareth?"

Before the Creeg could reply, a large bolt of lightning suddenly struck dangerously close by.

"Gareth?" Sarah called out. "Was that you?"

"Aye. Those bug things are forming a large mass. They're trying to find a way through my shield."

Steve rushed to Gareth's side and within moments, the rancid smell of burnt bugs wafted through the caverns, causing everyone who smelled it to cover their nose with disgust. Only Hedro appeared to be unconcerned. Steve returned and squatted down low, uncomfortably close to the Creeg's jaws.

"That'll only hold those bug things off for a bit. They're regrouping. They outnumber us by about a thousand to one, and I think they've figured out how to defeat Gareth's shield."

"I am sorry for all the trouble we've caused," Hedro hesitantly began.

"We?" Steve repeated, then frowned. "Who's *we*? You

said your real name isn't Hedro. What is it?"

"Eion."

Both Breslin and Athos gave a small gasp of recognition. Sarah's brow furrowed, then her eyes widened with surprise. She clutched Steve's hand tightly in her own.

"Oh, no way! Steve, do you know who this is? Honey, this is one of the four Ancients."

"What? No, there's no way. I think he's just messing with us."

The Creeg was slowly shaking his head. "I have been known by a great many names. The most recent, and perhaps well known, is Eion, Master of the Winds."

Breslin and Athos immediately dropped to one knee. Gareth blinked uncomprehendingly before he, too, dropped to one knee. Eion's eyes strayed over to Steve's and stayed there.

"I hope you're not expecting me to do that," Steve began, as he pointed at his dwarf friends. "You may be one of their Ancients, but you're not one of mine. I'm not from this world."

"I know you're not, Fire Thrower. Or should I say Steve Miller, from Coeur d'Alene, Idaho. The northern panhandle is very picturesque this time of year, don't you think? Oh, do not look so surprised. Your name is familiar to me."

"He knows where we're from, Steve," Sarah incredulously said. "If ever there were a candidate for a Lentarian deity, Hedro would definitely fit the bill. Oh, sorry. I meant Eion. Wait, you've been to Idaho?"

"On more than one occasion," Eion admitted, with exasperation in his voice. "I have been to a great many places. It's one of the consequences of having lived so long."

Steve's eyes widened as several rusty wheels upstairs began grudgingly grinding together. "Wait. The other dragon. Who was he? Was he another Ancient?"

Eion nodded. "Aye. One that you have encountered before, Fire Thrower."

Memories of ducking the fireballs spat at him by the other dragon flooded through his mind. There was only one Ancient—prior to today—he had ever had the misfortune of crossing, and that was none other than the Earth Guardian, Usol. Steve groaned aloud.

"Just tell me that wasn't Usol."

Eion grunted once and then nodded.

"I thought we made our peace with him," Steve grumbled. "We even saved the life of an infant griffin cub. That must count for something, doesn't it?"

"Did you, or did you not, step foot on his griffin isle?" the Ancient bluntly asked. "Not even we Ancients will violate one another's sacred retreats."

"Oh, good God, is he still angry about that?" Sarah demanded. "Steve's right. He has no business being angry with us. We saved the life of a baby griffin. We're raising him back on our home world. We've even apologized outright to him. What more does he want us to do?"

"That is up to you to figure out," Eion informed them. "All I will tell you is that Usol has not accepted your apology."

"You think?" Steve snapped. "He appears down here as a winged dragon and spits fire at me."

"Can Usol gift powers to humans?" Breslin asked. "If I didn't see it with my own two eyes, I would not have thought it possible. I saw humans, the same pirates we are pursuing, jumping nearly thirty feet into the air."

"I have never heard of Usol granting special abilities to humans," Eion admitted. "But, I know he was responsible. I could smell his power all over those humans."

"I knew it," Steve muttered to himself. "I knew there was something fishy with those guys. Why help them? I don't get it."

Eion nodded. "To use your vernacular, I will say that makes two of us."

Steve felt a nudge on his right elbow. Breslin was there, and he was twisting his beard into knots with his hands.

"What is it?" Steve softly asked.

"Would you kindly ask what he's looking for in Foronlir? Perhaps we could help him."

"Why don't you ask him yourself?" Steve asked, curious. "I mean, I know he can hear you."

"Very well. Er, Eion, would you tell us what you're

looking for? Is there something hidden in the rock that you seek? Perhaps it's in our nearby sister city of Borahgg?"

"I search for my Stone, Master Dwarf."

"Your stone?" Breslin repeated, confused. Then his eyebrows shot up. "Are you telling me there's an Alchos Stone buried in the ground somewhere nearby?"

"Here, or the mountains you people call the Selekais, I really don't know. I cannot remember. So, I search for my missing stone."

"How do you know it hasn't already been found?" Steve asked. "Take Captain Flinn. He's clearly found one of the stones. Do we know which one it is?"

"The human known as Captain Flinn holds the *Essence of the Sea*. It belonged to Aeia. I have vowed to return it to her possession."

Steve's eyebrows shot up. "*Her* possession? One of the Ancients is a female?"

"There are two males and two females," Eion answered. "Aeia and Aura."

"I thought for certain all the Ancients were male," Sarah said. "I trust my memory better than that. Does Aeia go by any other name? Perhaps Aeus?"

Eion shrugged. "She has before, aye."

"Can she appear as a man if she wanted to?"

Eion nodded. "Of course."

"What was the other one?" Steve asked, turning to Sarah. "What's the name of the Ancient who meddles with fire?"

"I thought it was Oros," Sarah answered.

"Oros, Aura. It's a matter of personal preference."

"I cannot believe I am in the presence of an Ancient," Breslin breathed. "My father will go insane with jealousy."

"Can you heal yourself, Eion?" Sarah asked. "Your leg looks terrible. I might not be an expert in Creeg physiology, but that has got to hurt."

"It does," Eion admitted.

"I wish I could help," Sarah added.

"Your kind regards are welcoming," the Ancient informed Sarah. "However, I believe there is nothing you can do."

"You never answered her," Steve pointed out. "Can you

heal yourself?"

Eion shook his head. "No. At least, not while I am in a foreign form. Usol knew this and deliberately attacked me, hoping he'd be able to lock me in this form. Unfortunately, it looks like he succeeded."

Sarah groaned. "Let me guess. You can't change back while you're injured?"

"I have sustained injuries to my various forms before," Eion contradicted, "but this time is different. My leg has become damaged. Since the physiology of each form I assume is different, I am forced to remain in this form until such time I can safely change without it affecting my new form."

"I don't get it," Steve complained.

"Do all beings walk around on two legs?" Eion calmly asked.

Steve shook his head no.

"If you damage the right rear leg of a biped, like what has happened to me, then you cannot change to a quadruped, since the method of locomotion differs significantly."

"So, you can change to another biped?" Steve hopefully asked.

Eion sighed. "I see I haven't made myself clear enough."

Sarah suddenly placed a hand on Eion's Creeg form, drawing him up short. She shot a look to Steve, which said 'zip it' in any language, and gently patted the Creeg's nose.

"You have, Eion. I'm sorry about my husband. I would have thought he'd be more understanding about changing forms, since he's personally been changed to a dragon and a huge centipede monster."

"How *was* that accomplished, anyway?" Eion curiously asked. "I didn't think humans had strong enough jhorun to execute a shifting spell on their own. Not without a talisman of some sort."

"That's Gareth for you," Sarah proudly announced. "He's the young man you see over there, next to the guur."

Two Creeg eyes focused on Gareth. The teenage wizard fidgeted uncomfortably from one foot to the other as soon as he noticed he was being watched. Deez remained unconcerned, and returned Eion's frank stare.

"Ah. I had forgotten about the half human, half shealk wizard. You are powerful indeed, young Gareth."

"You know about me?" Gareth incredulously asked.

Eion nodded. "Of course. I am glad to see you on the right path after all the dastardly deeds you wrought unto others during your younger years. Aura and I had an ongoing wager on whether or not you'd be clapped in irons by your eighteenth birthday."

Gareth's mouth fell open. "Two Ancients were betting? On me??"

Sarah laid a protective hand on the teenager's shoulder. "Gareth has come a long way. He has seen the error of his ways and now only uses his power for good. Isn't that right?"

Gareth nodded. "Uh, yeah. It is."

Eion shifted to stare at Steve. "Tell me something, Fire Thrower. What did you do to Usol to irritate him so? I was misinformed. I thought only Ancients could anger another Ancient that badly."

"It's a long story," Sarah said. "We couldn't possibly take the time to tell you everything that happened."

"Then sum it up for me," Eion suggested.

Steve went into the story of how they'd found the island of Ranal to find a special flower to save the Fae people, and ended up adopting the orphaned baby griffin.

"I should have known a human stepped foot on his blasted floating isle," Eion said. "Nothing would have angered him more than that. He favors the griffins and despises humans."

"That's just swell," Steve grumbled. "And here I thought I was done worrying about that guy."

"We'll have to worry about Usol later," Sarah told him. "Right now, how are we supposed to help him? Do you know anything about how a Creeg's leg works? We need a Creeg doctor. Does anyone know if such a person exists? Could you ask Pryllan?"

Pryllan? Did you hear any of that? Do you know who we have in our midst at the moment?

I did hear and I have relayed this to Kahvel. He is beside himself with amazement that one of the Ancients

has revealed himself to you.

Within minutes, Steve had the answer. "Kahvel says there isn't anyone he's aware of who could help us."

"Damn," Sarah swore. "What about... what about someone from our world?"

"You think there are dragon doctors in Idaho?" Steve scoffed. "Seriously?"

"Can you think of a better idea?" Sarah challenged.

"Who do you have in mind?" Steve asked, genuinely curious.

"I don't know. There must be someone out there who can help."

Steve was silent as he considered Sarah's suggestion. Was there anyone they could turn to? Would they be able to help? Better yet, would they be willing to come to another world to administer aid?

"Your idea has merit," Steve began, "but has all kinds of problems associated with it."

"I know there are," Sarah said, nodding. "I was just brainstorming. Do you really think we could find someone?"

"Well, let's think this through," Steve began, as he rose to his feet and started to pace. "We can definitely rule out veterinarians. I can guaran-damn-tee you they didn't cover this type of thing in any of their animal wellness classes."

"What about zoos?" Sarah asked. "Perhaps we could ask a zookeeper?"

"There are no dragons in our world," Steve pointed out. "And there certainly aren't any dragons in any zoo on our world. That wouldn't do us any good."

"I'm not talking about dragons," Sarah sighed, exasperated. "I'm talking about reptiles. Maybe we could find a reptile keeper. A herpetologist. He might have an idea what we need to do."

Steve suddenly snapped his fingers. "I've got it! We need to go to a museum!"

Sarah blinked at him a few times, clearly confused.

Steve pointed at the Creeg. "Haven't I said several times now how much I think the Creeg look like dinosaurs?"

Sarah's eyes widened. "You want to ask a paleontologist

for help?"

"One specializing in Tyrannosaurus Rex. Well, what do you think?"

Sarah shrugged. "It's a plausible idea, but how do we find one?"

"There are dinosaur bones at the Phoenix Museum in Arizona. Someone on staff must know more about them than we do. I say we find out who that person is."

Sarah looked at the two dwarves. "Will you guys be okay for a while? We need to go find some help. Gareth? How are you doing? What are those bug things doing now?"

"They're still experimenting with different tactics to defeat my spell. Nothing has worked for them, thankfully. But hurry—I think these bugs are smart."

"Can you hold them off for a little bit?"

"I heard. You and Steve need to go to your world? One of these days I'd love to go there, too, just to say that I've been there."

"You'd love it," Steve confirmed. "Maybe a vacation to Disneyland again? I think it's time."

Sarah clapped her hands, trying to hurry him. "Once we solve this. Okay, let's get going. Ready?"

Steve unbuckled Mythrin and handed it to Breslin. "Here. Hold on to this for me, would you? The people of my world kinda frown on a person walking around with a magical broadsword on their back."

Breslin nodded and accepted the sword.

"Eion?" Sarah called. "We'll be back as soon as we can."

"Unless those carnivorous insects break through, something tells me I'll be right here," the Ancient dryly responded.

Chapter 14 — Dino Doctor

W hat's that smell?" Steve asked, ten minutes later. "Are you sure you took us to the right place?"

"I think we're in a janitor closet," Sarah quietly answered. "I can smell bleach. And yes, we're in the right place. It's just odd. I've never been in this closet before."

"Where was your safe zone?" Steve wanted to know.

"The gift shop. I've purchased a few things from this place."

"Maybe they remodeled," Steve suggested. "We could be standing where the gift shop used to be, you know."

"I suppose," Sarah agreed. "It's been a few years. Come on. I think the museum might be getting ready to close. We don't have much time."

"You ain't just whistlin' Dixie, lady," Steve chuckled.

Sarah eased the door open and checked the surroundings. They were in a semi-darkened hallway, which brightened as soon as they emerged. Apparently, the museum installed motion sensors in an attempt to conserve energy.

"Look!" Steve hurried over to a wooden kiosk and gazed up at the display.

Sarah nodded approvingly. "Fantastic. A map. It's just what we need. I don't remember it being this big, do you? How are we supposed to find anyone in here? Can we say, 'needle in a haystack'?"

The Arizona Museum of Natural History was the only natural history museum located in the greater Phoenix area. The museum's complex encompassed some seventy-four thousand square feet, with over forty-six thousand square feet dedicated to collections. Spread across four floors, the huge complex included a three-story indoor waterfall on Dinosaur Mountain, Dino Hall, a real territorial jail, and even an authentic recreation of the Lost Dutchman's Gold Mine.

Laid out across the informational kiosk were floorplans of the four different floors. A color-coded key indicated which halls were dedicated to various collections. Steve tapped on the orange dot.

"Here we go. Fossil Halls. We're looking for orange."

"Figures," Steve grumbled. He pointed at a serious of orange rectangles. "The fossils are on the top floor."

Sarah took his hand. "Come on. We need to get going."

They followed a hall, which turned to the left, then immediately to the right. They were now standing in the Grand Gallery, just inside the main front doors. They also nearly bumped into a pair of museum security guards.

"Can we help you find anything?" one guard asked. Both were young, presumably in their mid-twenties.

Steve nodded. "You guys have a T. Rex skeleton here, don't you?"

"And my second question, are there any actual paleontologists on staff here?"

"I saw Dr. Benz here earlier today. She'd be a good one to ask."

"Where can we find her?" Steve asked.

"Top floor is where you'll find all the offices. I forget which one is hers, but you'll be able to see their names on the doors."

"Thank you so much," Sarah gushed. "This should really

help my paper."

Both guards nodded politely and moved on.

The fourth floor, as promised, housed all things dinosaur. They saw impressive exhibits, featuring pterosaurs, mammoths, and even the multi-horned triceratops. Steve nudged Sarah and pointed in the far corner of the Hall of Ornithischian Dinosaurs. There, standing on two massive hind legs, was the Tyrannosaur.

"Impressive, isn't it?"

Steve and Sarah glanced over and saw a short young woman with long curly blonde hair. She was wearing a Polo shirt with the museum's logo, khaki pants, and white sneakers. She couldn't have been more than twenty years old, probably a docent.

"Yes, it is," Steve agreed, looking up at the fossilized skeleton. "I certainly wouldn't want one of those things on my tail."

"First time in our museum?" the girl cheerfully asked.

"I've been here a few times before," Steve told the girl, "but I will admit it's been a year or two. Hey, listen, is there any chance you can tell us where to find a Dr. Benz? We were hoping to talk with her."

The girl nodded, and surprisingly, held out her hand. "Dr. Emily Benz. It's a pleasure. And you are?"

A look of disbelief washed over Steve's features. He automatically took the doctor's hand and noticed it was heavily callused. "Steve Miller. Okay, you caught me off guard. I wasn't expecting someone so young. This is my wife, Sarah."

Sarah shook the paleontologist's hand and smiled at her. "It's nice to meet you, Dr. Benz. You'll have to forgive my husband. He's easily surprised."

"Could we speak to you in private, Dr. Benz?" Sarah asked.

"Could I ask what this is about?" the paleontologist asked. Her smile became guarded.

"We need to run something by you," Steve began, "and we'd just as soon do it in private, 'cause it's gonna sound a little crazy."

Dr. Benz regarded the two of them for a few seconds before shrugging. "Sure. I've been having a strange week so far, so I doubt anything you say could surprise me at this point."

"You might want to hold on to that thought," Steve softly muttered, as he turned to follow Dr. Benz and his wife.

Dr. Benz unlocked the second door from the far right and held open the door, inviting the two of them in. She was smiling, but the smile was still guarded. Leaving the door open, Dr. Benz walked around her cluttered desk, pulled out her chair, and sat down. Steve and Sarah did the same.

"Now, what is it you wanted to talk to me about?"

Steve looked at his wife and nodded. Sarah steeled herself, took a breath, and faced their new friend.

"We need you, no questions asked, to come with us to help out a friend of ours, who's been hurt."

Emily frowned. "If someone has been hurt, shouldn't you be calling for an ambulance?"

"There are no ambulances there," Steve told her. "No ambulances, and unfortunately, no doctors."

"And which Third World country would that be?" Emily asked, confused.

Steve looked over at Sarah. "Do you want to take it from here?"

Sarah nodded. "Umm, let me ask you something first. How open-minded are you?"

Emily's brow furrowed. "What's that supposed to mean?"

"It means just that," Steve said. "How open are you to experiencing something that isn't supposed to be possible? Can you keep such a thing secret and never tell anyone?"

"I'm not sure I want to get involved with whatever is going on with you two," Emily began, rising to her feet. "I think I'd like you to leave now."

Steve looked up. He smiled. He couldn't see any smoke detectors, or fire suppression systems anywhere in the small office. Ordering his jhorun to remove all heat, he held up his right hand and ignited it.

Emily gasped with alarm and fell back into her chair. She stared, open-mouthed, at his burning hand and lifted a shaky finger. Steve extinguished his hand and leaned forward to rest his elbows on her desk.

"That was just the tip of the iceberg, Dr. Benz. Sorry, I mean, Emily. Look, we're running out of time. You want us to be honest? Fine. Here it goes. We have a friend, who's a Creeg, a creature that looks very much like a T. rex. He has a dislocated leg and it needs to be set. None of us know how to do that. No one on that world does either, for that matter."

"*That world?*" Emily shakily repeated. "You're telling me you've been to another world? That's not possible."

Steve nodded. "Oh, but it is. We've been there quite a few times. Forget about that for now. The simple fact is, our friend is hurt. We think you might be able to help. So, will you? Will you help us?"

"You're suggesting you want to take me to another world and have me medically treat a T. rex? Are you serious?"

Sarah nodded. "That's exactly what we need you to do. Please, Emily, we're in a serious time crunch. We left our friends protecting Eion, and we're not sure how long they can hold out. We need to get back. Please, if you don't want to go, that's fine, but could you recommend someone who would be willing to help us?"

Emily rose to her feet once more. "Omigod, you're serious about this, aren't you? And you. Your hand? Were those real flames?"

Steve nodded.

"And you?" Emily asked, turning to Sarah. "You have a magical ability, too?"

Sarah nodded. "Yes. That's why we're here, Emily. I wasn't kidding when I said we had *just* left our friends. They're there, waiting for us. We have to get back to them. Are you with us?"

Emily reached for the phone on her desk and punched a few buttons. "Dr. Rosenbaum, this is Dr. Benz. I have a family emergency, and I need to take a leave of absence. No, I'm not sure how long I'll be gone." Emily thanked him and replaced the phone. She looked up at Sarah. "At least, I think I'll be in touch. Do they have phones there?"

Both husband and wife shook their heads no.

"But," Sarah added, with a smile, "I can literally get you back here in the blink of an eye."

"Her jhorun is way cooler than mine," Steve quipped, offering the paleontologist a smile.

"Jhorun?" Emily repeated, confused.

Steve cringed. "Oh, sorry. That's what the locals call their magical abilities. Not everyone has it. I mean, all humans do, but not all the species. Dragons, yes. Dwarves, no."

"Some do," Sarah reminded him. "Don't forget about the guur."

Emily's eyes had widened with alarm. "Dragons?"

Steve nodded. "Yep. They're just as big and intimidating as you can imagine, only most are friendly. I have a good friend who's a dragon."

"My mind is spinning," Emily admitted, as she sank back down. "What … what do I need to bring? You say this creature has a dislocated hip? We will need to find a way to stabilize the leg so that it can't move. Will there be anything there that we can use?"

"If there isn't, the dwarves will be able to get it for us," Sarah promised. "Or I can, even if I have to come all the way back here to get it."

Emily nodded. "Very well. What now? What do we have to do?"

Steve pointed at the door. "Should we lock it? We need to maintain the illusion that you are away."

Emily nodded. "Yes, thank you."

Steve offered his hand to his wife, who placed her right hand over his. Together, they looked at Emily.

"What? Do you need me to place my hand on yours?"

"Physical contact," Sarah explained.

Emily came around her desk, approached husband and wife, and hesitantly placed her hand over Sarah's. "Okay, now what?"

Steve grinned at her. "Brace yourself for one helluva jolt."

Emily's eyes widened. "A jolt? How much of a… aaahhh!"

The world winked out and was replaced by the darkened, subterranean cavern once more. Steve immediately pulled his hand free and checked the surroundings. Gareth was sitting on a rock and warily eyeing the horde of black insects that were kept at bay by his spell. Catching sight of their return, the young wizard looked relieved.

Sarah led Emily over to the Creeg, who was lying motionless on the ground. Eion's eyes opened and watched the two of them approach. The paleontologist's eyes were wide.

"You weren't kidding!" Emily exclaimed. "Heavens above, it's a live Tyrannosaurus rex, in the flesh! Only ... this one is different. He doesn't have vestigial arms. And his face is..."

"While similar in structure to the theropods you are familiar with, Emily Benz," Eion interrupted, as though he was having a scholarly debate amongst old friends, "this form is not a Tyrannosaurus rex. Since it has yet to be discovered by the paleontologists of your world, there is no technical name."

"Seriously?" Emily squeaked with surprise. "It speaks? How is this possible?"

Steve cleared his throat. "Umm, there might have been a few things we left out."

Emily shot him a dark look. "Would you care to fill me in? I trusted you. Based on what I see before me, it's easy to believe I'm no longer on my world. I think I am entitled to the truth. Who is this creature? How did it know my name?"

Eion interrupted. "Are you knowledgeable enough in, as you would say, theropod anatomy, to fix my leg?"

Emily knelt down, next to Eion's distended hip. She gently poked and prodded. Then she ran her hands along the length of Eion's reptilian leg. After a few moments, she grunted.

"You probably have different terms for the words I know, so I'll just use my own. Just by looking at your leg, I can see that your femur, er, leg bone, is no longer sitting in its socket. In fact, it's nowhere close to where it's supposed to be. That's why your leg is so swollen right here. Much of that is the bulge from the end of the femur. This," Emily gently tapped the bulge in Eion's scaly skin, "needs to move, ah, I'd say about eighteen inches toward your hip."

Eion nodded. "I deduced as much. What needs to be done?"

"We'll need helpers. Look at the size of his leg. The femur alone is bigger than the two of us put together. We're going to need a lot of people to lift that leg."

"Where's Breslin?" Steve asked, as he turned to inspect the surroundings. "And Athos? Were they called away?"

Gareth, overhearing the question, pointed back toward the unfinished tunnel, with the now broken Gate.

"They're inspecting the wall you smashed through."

"Never mind," Steve said to Emily, then turned to his wife. "Would you bring Breslin and Athos back here? We need some more hands. I think I know where we can get some."

Sarah nodded, winked at Emily, and vanished.

"Whoa! Where'd she go?"

Steve pointed at the far southern wall of the cavern.

"The tunnel on the left leads down, to the dwarf cities of Borahgg and Foronlir. Our two dwarf friends are there, inspecting the damage I inflicted on it earlier. That's where Sarah…"

Sarah suddenly appeared, with a dwarf on either side of her.

"…was," Steve slyly finished.

Sarah introduced the newcomer to the dwarves and told Breslin to help her recruit more help. "We'll be right back. Oh! Emily? What supplies will you need?"

Emily returned her gaze to the injured Creeg and considered. "Well, let's see. We'll need something long and sturdy, to make a splint. Firm, strong bandages so we can strap the leg to the splint. I think that ought to do it."

"You got it."

Sarah and Breslin vanished. Emily turned to look appreciatively at Steve. She then lowered herself to the ground, sat back on her haunches, and laughed out loud.

"What's the matter?" Steve asked. "Wasn't this what you were expecting you'd be doing when you woke up this morning?"

"Heavens, no," Emily admitted. "You and your wife have

given me a lot to think about. I…"

"Watch out!" Gareth suddenly shouted.

Steve whipped his head around to see Gareth gesturing frantically in the air. Lightning bolts appeared out of nowhere and repeatedly struck the ground. Steve quickly pulled Emily to her feet, positioned her behind him, and then ignited both hands.

"Stay behind me! Gareth, get out of the way!"

The young wizard reached into a pocket, pulled something out, and in a brilliant flash of white light, vanished. Once he was out of the way, Steve could see what was happening. The chra horde had gathered itself together again, forming a large ball of tightly packed insects. The large sphere of bugs had breached the protective spell.

"Cover your nose," Steve told Emily. "These things stink when they're burning."

He generated a huge wall of flames and torched the ball until it was nothing but ash. Twin jets of fire then targeted various places on the ground where he could see the squirming black horde of insects. After a few minutes of incessant torching, Steve extinguished his flames. The seething black mass of chra had been driven back, but it was only a matter of time before they more than likely would try again.

Steve fanned the air in front of his nose and turned to Emily. "See? I told you they stink."

"I think I like your magical ability more than your wife's."

Steve shook his head. "There's no way. I don't think you realize how her jhorun works. She can literally return to any place she's previously been. Think about that. We live in northern Idaho. Her mother lives in Sacramento. She can literally teleport the two of us to her mom's house in the blink of an eye."

"What's her range?" Emily curiously asked. "Is there a limit to how far she can go?"

Steve held out an arm and swept it around the cavern. "Well, you're here, aren't you? That's a jump from one world to the next. I would think that's about as far as you can go."

Sarah appeared, along with a dozen dwarves. She instantly wrinkled her nose and frowned. Then she saw sections of the ground still burning and her eyes widened with alarm.

"Did those cockroach things attack?"

"They're getting smarter," Steve acknowledged. "They just formed themselves into this big ball and got through Gareth's shield."

"I've modified the parameters of my spell again," Gareth announced. "I added another layer. This time, only humans and dwarves will make it through. I'd like to see them figure out how to get through that now."

Sarah gave her husband a peck on his cheek. "Be right back. There are two more groups waiting to go. Something tells me we're going to need all the help we can get. Plus, I'll need to have energy left to return them home."

"They can always walk back to the city," Breslin interjected. "You will not be taxing your jhorun on our account, thank you very much."

Sarah gave Breslin a beaming smile and then vanished. Steve watched Emily give the dwarves a speculative look. She had to be no taller than five foot two, yet the dwarves only came up to the top of her shoulder. It was yet another culture shock she was going to have to get over, whether she liked it or not.

Less than five minutes later, nearly thirty dwarves, several stacks of lumber, a large pile of what looked like burlap, and a wide variety of tools were sitting next to the Creeg. Just then, Eion's head turned and locked eyes with Steve's. The Creeg gave a very perceptible shake of his head. The Ancient didn't want his identity revealed to anyone who didn't already know it! This time, Eion nodded. The Ancient was clearly telepathic, too!

Breslin turned to Emily and nodded. "Lady Emily. How would you like to proceed? What do you need us to do?"

Emily sucked in a breath and stared at the large group of strange, bearded, small beings who were staring at her with equal fascination. Steve appeared next to her and laid a friendly hand on her shoulder.

"They're here to help. Whatever you said before, just say it again."

Emily released the breath she hadn't realized she'd been

holding. "All right. Okay, here's what we need." She began giving instructions.

Breslin immediately turned and issued orders. Dozens of dwarfish hands got to work. Tools were gathered, hammers were readied, and saws were sharpened. Within moments, two long planks, reinforced with layers of timber, were assembled and adjusted to the length of Eion's leg.

"Now what?" Breslin inquired.

Emily took a deep breath, swept up her hair and tied it into a bun to get it out of her face. She slowly let her breath out. "We need every single person on his leg. It'll need to be lifted and extended straight out, as though he was doing a high kick, like a cheerleader."

A sea of blank faces stared at the paleontologist.

"Er, we need to stretch the leg up as high as it'll naturally go. Then, we'll rotate it left, and then right, until the bone pops back in its socket. Does everyone understand?"

There was a chorus of 'ayes'. Thirty dwarves rushed forward and prepared to lift the Creeg's leg. Breslin, Athos, and Steve joined in as well.

Sarah held up a hand. "Excuse me, but isn't this where the patient is typically sedated? I mean, isn't this going to hurt?"

Emily hesitated and looked questioningly at the Creeg. "Umm, I'm sorry. I hadn't thought of that. She's right. We should probably put you down."

"You have no way to render me unconscious," Eion told her. "You may proceed. I will be fine."

Sarah looked over at their young wizard companion. "Gareth? Is there anything you can do to help him to ignore the pain?"

Gareth sadly shook his head. "No, I'm sorry. I've tried several spells on him already, and none have worked."

Emily squeezed in between Athos and Breslin and placed her hands on Eion's upper right thigh. Yes, she could feel the muscles in his leg, but with the femur in the wrong position, the muscles were bulging outward, forming a disquieting enormous bulge in his leg. This had to work!

Emily glanced behind her to verify everyone was in place when she came face to face with the biggest, ugliest bug she'd ever seen. The scream she let out was guttural; primal, causing every single dwarf present to pull their weapons.

"Put those weapons away. The guur is an ally."

Steve felt a light tap on his shoulder. Turning, he saw Emily giving him a questioning look.

"Yes?"

"What was that thing?"

"I'll explain more later. Like others on this world, he's sometimes telepathic."

GRATITUDE

Emily turned to Deez and nodded. "I heard that. You just said 'gratitude'. It's a sentiment we both share right now. I'm very grateful to be included in this adventure. Come on, everyone. Let's get his leg fixed."

With nearly fifteen dwarves on each side of Eion's leg, they gently lifted and waited for the Creeg to roll over onto his left hip. Once he had, they carefully stretched the leg out. Steve kept watch on Eion's face. The Ancient may have said he wouldn't notice any pain, but his features said otherwise. Whether in his natural form or a borrowed one, evidently the Ancients felt pain, like any other creature.

"Is everyone ready?" Emily called out. "Here we go." She issued precise instructions.

Steve watched as everyone collectively swung the Creeg's leg back and forth. With careful ministrations, Emily directed the dwarves to either lift there, or lower there, or extend there. As soon as the leg was stretched as far as it would go, which to Steve, looked as though the Creeg was trying to jump over a hurdle, Eion gave a sharp grunt of pain.

"There!" Emily said excitedly. "I think we have it! Yes, it feels like the bone is back where it should be! Excellent work, everyone! Now we just need to wrap the leg tightly to these splints and I think we're done."

"That won't be necessary," Eion informed her. "What needed to be done, has been done. I am whole again. I thank you."

"Can you say for certain that you won't reinjure the leg

by prematurely walking on it? We need to immobilize your leg, period."

Eion nodded. "Very well, Dr. Benz. You may proceed."

Ten minutes later, with the splint securely in place, Eion rose to his feet. He took several clumsy steps, but was able to gingerly move about. After a few moments, the Creeg lowered himself to the ground and eyed the onlookers. Eion turned to Breslin and waited until the dwarf made eye contact with him.

"Master Breslin, would you thank your helpers for me? I am feeling much better."

Breslin gave Emily a bow and with Athos' help, rounded up the helpers. Sarah approached Breslin and gave him a smile. "I'm still feeling pretty good. I can get them back to the city."

Breslin eyed her guardedly. "Are you sure, Lady Sarah? I do not want to overtax your jhorun."

"We have plenty of mimets if I get tired. I'll be fine. Besides, I don't want you guys to risk running into that mass of chra over there. Granted, it's getting smaller, thanks to Gareth and Steve, but those are some persistent little boogers."

Breslin eyed the swarm of small black beetles and nodded. "Aye. You have a point. Very well. We're ready to go."

Once Sarah had vanished with the first group of dwarves, Steve wandered over to where Gareth was sitting, still keeping an eye on the bugs, and tapped him on the shoulder. "Want a break? I can drive them back for a while. That'll give you a couple of free moments."

Gareth nodded appreciatively.

Steve ignited both hands and incinerated the swirling sphere of bugs that were in the process of trying to re-enter the protective shield Gareth had created. Growing tired of the pesky bugs, Steve torched everything he could see. If it was small and black, it got burned. He felt another tap on his shoulder and found Emily beside him,

"Steve? Can I ask you something? Why wouldn't the creature tell me his name when I asked?"

"I got the distinct impression he didn't want his identity as one of the Ancients known," Steve answered.

"Correct, Steve Miller," Eion's voice came.

"Why not?" Emily asked, as she turned back to the Creeg.

"My own personal preference," Eion answered. "I prefer my privacy, as do you."

"You don't know anything about me," Emily accused. "You couldn't."

"Single, no desire for romantic entanglements, much to the chagrin of your sire, and--to use a phrase common on your world--a dedicated workaholic."

"How could you possibly know that?" Emily whispered; her face ashen.

Eion looked down at his leg and wiggled his three reptilian toes.

"You really shouldn't be trying to move anything," Emily told the Creeg. "I don't care who you are. You have to treat your body better than this."

Once Sarah had returned, and the only people in the cavern were husband and wife, Emily, wizard, guur, and the two dwarves, Eion turned to Sarah and bowed.

"Lady Sarah, could I beseech you to part with one of your precious drops of kaormac elixir?"

"But it won't heal your leg," Sarah protested. She pulled her medallion out of her shirt by its chain and opened the hidden compartment. "You told me that a little while ago."

"The elixir will mend broken bones, but will not move them. When you applied the first drop, I felt an immediate lessening of the pain, indicating it was soothing stretched muscles. Now, however, those same muscles have been overstretched again. They are quite painful. I do believe that, should you administer another drop, I might be able to change form."

Sarah nodded. She wet the tip of her finger with a single drop and touched Eion's scaly leg. The Ancient's eyes widened, and then a smile appeared on his face. Eion looked down at his immobilized leg and flexed his knee. The burlap wrappings creaked as they stretched, but held together.

"No pain," Eion reported. "My supposition was correct."

Breslin and Athos pulled out their daggers and quickly cut the wrappings off the splint. Eion rolled to his feet and shakily straightened to his full height. A few moments later, the Creeg's body shimmered with sparkles of white light and vanished. In its place was a bright white lizard the size of a Gila monster. It flopped around on the ground, like a fish out of water.

Steve squatted down next to the lizard and frowned. "Houston, I think we have a problem."

Chapter 15 — Trouble in Paradise

"What happened to him?" Sarah wanted to know. She rushed over to Steve's side and looked at the upside-down lizard, who was struggling to right itself. "Is that Eion?"

Emily squatted down next to the lizard and gently helped flip the reptile over. "I told you, you have to treat your body better than this. Clearly, your body has been hurt, and your injuries are being transferred to your other forms."

The lizard glared angrily up at Emily before giving a loud, audible hiss.

"Try changing to a biped," the paleontologist suggested. "And when you do, don't try to move. Just stand still and wait for your body to acclimatize."

Steve came up beside her and grinned. "For someone who never would have believed magic existed, or other worlds, for that matter, you certainly are fitting in quite nicely."

Emily shrugged. "Either I accept what I'm seeing, or I'm going to need extensive therapy when I return home. I'm a scientist. I trust my senses."

The lizard glowed again then disappeared into a brilliant flash of white light. When the light faded, they could see that, in its place, was a humanoid figure wearing white robes. The figure clumsily pulled the hood off his head and faced his helpers. Steve sucked in a breath. The face was human, but the eyes were not.

Both of the figure's eyes were glowing white, with no discernible iris or pupil. The man was slightly shorter than Steve, had a thin build, and was sporting a full brown beard. The figure turned to Emily, blinked his eyes a few times, which had the unsettling result of turning off the light emanating from his eyes, and nodded again.

"This, Emily Benz, is a form I seldom use. I should have followed your advice and chosen a bipedal creature first. And no, before you ask, this isn't my natural form. Come. All of you. We have much to talk about."

"Where are we going?" Sarah wanted to know. "And I should probably return Emily before we go any further."

Eion turned to the paleontologist and bowed. "Of course, if that is your desire. Otherwise, if you'd like to join us, you are welcome."

Emily nodded. "I'm staying right here, thank you very much. Do you really think I'm that anxious to get home? Knowing that there's this other, fantastic world out there that I have a chance to explore? I'd have to return my doctorate to the university should I ever give up a chance like this."

Eion nodded. "Very well. Come with me. There are things all of you need to hear."

"Where do you want to go?" Breslin hesitantly asked.

"A place where we can talk without fear of being overheard," the Ancient replied.

"And where's that?" Steve wanted to know.

"You'll see."

In literally the blink of an eye, bright light was pouring down on them, bathing them in warm sunshine. The chirps of countless kytes sounded from all directions. Directly before them was a grassy clearing with a ring of huge trees to the north, the base of a small mountain to the west, and a wide open expanse to the east. A tiny pool of water bubbled up from the earth near the base of the mountain and traveled south as a creek, snaking around rocks, trees, and anything else in its path.

"Where are we?" Sarah asked, as she looked around. "Wherever this is, I like it."

Steve shaded his eyes and gazed east, out into the open expanse of air. Were they standing on a cliff? If so, this couldn't possibly be Lentari. He wasn't aware of any cliffs as high as these.

Eion spread his arms in welcome and smiled at them. "Welcome to Astral. You are the first visitors here since ... forever."

The Ancient rubbed his right leg and, with the injured leg held straight as a board, lowered himself into a sitting position. Sarah noticed there wasn't a chair beneath him and started to say something, but hastily shut her mouth as a large, flat rock appeared. Eion looked over at Emily and grimaced.

"You were right, Emily Benz. The injury may be gone, but the pain is still there and the flexibility I am used to is absent. That must be why I floundered as the lizard."

"Give it some time," Emily patiently told the strange man with the glowing eyes. "You may be immortal, but that form is not."

"Understood."

Steve held up a hand. "Er, excuse me? Where is Astral? Are we still in Lentari? Ranal?"

"You're on *my* island," the Ancient clarified. "I have no business in ever stepping foot on my brother's island. Ever."

"Do all the Ancients have their own personal islands?" Sarah curiously asked.

Eion nodded. "Aye. We each crafted our own sanctuaries with the explicit intent to never step foot on one another's islands. I don't often use my isle, so I figured this would be a great place to talk unhindered."

Steve wandered over to the grass-covered clearing and sank gratefully to the ground. "I have been on my feet all day. This feels good. Thanks, pal."

Eion nodded.

The others joined him.

"You have helped me more than I thought possible," Eion began. The Ancient leaned back and closed his eyes. "Long have I watched you humans. You've fought wars, brokered peace, and explored distant lands. You've created bonds with other worlds, invited strangers to look after family, and placed your trust in former adversaries. If ever there were a species to be commended, it would be yours."

"I'm not sure how to respond to that," Steve quietly admitted to his wife. Sarah promptly shushed him.

"Now, the humans I've admired for so long have been given one of the Alchos Stones."

"By Usol," Steve guessed.

Eion nodded. "Correct."

"Why?" Sarah asked. "Why would he do it?"

Eion sighed. "When you have been around as long as we have, unfortunate side effects can and do appear."

"Such as?" Breslin asked.

"Boredom," Steve guessed again.

Eion nodded appreciatively at Steve. "Precisely. Whereas I, myself, refuse to meddle with human affairs, my brother cannot say the same. He craves attention-- power. He enjoys interfering with human lives for his own entertainment."

Sarah shook her head. "Wait a moment. I thought the Alchos Stone Captain Flinn was the *Essence of the Sea*. Wouldn't that belong to the Ancient who oversees water? Aeus, I think?"

"Aeia," Eion corrected. "Aeus is just one of the names she has been known to assume."

"How did Usol get his hands on Aeia's stone?" Steve asked.

At this, Eion frowned. "How else? He stole it. He has demonstrated time and time again that he has no scruples. Believe me when I say we must get the Stone away from the humans. Of course, I mean no offense."

"None taken," Steve assured the Ancient. "Trust me, I know what we humans can be like. No human should be given that much power."

"You're an Ancient," Sarah began. "You're telling me you don't suffer from boredom? Why bother helping us out?

What do you get out of helping us?"

"I hope to make peace with Aeia," Eion sadly answered. "I hope to be able to count her once more as an ally and a friend."

"She doesn't consider herself your friend?" Breslin asked. "May I ask why that is?"

Eion hesitated a few moments. "Because … well, I'm the one that gave Usol her Stone in the first place."

"What in the world did you do that for?" Steve demanded. "Are you trying to land your sorry butt in the doghouse?"

"I don't think he'd know what that means," Emily softly said.

Sarah smacked him on the arm. "I don't think he did it on purpose, dear. You didn't, did you?"

Eion shook his head no. "I never dreamed Usol would betray me the way he did. Aeia gave me her Stone for safekeeping. Reflecting back on that day, I can only assume my brother knew this. He wanted to know if I had recently seen a large sapphire and wondered if it was her Stone, which was known to be blue in color. I told him it was, and that she had entrusted it to me while she was away."

Steve raised a hand. "I have a question. You said the Ancient responsible for water was away? Where did she go?"

Eion shrugged. "I know not. I did not ask. Wherever Aeia chooses to go is up to her."

"How long ago did she leave?" Sarah asked, curious.

Eion waved a dismissive hand. "Over five thousand of your years. That's not important. The fact that she entrusted her Stone to me, and I foolishly showed it to Usol, is what matters."

"So, you showed this Stone to Usol," Steve replied, frowning. "How does that make you a bad person? It's not like you just dropped it into his hands and said, 'Guess what I have here?' right?"

Eion was silent.

"You didn't," Steve groaned.

"I was foolishly trying to impress him," Eion admitted.

"Did he take the Stone and run?" Gareth asked. "If given enough time, I might be able to write a spell which would take the Stone away from the pirate captain."

Eion shook his head. "Your spells would be futile against the power of a Stone."

"What about persuading Usol to steal it away from Flinn?" Steve asked. "Could Gareth do something like that?"

"I'd be willing to try," Gareth announced.

"Impossible," Eion disagreed, shaking his head. "If you think your powers are feeble against a Stone, then please remember the Stone is just a fraction of the power an Ancient commands. Your jhorun is useless against us, young wizard. That's why all your spells were ineffective while I was a Creeg."

"Have you ever meddled with human affairs?" Sarah suddenly asked, growing suspicious.

"No. I believe the fate of the humans should be left to their own doing. I have never yet tried to influence anyone to do anything, and I intend to keep it that way."

"We already know Usol doesn't feel the same way," Steve began. "What about Aeia? Or ... or ... the fire chick?"

Sarah groaned. "Fire chick? Did you really just say that?"

Emily snickered loudly, eliciting grins from both the dwarves and Gareth.

"I like you two," the paleontologist decided.

"Aeia and Aura feel it is beneath them to interact with humans. That isn't to say they won't, but I do believe neither will willingly cross that line."

"What did Usol do after he stole Aeia's Stone?" Gareth asked. "Did he go straight to Captain Flinn or ... wait. He went straight to the shealk, didn't he? Why? What did the water dragons ever do to him?"

"The shealk were part of Aeia's domain," Eion answered. "However, you are misinformed. Usol did not give Aeia's Stone to the shealk."

"Yes, he did!" Gareth insisted. "My father told me all about it!"

"Again, you are mistaken, young wizard," Eion patiently informed him.

"And if I can prove you wrong?" Gareth challenged. "What then?"

"Listen, pal," Steve whispered in the teenager's ear. "Are you sure this is a wise idea? You do know who you're facing, right?"

"He's getting the story wrong," Gareth insisted.

"And if I can prove otherwise?" Eion mildly inquired.

"You can't, but let's just say you can. I'll ... I'll ... hmm. I don't know."

"You will owe *me* a favor, young wizard. You will do whatever I ask you, whenever I ask it. Do we have an accord?"

"What about if I win?" Gareth asked. "What do I get?"

"What do you want?" the Ancient asked.

"Three wishes," Gareth suddenly blurted. "Just like in the books from their world."

"One wish," Eion amended, "and I am not a genie."

"Fine one wish."

"Very well, we have an accord. Now, make your case."

"Gareth, you fool," Sarah softly scolded, shaking her head. "You're smarter than this. What in the world are you doing?"

"Earning myself a wish. Watch this."

Gareth wandered over to the small pond, scooped a handful of water from the surface, and slowly let it escape through his fingers.

"Father," Gareth solemnly said.

The drops of water that had fallen to the ground suddenly sizzled, as on a scalding hot surface. After a few seconds had passed, a small cloud of steam formed. It quickly molded itself into a familiar humanoid face: Balthor. The shealk wizard's face spun in place until it was looking straight at Gareth.

"Son, are you well?"

Gareth nodded. "I am, Father. I'm sorry to contact you this way, but..."

"Are you being held against your will?"

"What? No, Father, I'm not."

"Where are you? I cannot sense you anywhere on Lentari. Who are you with?"

Gareth stepped out of the way, revealing Steve and Sarah, who smiled and waved meekly at him. The head slowly spun to Gareth's left and focused on the two dwarves. The young wizard performed introductions all around, then paused. "Father, can you come to my present location? There's someone here you need to meet."

"You're certain you are safe?"

"Perfectly, Father."

"Very well. Is there water nearby?"

"Aye, over there. There's a small pond."

"That will do."

The steam quickly dissipated.

The surface of the pond suddenly rippled, as though someone had dropped a rock into the water. A few moments later, the ripples turned into roiling bubbles. A large, delicate bubble emerged from within the depths of the pond. Inside was a tall, humanoid figure. The bubble drifted over to the ground and popped, depositing the figure onto the grass.

"Father!" Gareth called. "I'm over here!"

Balthor straightened as he looked for his son. He caught sight of Steve and Sarah and formally bowed. As he continued to turn, his eyes caught sight of Eion. The shealk wizard stared at the figure in white robes for a few moments before his eyes widened with recognition.

"You! I remember you! You came to me, in a dream, telling me about the Alchos Stones. You were able to describe the sapphire belonging to Aeus, the Water Ancient. With your help, I managed to locate it."

"And lose it," Eion dryly replied.

"Who are you?" Balthor asked. "You wouldn't tell me your name before."

"How do you know him?" Sarah asked.

Balthor sighed as he looked at his son. "I assume everyone here knows of the thriper?"

"The what?" Steve, Sarah, and Emily asked, at the same time.

"I know what it is," Gareth proudly announced. "I helped Mikal defeat it."

"It's the creature that fed off of jhorun," Balthor explained. "It had been imprisoned deep beneath the ocean, only it escaped. After thousands of years, it was starved, and

I was the first person it came across. It stripped me of all my power. Imagine, a wizard who is unable to do his duties."

Sarah was nodding. "The thriper. I've heard that term. Isn't that the creature who drained the jhorun from the Fae's tree?"

Steve shrugged. "I think so."

Sarah sighed. "You and your memory."

"I'm envious of the stories you two must be able to tell," Emily ruefully said. "I would love to hear them all."

"That can probably be arranged," Sarah told their new friend.

"I never realized who you were," Balthor continued, as he looked with fond reverence at the Ancient. "I even thought I might have imagined it."

"Imagined what?" Gareth softly asked.

"After my unfortunate encounter with the thriper, and I regained consciousness, I found myself on the seabed floor, unable to move, and barely able to breathe. *He* appeared and encouraged me to swim for help, to not give up. So, again I ask you, friend, who are you?"

"Be prepared for a shocker," Steve cautioned, from the side.

"Can I tell him?" Gareth suddenly interrupted, before Eion could speak.

The Ancient smiled and nodded.

"Father, you're not going to believe this. This is Eion! He's the…"

"…Master of the Winds," Balthor breathed, amazed. "You are one of the Four Ancients. I never would have guessed it. What are you doing here?"

For the first time, Eion smiled. "Believe it or not, settling a bet."

"With whom?" Balthor cautiously asked.

"With me," Gareth proudly announced. "I'm about to earn myself a free wish from an Ancient. How cool is that?"

"You … made a wager … with *him*?" Balthor incredulously asked.

"I say that Usol gave the shealk Aeia's Stone, the *Essence of the Sea*. Eion says I'm wrong, but I know I'm right."

"What did you wager?" Balthor asked, growing angry.

"A wish for a favor," Eion answered. "If your son wins, I grant him a wish. If he loses, he owes me a favor. So, young wizard, would you care to tell your father? It would be more entertaining if it came from you."

"I thought you don't like to meddle in human affairs?" Sarah asked as she turned to regard the Ancient.

"I don't. However, this particular scene is not of my doing."

Balthor turned to his son and sighed. "Gareth, the shealk were never in possession of an Alchos Stone."

"What?" Gareth sputtered, growing pale. "You were, too! You said you..."

"I said no such thing, son. If you remember correctly, I stated I had located one of the Stones, but found it in the possession of a wealthy human. That human placed it into the cargo hold of a ship, with the intent to move it to a more secure location. However, Captain Flinn, of the *Seven Kingdoms* attacked. He took possession of the Stone, and the rest, as they say, is history."

"But ... but..."

"You lost, kiddo," Steve jovially told the teenager. He looked over at Eion, who had a smug smile on his face. "Go easy on him, okay?"

"The task I have for him has yet to be decided. When I do, it will be well within his power to accomplish. That is the only stipulation I will agree to."

"You mentioned Aeia," Balthor recalled, as he looked at his son disapprovingly. "Who is that? Someone else you lost a wager to?"

"Aiea is another Ancient," Steve told the shealk wizard, eliciting a squawk of surprise.

"But ... there is no Ancient by the name of Aeia," Balthor pointed out. "Aeus, Eion, Oros, and Usol. Those are the Four Ancients."

"They sometimes go by other names," Steve helpfully offered. "In this case, Aeus is Aeia. Oros is Aura."

"Aeia governs the water," Eion explained. "The shealk are to her as the griffins are to Usol."

Steve nodded knowingly. "I did not know that."

"Nor did I," Balthor admitted.

"How does this help us?" Steve asked, looking around at his companions before settling on Eion.

"It doesn't," Eion informed him. "At least, not yet. You should know, Usol pursued Aeia, but she refused his advances.'

"A lover's spat," Steve grumped. "That's just great. Emily, are you sure you don't want to get out of here? These types of situations never play out the way anyone wants."

Emily vehemently shook her head, knocking her bun loose, which sent her blonde curls tumbling about. "No way. I haven't come this far to chicken out now. I want to see how this plays out."

"She likes us," Steve snickered. "Welcome to the Dark Side, Dr. Benz."

Sarah smacked him on the left arm at the exact same time Emily hit him on his right. Both had unerring aim. Both of his arms now stung like crazy.

"You hit the funny bone," Steve complained. "Both of you. Is that a skill they teach girls in school?"

Sarah and Emily gave each other high fives.

"I do not believe we have met," Balthor formally said, as he turned to Emily. "I am Balthor, of the shealk. And you are?"

"Dr. Emily Benz, of, er, Phoenix, Arizona."

"She helped Eion out when he was hurt," Gareth explained.

"Ah. In that case, you have my thanks, Doctor Emily Benz."

"Please, call me 'Emily'."

"As you wish."

Sarah waved her hands in the air, attracting everyone's attention. She then pointed at Eion.

"Can we get back to the problem at hand? The pirates are still out there. They have Aeia's Alchos Stone. What are we going to do about it?"

"What *can* we do about it?" Steve sputtered. "We've known for a while now that someone has been helping the pirates. Someone had to be feeding them information. How else would they have known where to look for the oskorlisk fang? Or how to find the door leading down to the dwarves?" Steve continued.

"Is this how that human piece of trash was able to wield my hammer?" Breslin demanded. "Because of Usol?"

"What hammer are you referring to, dwarf?" Eion politely inquired.

"The Narian Power Hammer," Breslin answered. "Only a person with Narian blood may properly wield that hammer. Flinn is neither."

"That was what he meant," Eion muttered to himself. He scowled and shook his head. "The enchantments on that hammer would not be difficult to overcome, especially not for one of us. My brother must've removed the requirement to be a descendent of Nar from the hammer."

"I've seen others try to wield it," Steve argued. "They couldn't. Only he could."

The Ancient shrugged. "Then the reverse has happened. Usol has given your pirate Narian blood, or whatever else the hammer needs from its wielder."

"How is Usol giving all this help to the pirates?" Steve wanted to know. "Can he communicate through the Stone?"

Eion shook his head. "If it was Usol's Stone, then it would be possible. As it is, that Stone is Aeia's, and only she can communicate with it in that manner."

"Then my question stands," Steve continued. "How is Usol helping the pirates? If not through that Stone, then how?"

Gareth suddenly let out a yelp of surprise and pointed straight at Eion. "I think I've figured it out."

"I'm all ears, kid," Steve said. "Let's hear it."

"I would like to know, too," Eion admitted.

"He's one of the crew," Gareth proudly answered. "We know the Ancients are capable of changing their forms. We know Eion can assume human form, so why can't Usol? I'm willing to wager he's part of the crew."

Balthor cringed. "Another wager, son? Must we seek you out some help? This is not a healthy way to live."

"I'm fine, Father. There's no need to worry. It's just harmless fun."

"Harmless fun? You now owe a favor to one of the Ancients! Do you think that's harmless?"

Gareth's cheeks reddened. "Can we talk about this later?"

"You had better believe we'll be talking about this later," Balthor vowed.

"Moving on," Steve said, "if Gareth's suggestion is correct, and Usol has disguised himself as one of Flinn's crew, what do we do about it? Do we warn Flinn?"

Sarah shook her head. "Chances are, Captain Flinn knows who he has been talking to. More than likely, he doesn't care, because of all the benefits he's been reaping. From what I hear, his ship is the terror of the seas. He's never been caught. And, he's so rich that he's bored out of his skull. I'm quite sure he doesn't care where his information is coming from."

"Well, should we go after the pirates?" Steve asked, glancing around the room. "I can't believe we're going to give up after coming this far. Granted, our success rate isn't looking too good. They still have the stone and the fang, and they now have the Power Hammer. Plus, they have a sizeable lead on us."

Sarah nodded. "You're right. We really should get going. I can drop us all in the valley, right in front of the dwarf door. We might even be able to get the dragons to help us."

"They would, in a heartbeat," Steve agreed. "Kahvel is still holding a grudge against Flinn for stealing Pryllan's fang."

Sarah held out her hand. "All right then. All those going to the surface, get ready to go."

"You should undoubtedly pursue," Eion's calm voice suddenly said, drawing everyone's attention. "However, thanks to the teleporter, time is on your side."

"How can you possibly say that?" Sarah demanded. "If the pirates make it Topside, and it turns out you're correct and Usol is helping them, how will we catch them? No, we need to be ready for them, just as soon as they enter the valley."

"Preparation is the key to everything," Eion calmly told them. "In this case, we know where they're going. Therefore, we, namely *you*, can prepare for their arrival."

"Of course we know where they're going," Steve said. "They're headed back to their ship."

Eion was shaking his head. "No, not yet they aren't."

"Why?" Breslin asked. "If you know something that can help us, then please tell us. We will be forever in your debt."

"Your pirate friends will be heading to the human castle."

"Castle R'Tal?" Sarah asked. "There's no way they're going back to that castle. The last visit didn't end well for them, so that can't possibly be right."

"That's where they're going," Eion insisted.

"Why?" Steve asked.

Eion cocked his head as he stared at Steve. "Why, didn't I tell you? There's an Alchos Stone in Lentari."

Chapter 16 — Angry Ancient

Didn't I say that from day one?" Steve exclaimed, as he turned to regard his companions. "I knew it. Man alive, I just knew it!"

"Don't gloat too much, dear," Sarah cautioned. "It doesn't become you. Okay, Mr. Ancient, you say there's an Alchos Stone in Lentari and it's hidden in the castle. Does the king know?"

Eion was shaking his head. "I never said the Stone was in the castle."

Steve frowned. "Beg to differ, amigo, but that's exactly what you said."

Sarah sat back and was silent for a few moments.

"Wait. The only thing you said was that you knew where the pirates were going. So, my question is, if there's no Alchos Stone hidden in the castle, why would the pirates want to go there?"

Eion gave Sarah an appraising look and eventually nodded. "Your powers of recall are excellent, Sarah Miller."

Sarah pointed at Steve. "Tell him that, would you?"

"Snot," Steve laughed, shaking his head. "So I was a little bit off."

"You weren't even close," Emily told him.

"Thanks, for the recap, Judas."

Emily laughed.

"So, where is it?" Sarah repeated. "Can you tell us?"

"The Stone is safe and secure in the Temple of the Alchos," Eion answered.

"The Alchos Stone is in the Temple of the Alchos," Steve repeated. "Not very original."

Eion shrugged. "There are way too many Temples to name them all. Temple of the Alchos will have to do."

"How many Alchos Temples are there?" Gareth asked. "I've never heard of any temples being in Lentari."

"Nor have I," Breslin admitted.

Eion held up a hand with three fingers splayed out.

"Three?" Sarah asked. "There are three of your temples in Lentari? Is that why the pirates are going to the castle? To find out where they need to go?"

Eion shook his head. "The pirates are headed to the castle, because that is where Usol is recommending they go. As for knowing the location of the Temples, well, that's different. The only way to find the first Temple is to gain possession of the key. The second Temple can only be found after solving the first. And the third after the second."

Steve held up his hands in a time-out gesture. "Wait. Wait a minute. Did you say 'solve the temple'? What does that mean?"

"There are puzzles that need to be solved," Sarah groaned. "Obstacles. Tell me I'm wrong."

"You are not wrong," Eion told her, with a smile. "I meant what I said earlier. The Stone is in the single most secure place in all of Lentari. Acquiring the Stone would be impossible for a human."

"How about a human with an oskorlisk fang, a Narian Power Hammer, and an Ancient as a companion?" Steve dryly asked. "Then would they stand a chance?"

Eion sadly nodded. "It is clear Usol has been schooling

your pirates on what tools will be needed in order to defeat the obstacles at the Temples. With Usol personally there, offering guidance, I'm sorry to say, it is possible the Temple defenses can be defeated."

"Why doesn't Usol just give the damn stone to Flinn?" Steve grumbled. "Why put them through all of this? Could he really be that bored?"

"Usol cannot give the stone away until he takes possession of it once more," Eion cryptically answered.

"What does that mean?" Breslin asked, confused. He turned to Athos, who shrugged. "He clearly has the power to simply reclaim his stone. Why doesn't he?"

"Because the vast majority of his powers were stripped from him," the Ancient explained, eliciting gasps from Sarah and Emily. "I should know. I'm the one who took them from him."

"You?" Sarah echoed, incredulous. "Why?"

"Allow me to explain this in terms you would understand. Hmm. It was for the same reason you would take a toy away from a bully. He was misusing his abilities, causing more strife than he was alleviating. He repeatedly violated his warnings, and then uses the 'I didn't mean any harm' defense. Well, after several millennia of reckless behavior, an intervention had to be given."

"So, what happens if he gets his Stone?" Sarah asked. "Will he be given back his powers?"

Eion nodded. "Aye. Speaking for myself, and for Aeia and Aura, that is something we wish to avoid."

"No wonder Usol is so keen on helping Flinn and his crew," Steve said, more to himself than to anyone. "Okay, Eion. Clearly you don't want Usol to get that stone. We're right there with you on that. What are we going to do about it? You can't possibly sit this one out. We're going to need your help."

"You're getting my help right now," the Ancient curtly replied.

"So, if we can get Usol's Alchos Stone before he does," Steve began, "that would solve a lot of problems, wouldn't it? How do we do it? What's our first step?"

"The first step is obtaining the key," Eion reiterated. "Locate the key and find the Temple. I will meet you inside."

"Can't you just take us there?" Gareth asked, dismayed. "I mean, what if we can't find the key?"

"Can you at least tell us what it looks like?" Sarah asked.

"All I will tell you is the key has been enchanted to look like whatever is next to it."

"What?" Steve demanded. "Can you be a little more specific than that?"

There was a brilliant flash of white light. When the light faded, and after the spots were rubbed out of their eyes, the companions looked around. They had been returned to the Gate Cavern and were staring at the mouth of a tunnel. Visible through the tunnel was a set of stairs that stretched endlessly up before fading away into the darkness.

"I guess not," Steve grumped.

"My legs are aching just looking at all those steps," Emily moaned.

Sarah held out her hand. "Not to worry. We went down those steps once, and only once. I can get us all the way to the castle. Is everyone coming? Emily, are you sure you don't want us to take you home?"

The paleontologist fervently shook her head. "I want to stay as long as you're willing to have me. I think this land is absolutely fascinating."

Sarah turned to the dwarves. "Athos? Breslin? I realize your responsibility lies here, but if you'd like to come and lend a hand, I certainly wouldn't turn down the help."

"Nor would I," Steve informed his dwarf friends.

"I will come," Athos stated, looking over at Breslin, who nodded.

"As will I. I will not abandon you in your time of need."

Sarah looked over at Gareth, with Deez next to his side. "Are you two coming?"

Gareth nodded. "Aye."

DESIRE TO REMAIN WITH HIVE

Surprised, all seven companions, plus one paleontologist,

turned to regard their guur friend.

Steve nodded. "We're glad to have you, Deez. We're ready when you are."

Hands were placed on top of each other, with Deez placing the tip of one his front forelegs directly on top. As before, the world winked out and was immediately replaced by the main wall surrounding R'Tal. There, directly before them, was the open drawbridge leading in to the West Gate. People were milling about, exiting and entering through the gate, while armed guards stood diligently by, keeping an eye on everyone.

Two of the five guards noticed the sudden appearance of their group and immediately headed toward them.

"Halt! Identify yourself and state your … Lady Sarah! Sir Steve! A thousand apologies, Nohrin. Make way! Let the Nohrin and their party through!"

The guards immediately shooed everyone to the side, allowing unencumbered access through the gate. Sarah was all smiles, having finally been recognized before Steve. She looped her arm through his and together, entered the city.

"Still with us, Emily?' Steve called, looking back at the short blonde woman.

"I am. This is amazing! Look at the street vendors! Look at the people! This is right out of a Renaissance Fair!"

"This is the real thing," Sarah assured her, turning to look back at their new friend with a smile. "These people have been here a long time, and if I have anything to say about it, they will continue to be here long after we're gone."

"I'm glad to hear it," Emily returned. "Where are we headed?"

Overhearing, Steve pointed at the imposing castle. "We're headed there. We need to check in with Mikal and Lissa."

"Who're they?" Emily wanted to know.

"Mikal is the current king, filling in for his parents while they're away," Steve answered. "Lissa is his wife."

"We were once Mikal's bodyguards," Sarah added. "During our first visit here, we were told we were the pre-ordained protectors for Mikal."

"How did you first find your way here?" Emily wanted

to know.

They wound their way through the streets, on a direct course for the castle as husband and wife recanted their tale. They received their fair share of looks, especially since Gareth and Deez were bringing up the rear. The young wizard had his hands full keeping his guur companion's attention on him, and not on the myriad of sights and smells found on every street corner. In fact, several vendors had tried approaching their group, only to be discouraged the moment Deez looked their way.

Word of their arrival must have spread like wildfire because a welcoming party was waiting for them at the castle drawbridge. Steve recognized Captain Pheron, Lieutenant Darius, and a few other soldiers, who immediately approached them on the open bridge.

Captain Pheron held up a hand, signaling everyone to halt. "Greetings, Sir Steve, Lady Sarah! Kre'Mikal has asked for you to be sent to the Antechamber just as soon as you returned."

Steve nodded. "That'll work. We've got a number of things to run by him. And Pheron? Might I suggest that you stay? We've got some trouble headed this way."

The tall captain nodded. "Very well. This way, if you please. I am anxious to hear … and who might this be?"

Husband and wife turned to see Pheron staring at Emily. Steve explained her presence.

Satisfied, Pheron nodded. "Any friend of the Nohrin is a friend of mine. Welcome to Lentari, Lady Emily."

Emily's eyes widened with surprise. "That's the second time someone called me Lady Emily. Ooo, I'm starting to really like this place."

Once inside the castle, Pheron lead the group straight to the Antechamber, where Mikal and Lissa were waiting. Steve noticed that several additional chairs had been added to the semi-circle in front of the main hearth. Leave it to Mikal to be fully prepared.

"Welcome back, everyone," Mikal formally announced. "It's good to see you all. I do see a couple of new faces."

After introductions were made, Mikal held his hand out

to Deez and waited for the guur to approach.

INTENT?

"He just wants to meet you," Gareth told the friendly guur. "He's not going to hurt you. Umm, I think you need to tell him you won't hurt him."

Mikal looked at the ten-legged creature and nodded. "I won't hurt you, Deez. I've never met a, er, guur before. I'm pleased to meet you."

COMPLIANCE

"Was that Deez's voice we just heard in our heads?" Lissa asked, amazed. "A telepathic bug. I didn't know such a thing existed."

"They don't," Steve corrected. "You're hearing Deez's thoughts, yes, but only courtesy of Pryllan, who presently has us all linked together."

Mikal looked up and acknowledged the dragon. "I was led to believe that the seven of you…"

"Eight," Lissa quietly corrected.

"…eight of you," Mikal amended, "have urgent business here in the castle. Can you tell me the nature of this business? Perhaps I can assist?"

Steve nodded. "Thanks pal. I'm hoping you can do exactly that. We're looking for a key…"

"To what?" Mikal asked, after Steve trailed off.

"To a temple…"

Mikal frowned. "Temple? What temple? In Lentari?"

"Well, that answers that," Sarah noted. She looked over at Lissa and smiled. "We were really hoping you'd have an idea where this key was, and that you had heard of the temple it allegedly unlocks."

"I did not know there were any temples to be found in Lentari," Mikal hesitantly admitted. He looked at his new wife and shrugged. "Did you?"

Lissa shook her head. "No, I'm sorry. What temple, Lady Sarah? Can you tell us anything about it?"

"You obviously remember the Ancients, right?" Steve began.

Mikal and Lissa both nodded. Steve quickly flicked his eyes over at Pheron, who also nodded.

"Well, as it turns out, there's an Alchos Stone hidden in Lentari."

"No way!" Mikal exclaimed, dropping formalities altogether.

"From what we've been told," Sarah continued, "this second Alchos Stone has been secured inside a temple. A, uh, Temple of the Alchos."

"A Temple of the Ancients," Lissa translated, nodding.

"That's what the pirates are after," Steve added. "They know this Alchos Stone is here, and that's why they won't leave until they get it. And trust me, we don't want them to get it."

Mikal looked at Lissa and nodded. "Agreed. What do you need from us? You're looking for a key? Do you know where it is?"

Sarah shook her head. "No. Here's the thing. We were told the key has been hidden inside this castle. The only clue we were given was that the key was enchanted to resemble whatever has been placed next to it."

The pro tem king frowned. "That means it could be hidden anywhere. And enchanted to look like whatever is next to it? That means it could be … well, it could be … You know what? I'm not sure."

Steve turned to point at the closest wall. "I'm thinking it's a stone. Think about it. It's the perfect hiding place."

Sarah was shaking her head. "That means there'd have to be several stones that are exactly alike. You heard what Eion said. The key would resemble whatever is sitting next to it. That would suggest that, in your example, Steve, the stones below, above, to the right, and to the left would all be identical." She strode over to the closest wall and inspected a couple of stones up close. "Look at this. From a distance, these stones look the same, only if you get up close to them, you'll see they're nowhere close to being identical. This one has a crack. That one has a couple of streaks of black running through it, and so on."

"I really, really, really hope I'm wrong," Steve was saying, as he looked around the room. "This whole castle is built from stones and it's too damn big. We could spend days in here, searching for identical rocks."

"What about a drinking glass?" Sarah asked, raising a hand. "Or a plate? They're always stacked, or stored, together, aren't they?"

"If so, it'd have to be a piece of china that hasn't been used in a long time," Lissa decided. "Otherwise, as soon as you move this 'key' off by itself, then wouldn't it revert to its true form?"

Steve turned to his companions. "Gareth? Any ideas? What about you guys, Breslin? What do you two think?"

"I think it could be flatware," Gareth said. "Maybe a knife or a spoon? This is a castle. They must have hundreds of knives or spoons. I would guess that not all of them have been used recently."

Breslin shrugged. "What about a weapon? A knife, or a spear?"

Athos shook his head. "I have no suggestions. I am sorry."

"That's okay, master dwarf," Mikal said. "Do we have any idea when this key was hidden here?"

Curious, Steve looked at Sarah, who shook her head. "Sorry, I should have thought to ask that. No, he never did say."

"But," Sarah interjected, raising a finger, "he did say that *you-know-who* did lose his powers many centuries ago. That would suggest the key has been here for a very long time."

Steve groaned and rubbed his temples. "I feel a headache coming on."

"So, it's a daunting task," Sarah chided. "You didn't think it'd be easy, did you?"

"That's the problem," Steve said, exasperated. "We only have a few hours to search before those pirates will be here."

Mikal stiffened in his chair. "The pirates are coming back here? How do you know this?"

"Because that key is what they're looking for," Sarah

explained. "We really need to find it first."

"And then what?" Lissa wanted to know. "What do you plan on doing with it?"

"What else?" Steve said. "We're going to use it to find this damn temple, and then claim that Alchos Stone before the pirates get it. If the pirates get their hands on it, then Usol wins, and he'll more than likely get his powers back. And trust me when I say that this Usol guy really knows how to hold a grudge. Wait a moment. Get his powers back? Doesn't he already have his powers? I mean, hasn't he been using them against us?"

Sarah shrugged. "That might be considered so minor that, to an Ancient, it's not worth mentioning. I don't want to even imagine what he would do if he had his full powers back."

"You and me both," Steve agreed.

Mikal turned to Gareth and nodded. "What about you? Do you think you could come up with a spell that could locate this key? I've seen you do some amazing things, my friend. Impress me again."

Everyone in the room turned to the teenager.

"I don't think I can," the young wizard reluctantly admitted. "Eion himself said that my spells were useless against him."

Steve held up his hand. "Wait a minute. He said that, yes, but he was also referring to himself or the Stones. We're not looking for an Ancient or an Alchos Stone. We're just looking for a simple key. What do you say? Think you can do it?"

Gareth blinked with surprise. "Oh. I didn't even think about that. All right. Give me some time to see what I can come up with."

"In the meantime," Sarah added, "I think there might be someone here whom we can consult with that might be able to help us out. Or, possibly shed some light on the situation?"

"Who?" Steve and Mikal asked, at the same time.

"Your favorite person in the whole wide world," Sarah happily exclaimed. "You know what? That goes for the both of you. It might give her a chance to feel important."

Lissa giggled and looked away. Mikal's face immediately

soured, as did Steve's.

"Oh, hell no," Steve began. "I'm not asking that old crone for anything."

"I'm with him," Mikal added, pointing at Steve.

"Who?" they heard Emily quietly ask.

"Miss Andra Alwyn," Sarah answered. "She's the keeper of the Archives. Think of her like a librarian."

"A pain-in-the-butt, know-it-all librarian," Steve corrected, "with the personality of a dust mop."

"She can't be that bad," Emily teased.

"She is," Steve, Mikal, and Pheron all echoed.

"Nevertheless," Sarah said, "we should include her. Lissa, I seem to remember you being able to work your magic on her. Do you think you could help us out?"

Mikal's smile was back. "What a splendid idea. My dear, would you? That would be a tremendous help."

"You just don't want to deal with her," Lissa accused, but she did have a smile on her face.

Mikal grinned. "Guilty as charged."

Lissa nodded. "Very well. I'll take you to her."

"Should I accompany them, Your Majesty?" Captain Pheron asked.

Mikal glanced over at Steve, who promptly nodded.

"Aye, I would prefer it, Captain. If this will help us prepare for the arrival of those infernal pirates, then you have my full blessing to aid and assist as needed."

"If it's all the same to you," Breslin began, "I would prefer to stay here. An Archives holds no interest for me."

"That goes for me, too," Athos agreed.

Both dwarves jumped up onto the closest set of chairs and settled down to wait.

Pheron nodded. "Consider it done, Your Majesty."

"Can I come?" Emily hesitantly asked. "I'm a scientist. I would love to view your Archives."

Mikal nodded. "Permission granted, by order of the king."

"Uh, thanks?" Emily offered. She looked at Sarah. "Do I curtsy?"

"Can you?" Sarah returned.

Emily faced Mikal and executed a perfect curtsy.

"That was pretty good," Steve confided to Emily, the moment they left the Antechamber. "Where'd you learn to do that?"

"I grew up in the South," Emily explained. "They've got something down there that's called Cotillion, and my mother thought it best to expose me to it."

"I've heard of that," Sarah said. "Isn't that where the young girls are all dressed up and go through some type of social training?"

"It's an English tradition, dating back to the eighteenth century," Emily explained. "Why they'd make a frightened young girl suffer through all those horrors is beyond me."

"Didn't enjoy it, huh?" Steve quipped.

Emily shook her head. "Not on your life."

"Here we are," Lissa announced, as they entered the castle's north wing. The entire area had been dedicated to the storage and cataloguing of books, scrolls, papers, and other important information. Census information, tax records, jhorun classification, it was all there. Overseeing the entire collection was none other than Miss Andra Alwyn, a cranky octogenarian who typically didn't get along with anyone. Steve and Sarah had crossed paths with the argumentative archivist on a number of occasions. Most recently, Lissa revealed she had the skill and patience to persuade Andra Alwyn into doing practically anything, all without it appearing like she was requesting anything.

"There she is," Steve grumped, as he caught sight of the archivist at her desk.

"She doesn't look too bad," Emily decided.

"Oh, but she is," Captain Pheron softly muttered.

"Let me do the talking," Lissa instructed. She strode up to the desk, smiled at Miss Alwyn, and waited for the archivist to say something.

"Well, well, what have we here?" Andra asked, as she peered over her spectacles at the procession before her.

"Good afternoon, Ms. Alwyn," Lissa formally announced.

"Kre'Lissa," Andra Alwyn acknowledged, with a smile. Her gaze fell on Steve and she instantly scowled. "Is there something I can do for you?"

Lissa turned to Steve and waved him forward. Taking a deep breath, Steve faced the archivist and tried his hand at giving out a forced smile. Andra's lips thinned as she regarded him.

"We were hoping you'd be able to help us out," Steve began. "What I'm about to tell you has to remain confidential, all right?"

A look of surprise washed over the archivist's face. Steve grinned. Andra was intrigued, whether she wanted to admit it or not.

"Somewhere in this castle, there's a key."

"What key?" Andra asked, as most of her anger evaporated at the first mention of 'confidential.' "What do you know of this key?"

"Only that it's going to look like everything else around it," Steve told the frizzy-haired records keeper. "We were told it would look exactly like whatever it was next to."

"What does this key unlock?" Andra wanted to know.

"That's why we're here," Sarah said. "This key allegedly unlocks an Alchos Temple located somewhere here in Lentari."

Andra's thin white eyebrows shot up.

Steve nodded. "That's what we said. Nevertheless, the temples exist, as does this key. My question to you is this: have you ever heard of any temples in Lentari? Their official name is Temple of the Alchos, and from what we've been told, there are more than one."

"Three," Sarah added.

Andra thought long and hard. The scowl on her face threatened to return when she looked at Steve, but she quickly glanced over at Lissa and smiled. Wordlessly, she walked around her desk and through the hall, into the vast holding room in the Archives.

Working quickly, Andra made several selections from the shelves, without even stopping to see if she was selecting the right book. Once the books became too heavy for her to lift, she simply held the books behind her and waited for someone to take them. Within ten minutes, Steve was holding nearly a dozen books.

"Sit there," Andra instructed, pointing to an open table in the middle of the room. "The Temple of the Alchos. I have heard of its existence, and I do know one is rumored to be in Lentari, but no one has ever laid eyes on it. You say there's a key involved with it?"

"That's right. We were told that the only way to find the temple was to be in possession of the key."

"Who told you this?" Andra wanted to know.

Sarah looked at Steve and shrugged. "How much do we tell her?"

"She's helping and not making a scene," Steve decided, ignoring the frown that had appeared on the archivist's face. "I say we tell her. We weren't told to keep it to ourselves, were we?"

Surprisingly, Andra Alwyn's face softened and, at long last, she smiled at Steve.

"Eion told us," Steve quietly announced.

Andra's head cocked to the side, as though she had heard a funny sound. "Eion? You must be mistaken."

"Uh, we aren't," Steve assured her. "He took us to Astral, and then took us back."

Much of her skepticism evaporated at the mention of Eion's private island. "You've really been there? To Astral?"

Everyone nodded; a fact not lost on the tiny, withered woman.

"You all have? What ... what was it like?"

"Help us find that key and we'll tell you all about it," Sarah promised.

Andra nodded and immediately flipped open the first book. Pulling out a chair, she sat, without breaking eye contact with her book. After a few moments, she discarded the first and moved on to the second. Working quickly and efficiently, Andra skimmed through all twelve books, jotting notes, before she looked up. She held up the note paper.

"There were six references to a temple," the archivist reported. "None of the books specify which temple it's referring to, but I feel we're working in the right direction. I should also mention, however, all six were reported to be in different locations."

"Well, it's a start," Steve told the archivist. "We appreciate the help."

Andra formally nodded. "Of course. Now, is there anything ... oh, sweet mercy! No! No!! Help! Make it go away!!"

Not knowing what to expect, Steve whirled around and ignited his hands. Emily immediately scooted behind Sarah, while Pheron drew his sword. Steve saw what had spooked the records keeper and snuffed out his hands.

Gareth was standing there, alongside their ten-legged companion, Deez. The guur was softly chittering, while slowly turning his head to inspect his surroundings. At the sound of the outburst, the chittering became louder and he immediately moved in front of Gareth.

"Why, I do believe he's trying to protect you," Sarah told Gareth. "That must make you feel good!"

Gareth patted the guur on his head. "It's okay, Deez. There's no danger. Ms. Alwyn was just surprised to see you, that's all.

NO THREAT DETECTED

"Yeah, we know," Steve told the guur, drawing a questioning look from the archivist. "She thought *you* were the danger."

"You're talking to that creature as though it can understand you?" Andra asked, appalled.

"That's because he can," Steve told her as he tried valiantly to mask the disgust he was now feeling at the old woman. "I know he can be frightening to look at, but he's our friend. He's come to our aid just as much as we've come to his."

"But ... but ... it's a guur!" Andra reiterated. "I simply cannot stand bugs!"

NO HARM INTENDED FOR MANIACAL HUMAN FEMALE

Steve snorted with surprise. Sarah giggled, while Emily's

eyes widened with surprise. Gareth had to clap a hand over his mouth and look away. Andra looked at Deez and bristled with annoyance.

"Did that thing say something about me?"

"Only that he wasn't planning on harming you," Steve answered, wisely leaving out the 'maniacal' bit. Deez was developing a sense of humor? How cool!

"What are you doing here, Gareth?" Sarah asked. "Do you have some good news for us?"

The wizard nodded, but looked depressed.

"Why so glum, chum?" Steve quipped, eliciting a smile from their teenage companion.

"I have an answer for you, about the key," Gareth began, "but clearly you already know."

The rest of the group eyed each other. They knew? About what?

"Care to fill us in?" Sarah asked. "We know about what?"

"About the key, obviously," Gareth reported. "I haven't found it yet, but did learn roughly where it was hiding. Here. It must be a book, but you guys already knew that."

Sarah shook her head. "No, we didn't. We just came here to get some confirmation about the temple. Andra here has been a big help. She's verified there is a temple in Lentari, but there aren't any clear references to its location."

"The key is here?" Andra repeated, looking around at the shelves of books and scrolls. "In my Archives?"

"Clever," Steve decided. "Well, we can deduce a few things."

"Like what?" Pheron asked, as he looked helplessly at the thousands of books.

Andra started to wander away when Steve called her back. "Hang on, Ms. Alwyn. We could really use you right about now."

Intrigued, Andra returned to their table.

"Thanks to Gareth, we now know this key is a book. But, remember what we said about it being disguised? That means this key is going to look like the book to the left and right of it. So, we're looking for three somewhat identical books, sitting next to each other."

"Hmm." Andra murmured, as she considered the possibilities.

"We can also add," Sarah continued, "that these books could not have been used in, what, at least several hundred years?"

"At least," Steve agreed.

"Are there any books here that you have never seen used?" Sarah asked, turning back to Andra.

"Aye," the archivist admitted. "Unfortunately, for you, there's more than I care to admit. Section three, row four, for example, has nothing but census forms for the past five hundred years. I have not seen anyone touch those tomes in all the years I've spent here in these Archives."

"That'd be a good place to start," Sarah decided.

"There's also an entire section dedicated to tariffs and trade laws," Andra continued. "Section ten, rows seven and eight."

"I'll take those," Pheron announced, as he headed off.

"Then there are constable reports from each village, dating back five or six hundred years. They are in Section fifteen, rows one through five."

"Sounds positively unpleasant," Steve grumped. "I can take…"

"Hold up," Emily interrupted. She turned to Andra and offered a smile. "I can search that section, if you'd be so kind as to tell me which direction to go."

Andra glanced briefly over at Lissa, who nodded. "Very well. Section fifteen is back there, near the base of the north stairs."

"Are you going to be okay?" Steve asked their paleontologist friend, as she rose to her feet.

"Please," Emily scoffed. "This is just another library. I can't tell you how many hours I've spent in libraries. I'll be fine. We're looking for three identical books, sitting right next to each other? If it's there, I'll find it."

"Now, let me think. Section twenty-three, rows two through seven. There's nothing but business ledgers, from hundreds of years ago. They haven't been touched."

"I'm on it," Sarah announced.

"As for you, Fire Thrower," Andra began, "I…"

"Look, I know we haven't always gotten along," Steve interrupted, "but I'm hoping we can put that past us. Your help in this matter is critical."

"I was going to tell you to search section thirty, rows three through nine. It's over there, against the far wall. There's nothing but tax records and payments, going back to when we first began to record the information."

"Wow. You guys don't ever throw anything away, do you?"

For the second time, Andra smiled at Steve. "Tell me about it. I've petitioned the king relentlessly to permanently store the unused records, but he insists they should be here, available for perusal."

"I'll put in a good word for you," Steve promised.

Andra grunted once and returned to her desk. Since he hadn't been assigned a section to search, Gareth wandered over to Section thirty to help Steve. Deez followed quietly behind.

"Is it me, or is she getting nicer?" Gareth companionably asked, as he started inspecting book spines.

"She's getting nicer," Steve admitted. "I think that has to do with Lissa. She was right. A little respect goes a long way."

"These shelves are huge!" Gareth exclaimed, when, after fifteen minutes, he hadn't even reached the end of his first shelf. "It's going to take us hours in here to find this thing."

"Probably days," Steve agreed. "However, we need to find this thing before the pirates do, so we push on."

All in all, the search only lasted about an hour. That was when Emily excitedly announced she had found three identical volumes of constable reports sitting side by side. When everyone had crowded around row four of Section fifteen, including Andra, Emily reached for the thick black volume nestled between two identical volumes on either side.

"How do we know if this is it?" Steve asked, as he glanced over at Sarah.

"I would imagine the book should change to match whatever it's next to, like a chameleon," Emily answered. "Is it supposed to be instantaneous? If so, then I would have thought … oh, ewww!"

268   Jeffrey Poole

The book dropped unceremoniously onto the floor, only it no longer resembled a book, but what looked like a severed hand.

"Eww, gross," Sarah agreed. "But, this is good news! That means you found it, Emily! Good job!"

The hand shimmered, and practically disappeared.

"No one moves!" Steve all but shouted. "It changed again, only this time, it's taken on the appearance of the floor, so the damn thing is invisible."

"How do we do this?" Gareth asked, exasperated. "The key remains hidden, since anytime any of us touch it, it changes form again."

Sarah suddenly nodded and smiled. She nudged Steve on the shoulder and pointed at the ground.

"Pick it up, would you? I think I know how to deal with this."

Steve knelt and ran his hands along the surface of the ground. The white marble felt cool; slick. Then, several fingers popped their knuckles as they rammed into what felt like another slab of marble, sitting directly on top of each other. With a grunt, he pried the stone off the ground and held it up, like he was holding a trophy.

"Got it. Oh, gross. The damn thing is changing again."

Now he was holding on to two severed hands. The mass of the marble had reduced to that of his hands, so he easily shifted both grisly hands to his right hand and waited. Sure enough, the two hands became one.

He looked over at his wife and shrugged. "Now what?"

"Hold still," Sarah instructed. "Watch this!"

The hand suddenly floated several feet into the air, suspended in midair by Sarah's jhorun. The hand shimmered a few times as it tried to mimic the surroundings, but since there was nothing near, it had nothing to base the change on. Several seconds later, the enchantment was broken and the key's true form was revealed: a small glittering diamond, cut in the shape of a griffin.

"Usol favored the griffins," Steve quietly recalled.

Sarah strode forward and gently plucked the jewel from the air. She rotated the diamond griffin in her hands a few times until she was looking at the bottom. It had felt pads, as though the griffin should be displayed in such a fashion as to not damage the surface it would eventually be sitting on.

"That's an archaic map marker," Andra excitedly announced. "See the pads underneath it? It's designed to be placed on a map, to denote a specific location. I've never seen one in such good condition before."

"That's an awful big map marker," Gareth added, as he eyed the glittering jewel.

"The maps these type of markers were designed for were much larger than the maps of today. In fact, there are several, here in the Archives. Floor two, Section four, Row one. Wait here, I'll fetch one."

Steve turned to Lissa and grinned. "Thanks to you, she's a lot more tolerable now."

Lissa waved off the compliment. "Don't thank me, thank Shardwyn. He has had a hand in her reversal of attitude."

Steve cringed, Sarah groaned, and Gareth's eyes threatened to bulge out of his head.

"Didn't I tell you?" Lissa continued. "Shardwyn is courting Ms. Alwyn."

"TMI, TMI, TMI," Steve chanted, as he plugged his ears with his fingers.

"What's going on?" Andra asked the moment she returned. She was holding a thick, four-foot-long paper tube. She placed it on the table and began to pull out the old map.

"Oh, nothing," Steve insisted. "We were just talking about how much we, uh, appreciate your help."

"Hmmph."

Andra unrolled the map and invited people to gently hold down the corners. She looked over at Sarah and inclined her head toward the map. Understanding that she was expected to place the diamond griffin marker on the map, Sarah leaned forward and gently placed the marker over the tiny illustration of Castle R'Tal.

"Now what?" Steve asked.

About to answer, Sarah gasped, then her mouth snapped shut. The marker was slowly sliding across the map, heading northwest. Up and up, it moved, passing Donlari and entering Anakash Forest. The griffin finally stopped moving at a nondescript location west of the dragon valley, in what looked like heavily forested terrain.

"There," Andra proudly announced. "That's where you can find your temple."

As everyone crowded around the map to talk about the possibilities of what they would find up in the mountains, no one noticed one of the chairs slide quietly out of the way, all by itself. No one heard the footsteps hurrying for the exit, nor should they, since the person doing the running happened to be holding the *Essence of the Sea*.

"Ye do not disappoint, Fire Thrower," Flinn chortled, as he exited the castle, unseen. "We will find the temple first. We *will* get the second stone. Mark my words!"

To be concluded in:
These are Not the Stones You're Looking For
(Pirates of Perz #3)

Author's Note

Yes, I'll be completing the Pirates of Perz story arc next, with the final installment: *These are Not the Stones You're Looking For*. Flinn and his pirate crew think they have the drop on the hapless Lentarians, and the pain-in-the-butt Fire Thrower, but do they? Will Steve and the gang be able to reverse the trend and, for once, be one step ahead of the pirates?

If you want to find out, stay tuned!

Want to help me out? Did you enjoy the book? Please consider leaving a review wherever you picked up your copy. We authors love reviews! They're one of the few things that can help us become more easily discovered by other readers. They really do help.

Finally, if you want to make sure you never miss another announcement, or would like to sign up for my newsletter (I won't ever share your contact info with anyone else), then head over to my blog at www.AuthorJMPoole.com and sign up!

J.
June, 2018

ABOUT THE AUTHOR

Jeffrey M. Poole is a professional writer who writes in both the fantasy and mystery genres. His series are listed below. Jeffrey lives in picturesque Southern Oregon, with his wife, Giliane, and their Welsh Corgi, Kinsey. His interests include archery, astronomy, archaeology, scuba diving, collecting movies, collecting swords, and tinkering with any electronic gadget he can get his hands on.

In March, 2015, Jeffrey became a proud member of SFWA, the Science Fiction & Fantasy Writers of America! Jeffrey encourages readers to connect with him on Facebook (facebook.com/bakkianchronicles). Fans can also follow him online at: www.AuthorJMPoole.com. Sign up for his newsletter here.

BOOKS BY JEFFREY POOLE

Epic Fantasy
BAKKIAN CHRONICLES

The Prophecy
Insurrection
Amulet of Aria
Disneyland Debacle (short story)
Winter Wonderland (short story)

TALES OF LENTARI

Lost City
Something Wyverian This Way Comes
A Portal for Your Thoughts
Thoughts for A Portal
Wizard in the Woods
Close Encounters of the Magical Kind
The Hunt for Red Oskorlisk (short story)
May the Fang Be With You (Pirates trilogy #1)
The Hammer is Strong with This One (Pirates #2)
These are Not the Stones You're Looking For (Pirates #3)
Blast from the Past

DRAGONS OF ANDELA
Harness the Fire
Strike the Spark

Mystery
CORGI CASE FILES
Case of the One-Eyed Tiger
Case of the Fleet-Footed Mummy
Case of the Holiday Hijinks
Case of the Pilfered Pooches
Case of the Muffin Murders
Case of the Chatty Roadrunner
Case of the Highland House Haunting
Case of the Ostentatious Otters
Case of the Dysfunctional Daredevils
Case of the Abandoned Bones
Case of the Great Cranberry Caper
Case of the Shady Shamrock
Case of the Ragin' Cajun
Case of the Missing Marine
Case of the Stuttering Parrot
Case of the Rusty Sword
Case of the Secret Staircase (short story)
Case of the Unlucky Emperor
Case of the Ice Cream Crime
Case of the Hobbit Heist

www.ingramcontent.com/pod-product-compliance
Lightning Source LLC
Chambersburg PA
CBHW050152120726
47903CB00002B/596